In Bed with a Blackguard

Book 1 of Lady Knights series

Cara Maxwell

ARE YOU SIGNED UP FOR DRAGONBLADE'S BLOG?

You'll get the latest news and information on exclusive giveaways, exclusive excerpts, coming releases, sales, free books, cover reveals and more.

Check out our complete list of authors, too!

No spam, no junk. That's a promise!

Sign Up Here

www.dragonbladepublishing.com

Dearest Reader;

Thank you for your support of a small press. At Dragonblade Publishing, we strive to bring you the highest quality Historical Romance from some of the best authors in the business. Without your support, there is no 'us', so we sincerely hope you adore these stories and find some new favorite authors along the way.

Happy Reading!

CEO, Dragonblade Publishing

CHAPTER ONE

April 1817
Exeter, England

*H*E WAS A *surprisingly good kisser.*

Jacquetta had seduced enough lords to report credibly on the subject.

He was thorough but with a touch of spontaneity. His tongue explored every part of her mouth, then flicked downward and pulled her lower lip between his teeth in a tantalizing nip.

Most of the gentlemen Jacquetta kissed were sloppy—too wet, too eager. But despite his young age, Lord Andresen impressed her.

It was almost a shame that in a few minutes he would be nothing more than an unconscious puddle on the expensive Turkish rug.

Andresen's hand wandered up her arm toward her shoulder, palming the soft curve exposed by the wide-cut neckline of her gown. Jacquetta was vaguely aware of the path his hand was taking. If he decided to get too bold, she'd take evasive action. Most of her attention was fixed on the closed door of the study and the hallway beyond. She monitored the sounds beyond, listening for footsteps or the creak of a floorboard.

But the door remained stubbornly closed.

Which meant the farce must continue.

Jacquetta slid her hand up from where she gripped Andresen's shoulder to the nape of his neck. She wriggled her fingers into the neatly clubbed, pale brown hair... pressed herself into him... let her lips vibrate in a little *mmmmm* of pleasure. A carefully executed sequence to keep Andresen's attention focused on her, his mind pliant.

She'd done this a hundred times. The gentlemen of the *ton* were so mind-numbingly predictable. A well-placed glance, a spin across the dance floor interspersed with lingering touches, and they allowed her whatever she wanted.

There. She finally heard it. Footsteps that stopped at the door rather than drifting on down the corridor.

Nothing in her touch changed—Jacquetta showed the young lord no sign that she'd shifted into the second phase of her plan.

Phase one had gone off flawlessly. She'd lured Andresen out of the ballroom and into the study for a private tryst with ease. Jacquetta had selected the room intentionally. It was far enough from the festivities that no one was likely to stumble upon them. No one except for the gentleman who'd been watching her all night.

That thought almost made her snort. *Gentleman.* Grayson Thane was nothing of the sort. Gentlemen did not linger outside closed doors, waiting to interrupt evening trysts and kidnap unsuspecting young women.

Which was exactly what Grayson Thane was doing at that very moment.

Jacquetta pulled her mouth away from Andresen's, letting her lush coral-pink lips part slightly as she panted in excitement. Not feigned. But certainly not from Andresen's kiss. She watched his mouth curve into a self-satisfied smile as he took in her heaving bosom and the exhilarated glitter in her eyes.

He did not notice that those turquoise eyes barely met his, were intensely watching the door to the study, which was still closed.

Andresen lowered his mouth back toward hers, ready for the next round of exploration.

"Perhaps a moment…" Jacquetta flicked her gaze down coquettishly, mock innocence dripping from her. She pretended to scan the room, her eyes settling on the crystal decanter and amber cognac which filled it. "A bit of refreshment?"

He followed Jacquetta's eyes to the low-slung table positioned between two gleaming cherry brown leather chairs. He glanced back, finding her expression a perfect mix of flirtation and hesitation.

"Of course, Miss Lawson." He slipped his hand from her shoulder and offered it to her, palm up.

Jacquetta summoned a small smile, biting her bottom lip for a second to draw Andresen's eyes. He looked tempted to push her back up against the wall and claim those lips, but the gentleman in him won out. She knew it would. He was, after all, an earl's son. Chivalry was practically bred into his veins. It was exactly what Jacquetta was depending upon for this whole scenario to unfurl according to plan.

"Would you like to sit?" Andresen motioned to the chairs.

Jacquetta nodded through her smile as if her voice was too choked by emotion to escape. But instead of taking either of the seats he indicated, she swept around the table laden with decanter and glasses and seated herself on the matching sofa. She gracefully rearranged her cerulean-blue skirts and then raised her gaze to his at the same moment that her hand softly patted the empty leather beside her.

"Won't you join me?" she breathed.

Desire flashed through the young man's pale blue eyes.

The young lord took one long step around the table and sank to the sofa beside her. He perched close—not quite near enough to touch her, but much closer than would have been allowed with the prying eyes of a chaperone looking on.

But he did not reach for the decanter before them, instead turning toward Jacquetta and leaning in…

Damn buck has fire in his britches.

How long would Grayson Thane wait at the door before interrupting? He was a professional, just like Jacquetta. But the window of time that he could slip her out of the manor was closing. Eventually, someone at the party would notice Lord Andresen and Miss Lawson's absences.

Well, if he was determined to paw at her again, she could at least use the moment to her advantage…

Jacquetta artfully angled her jaw upward to expose the delicate, pale column of her throat. Andresen pressed his lips to the tender skin. Jacquetta emitted a delicate little moan as she slyly slid her hand into the pocket of her gown and withdrew the tiny, stoppered glass vial.

His hand went to her knee, sliding against the layers of chiffon to feel the shapely leg beneath. She met his hand with her own—the one *not* holding a tincture—and twined their fingers together intimately. Jacquetta felt the thrum of excitement, that subtle tightening of Andresen's body as he shifted closer to her. It was just the distraction she needed.

She leaned her body into his and simultaneously uncorked the vial, dumping its contents into one of the two empty glasses before chucking the evidence under the chairs opposite them.

By the time she drew back, Jacquetta was blushing prettily and panting with exhilaration.

"Refreshments?" she reminded him, darting her tongue out over her lips.

"Of course, Miss Lawson… Jacquetta." He tried out her Christian name, watching to see if she would protest.

Jacquetta widened her smile. "I have never heard someone say it quite that way," she purred. By which she meant that he'd mispronounced it. Nearly everyone did.

The door opened. Not wide enough for Andresen to notice. Just a sliver.

Every one of Jacquetta's senses screamed to attention.

It appeared that Grayson Thane was tired of waiting outside

to see what would happen. But he had not quite decided to interrupt—just to open the door enough to hear what was happening within.

The door itself made no sound. The movement of the hinges was imperceptible. It was the slight increase in the volume of everything happening beyond the door that alerted Jacquetta to the shift.

It was time to move things along.

Grayson Thane might not mind an audience, but Jacquetta's orders were to involve no one, save Thane himself. She needed Andresen good and unconscious by the time Thane worked up his nerve to strike.

"I am fairly parched from the… excitement." Jacquetta nodded again toward the glassware before them.

The heavy crystal decanter full of rich amber cognac gleamed, and the two glasses Jacquetta had placed there hours before waited at attention.

"Allow me." Andresen kept his eyes on hers as he took the decanter by its neck and poured.

Not his favorite drink, but hers. If she was going to set up the situation, she might as well have her drink of choice rather than the sickly-sweet claret favored by ladies of the *ton*.

Jacquetta watched carefully as he splashed the cognac into her glass and handed it to her. But no switch was made—he was completely unaware of her deception. And stingy with his pour. She resisted the urge to swig it all down at once and instead made a show of taking a dainty sip.

Andresen's own pour was more liberal. But he took no more than a sip.

She did not have time for this.

"A toast!" Jacquetta held up her glass. "To Lady Brothwilde, for this delicious country dalliance in the middle of an otherwise tepid Season." She held Andresen's eyes as she drained her glass.

The man's eyes widened in surprise, but he accepted the challenge. He could hardly be outdone by a debutante. He raised the glass to his lips and downed the liquid.

Jacquetta watched his throat contract as the spirit slid down his throat.

One… two… three…

She'd never seen a man hold his head up past twenty. Most were lolling by twelve.

A strange look passed over his face.

Jacquetta bit back a laugh. "Are you well, Lord Andresen?"

Seven… eight… nine…

"I feel rather queer." He hunched forward, nearly dropping the glass but somehow managing to get it upright and back on the table.

Twelve… thirteen… fourteen…

He was taking an irritatingly long time to respond to the—

Young Lord Andresen fell over sideways onto the arm of the sofa with a satisfying *thud*.

Jacquetta finally let a triumphant smile show. Her generous coral lips curved into a grin, and she flicked a stray curl of dark gold hair over her shoulder.

She reached for the decanter and began to pour herself a more generous portion of the expensive cognac she'd chosen for the occasion—

"Miss Lawson."

Her spine tensed. That reaction was genuine. The tightening on her glass, the dramatic freezing of her hand in the air… all a well-choreographed act.

Jacquetta jumped to her feet, dropping the decanter—*a damn waste of fine cognac—*

"What… Who… We were only—"

"I am not concerned with your illicit activities, Miss Lawson."

She had not seen Grayson Thane in years. Not since long before her debut, promenading with her family in Hyde Park. He was several years her senior, and he'd held little interest for a girl more interested in frocks and bonnets. But now… now he was far more interesting.

Disowned by his family, moving to the periphery of polite society, disappearing for months on end. He was very interesting. At least, the Crown thought so.

"I haven't any notion what happened to him!" She gestured to the slumped form of Lord Andresen. "We were… we were… Then he collapsed!" Jacquetta gripped the glass tightly, wondering if there might still be a chance for her to drink the contents discreetly.

Thane flicked his disinterested gaze over the young lord's hunched form. "At the rate he was drinking this evening, it's a miracle he remained on his feet as long as he did."

Jacquetta's eyes flared. A quarter second later, her mouth dropped open. "I… You were watching him. Us? Why?" She let her lower lip quiver. She had a role to play—he'd surprised her, but Jacquetta had a reputation among the *ton* for being sharp-witted and strong-willed.

He shrugged nonchalantly. "I am observant."

Her eyes narrowed. "It is hardly appropriate to stare, Mr. Thane."

"You do recognize me, then."

"I have an excellent memory for faces." That was true. It was the first and most natural tool in her arsenal. She could remember a page after seeing it once or recall the details of a painting on the wall where she'd taken tea a week ago. The skill had aided her work again and again over the past two years.

Grayson Thane's face had changed markedly over the past several years, but the remnants of the young man were there. The softness of his cheeks had sharpened, pulled taut by his muscled neck. His dark hair was shorter now, but still long enough that Jacquetta could easily thread her fingers through it.

That was a professional appraisal, she assured herself. She might need to use her womanly wiles on Thane before this quest was over.

His eyes were darker, cast in shadow beneath heavy, ridged eyebrows. And a scar snaked through his left eyebrow. A handsome man, to be sure. But a dangerous one.

"I am surprised you remember me, however," she said.

"I didn't."

Irritation flared inside her chest. "Charming."

"But you have certainly made an impression tonight, Jacquetta."

He did not mispronounce her name. It slipped off his tongue with quicksilver ease.

She squashed the trill of appreciation that rose in her chest and instead inclined her head sharply. "I do not recall giving you leave to use my Christian name."

"You did not seem to mind Lord Andresen's familiarity." He was stalking closer. A sentence, a step. Moving into position.

Her internal alarms sounded. This man was a predator. But tonight, she was meant to be his prey. So she held her position by the sofa.

"Lord Andresen and I are well acquainted—"

A chuckle. A mirthless bark. "*That* is quite evident."

She did not have to feign annoyance. "Conversely, you and I have never been introduced. And I think I would prefer it remains that way."

"That's a shame." He was less than a yard away from her, separated only by the sofa.

Jacquetta rolled her eyes. "I think I shall recover."

Thane's hand snaked out. Surprise shot through her—what kind of fool would try to pounce with a sofa still between them? But his hand did not reach for her. It landed on the back of the sofa and stroked along the curved edge with feline smoothness.

The room around them quieted suddenly. Thane's gaze was on her, but she could not bring herself to meet it. The intensity of that look combined with the movement of his hand… shocked her. And Jacquetta feared that if she lifted her eyes to his, she would lose track of the situation.

Distantly, as if through a fog, she could hear the mantel clock ticking, reminding her someone would be along to look for her soon. It was time to force Thane to act.

She lifted the glass to her throat and drank down the remaining cognac, savoring its decadent flavor. She was about to be kidnapped. Who knew how long it would be before she drank something so delicious again?

"If you will excuse me, Mr. Thane, I think I'd rather our acquaintance terminated here and now."

His lips curved. The first hint of a smile. "I thought this was going rather well."

"Pffft! A characteristic male misjudgment."

"I suppose that depends on the criteria one is using to judge." His hand reached the end of the sofa, and he stepped to the side of it, directly between Jacquetta and the exit.

Finally.

"I tremble at the thought of hearing your criteria," she said as she turned slightly to set the glass on the low table.

Another laugh from Thane. This one sounded almost genuine. "Why do I think it would take more than that to make you tremble?"

A long, languorous flame climbed up her spine at his words. The timbre of his voice, the slant of his mouth... she knew precisely what he implied. Rather than dwell on the heat it summoned in her, she seized the opportunity.

"This conversation has turned most inappropriate... my father will be most displeased." She made to step past him, but he caught her arm.

His fingers held her lightly. But the slight pressure promised steel.

She would not win against him in a physical confrontation. *That's fine,* Jacquetta reminded herself. Physicality was rarely her chosen weapon.

"You will not have a chance to speak with your father this evening, I'm afraid."

"Take your hand off me," she warned him.

She knew he would not. Could not.

Blazes, this was what she *wanted*. The whole purpose of this charade with Andresen was to draw in Thane and let herself get kidnapped!

But even so, Jacquetta fought every screaming instinct within her to jerk her arm back and flee. Because when she raised her glowing blue-green eyes to meet his, what she saw turned her soul cold.

And the next thing she saw was darkness.

Three days earlier…

"HE'S GOING TO ask you to dance," Marie hissed into her sister's ear.

"Then he shall be disappointed," Jacquetta said, lifting the glass in her hand to her lips.

Ratafia. Disgusting.

She forced herself to swallow down the heavily spiced cordial. But she did not bother to restrain the expression of distaste that ruffled her fine features.

"Your dance card is hardly full." Marie grabbed at the card around her sister's wrist for confirmation, but Jacquetta was faster.

She jerked her hand away, ripped the dance card free with a sharp tug, and shoved it into the half-full glass of ratafia.

Her sister rolled her eyes. "You are the most un-debutante-like debutante I have ever met."

"A compliment, indeed," Jacquetta quipped, a small smile curving her lips. "If you will excuse me, I require a visit to the retiring room—"

The young man her sister had pointed out earlier was nearly done threading his way around the ballroom. But he could not ask her to dance if she was not *there*.

"Coward," her sister said.

"I love you too, Marie."

Jacquetta ignored whatever her elder sister mumbled under her breath and slipped through the doors behind them into the corridor. Even the dimly lit, long hallway was busy with guests. The Duchess of Guilford never failed to attract a veritable army of attendees to her balls. This was precisely why the Lady Knights always chose her events as cover.

Jacquetta strolled down the hallway toward the retiring room, nodding and smiling at the guests she knew. Despite her very recent debut, she knew most of them. Nineteen was rather late to be presented to the queen, but Jacquetta's family was fashionably situated enough to bear the delay. Jacquetta's overly indulgent father hardly blinked when his daughter requested *another year* of delay.

But her mother would allow no further demurring.

Three months ago, Miss Jacquetta Lawson was presented at court before Queen Charlotte—the woman she'd secretly been working for the past two years.

The corridor ended in a T before fanning off into separate hallways. To the left was the ladies' retiring room. To the right was a flight of stairs.

Halfway down the corridor, Jacquetta spotted a buxom redhead in animated conversation. The woman shot her a scathing look of disapproval, which Jacquetta pointedly ignored. Her family had been feuding with the McGoverns for fifteen years. She would not cow under the gaze of their spinster eldest daughter.

She reached the end of the corridor just as another woman was rounding the corner. They both jumped, and Jacquetta's round reticule dropped to the ground and rolled away. The dark-eyed, dark-haired maid in her forest-green uniform curtseyed and mumbled an apology. Jacquetta waved her off and went down the hall to retrieve her reticule from where it had rolled to the foot of the stairs.

One swift glance behind her to ensure no other ladies were

coming or going from the retiring room and she dashed up the stairs.

From there it was easy. Her feet had memorized the steps. Down a hall, one right turn, up another flight of stairs. There was no one to encounter here—these were the Duchess of Guilford's private rooms. All staff were at work below, occupied with the ball. No guests would dare intrude above stairs.

At last, Jacquetta pushed open the door of a stately bedroom. Completely unoccupied. Sheets were draped over the furniture to protect it from dust. She strode through that room to the dressing room door so cleverly disguised to look like a wall panel. And there she met her fellow lady knight.

Miss Jane Jacobson lounged at the round table looking thoroughly bored. She was the youngest of the Lady Knights—plain brown hair, middle height, clever brown eyes often hidden behind spectacles. In her gray gown, she could almost have disappeared into the dim room with its wood-paneled walls and sparsely lit lamps.

"You're late."

Jacquetta slid into the seat on Jane's left. "If I had not escaped when I did, I would have been later still. Wiltshire was aiming for a quadrille."

Jane's brown eyebrows rose. "Wiltshire? You could do worse."

"I could do better."

"The others will be delayed because of you."

"I saw them both on my way up. I am sure they will be along momentarily—"

As if summoned by the discussion, the door opened again and the generously curved redhead from the corridor below stepped into the small room. She grinned at Jacquetta.

"Your scathing looks have turned positively savage, Red." Jacquetta batted at the other woman's skirt as she swished past to take the seat on Jane's other side. Two seats remained vacant.

Red's grin simmered down to a smirk. "My mother was

watching. I had to make it convincing."

Decades ago, Jacquetta and Ethelreda's mothers had been best friends. Like sisters. Before the falling-out that split their families asunder. Unfortunately for Jacquetta and Red, *after* their mothers had graced them with hideously medieval matching names.

"Is there anything to drink in here?" Red turned and scanned the room behind her. There was a sideboard, but as always, it was empty.

Jacquetta reached into the extra pocket sewn into her gown. She tossed the flask across the table. "I came prepared."

"Capital!" Red twisted the cap free and sniffed. "Cognac? Are you a sixty-year-old man or a twenty-year-old debutante?"

"Nineteen-year-old debutante," Jacquetta corrected her with a shrug.

Red rolled her eyes and took a sip, wincing at the taste. She held the flask out to Jane, who shook her head.

"You might want to rethink that, dear. My mother had just cornered the duchess when I left. We may be waiting a while yet," Red advised.

But quiet, observant Jane shook her head slightly and turned her eyes back to the door, which opened once again.

The maid swept in—the one who'd nearly knocked Jacquetta on her arse.

Dominique stalked into the room with none of the reticence befitting her outfit. Jacquetta could see her fingers contracting and then relaxing, itching to rip off the tightly pinned white cap on her head.

"Chafing a bit tonight, are we?" Jacquetta bit her lower lip to stifle her chuckle.

Dominique's eyes were daggers when she turned them on her friend. "I have worn many costumes. But of all the maids I've portrayed, the duchess has the most annoyingly exacting uniform protocols." Such as the tightly bound hair. "This cap is attached with no less than fifteen pins," she huffed as she dropped into the chair beside Jacquetta.

Leaving one chair empty—the one closest to the door.

"Drink?" Red offered helpfully, holding up the flask.

Dominique considered but ultimately jerked her head in negation. Red passed the flask back to Jacquetta. It was noticeably lighter in her hand as she accepted it.

Jacquetta observed her friends quietly as she lifted the flask to her lips. The smooth, expensive cognac slipped down her throat as she considered them. Her fellow Lady Knights.

Hand-picked.

Clever.

Razor-sharp instincts.

Lethal when required.

"I was supposed to be in York," Dominique was saying. "But then the invitation came and I had to ride hell for leather to make it here in time."

"Any inkling why we've been summoned so urgently?" Red licked her lips, her excitement barely leashed.

"You shall find out presently," Jane said with that uncanny sense, not ten seconds before the door to the dressing room opened for the final time.

The Duchess of Guilford herself stepped inside, closing the door behind her with an audible *click*. She did not bother to lock it; if someone made it to the door despite all of their precautions, the Lady Knights would rather they come bursting in and identify themselves than lurk outside.

The forty and four duchess's dark hair was liberally threaded with sparkling silver. She played up the effect by adorning every part of her in sparkling diamonds and dressing in gossamer that shimmered when she moved. She was beautiful and terrifying— to most of the *ton*.

But when she lowered herself to the last vacant seat, she was another lady knight at Queen Charlotte's round table. Valued. Respected. Equal.

"Red."

Despite the bit about equality, Ethelreda's spine straightened noticeably.

"Your mother is insufferable." The duchess shook her head and released a long, exasperated exhale. "Pass me that flask." She held her hand out expectantly to Jacquetta.

Jacquetta reached into her pocket with a sly smile and passed it over to her. The duchess took a hearty drink, shook it to see how much was left, and then tipped it back to finish off the last swig of cognac.

"Your father has fine taste," she said as she handed it back to Jacquetta.

"We have a shared love." Jacquetta grinned. "My sister will be looking for me soon. Why are we here, Matilda?"

The duchess—Matilda—shrugged her thin shoulders. "I do not know. I was not the one who called this meeting."

"I was," Jane said quietly.

All eyes shifted to her. Jacquetta chuckled silently. *Of course.* Jane had been here first, waiting. She'd been very quiet—though she was quiet by nature. But tonight she'd been even quieter than usual.

It was an important reminder, Jacquetta told herself. Not to make assumptions, to look for the anomalies. Around her, she could see her fellow Lady Knights coming to the same conclusions.

Dominique's arms were folded, her eyes cross. She now knew precisely who to blame for her uncomfortable attire. "Let's have it."

"Grayson Thane is back in London," Jane said.

Jacquetta leaned forward across the table eagerly, her excitement unchecked. "When?"

"I am not certain when he arrived. I heard my father speaking about it two nights ago," Jane elaborated.

"Where will he be? I can make an excuse to my father—"

"That is only if the Crown still wishes to pursue him," Jane stated calmly. Always the judicious one among them.

Jacquetta's eyes went to Matilda. The duchess was their conduit to the queen. The one who had first recruited them, called them together, sat them around this nondescript round table in a hidden dressing room to ask them to serve their queen in the most thrilling and dangerous way.

Matilda's mouth was tight as she spoke, her face pinched. "They do. The man he works for is very dangerous. Agents of the Crown have been trying—and failing—to identify the scoundrel for three years. To no avail. Which is how this matter ended up in the middle of *our* table."

Excitement was thrumming through Jacquetta's veins. Thane had been in her periphery for months. Now he was finally moving into place. She would finally have her chance.

She turned back to Jane. "Where?"

"Lady Brothwilde's country party, in Exeter."

"What's the plan?"

Jane and Matilda exchanged a hesitant look. Jacquetta tried to tamp down her annoyance.

"You don't think I can handle it," she said stonily.

Red rolled her eyes so emphatically that the others practically heard it. "Don't get so defensive, Jacquetta."

Jacquetta ignored her. "Whatever it is, I can manage. I have been waiting for my chance at him."

"Even captivity?" Jane said softly.

Jacquetta shifted her eyes between Jane and Matilda and then back again. She swallowed hard. No fear... but consideration entered her eyes. "I am to be his captive?"

"*If* we decide to go forward with this, we put it out that you've stumbled upon the secret of Thane's falling-out with his family all those years ago," Matilda began.

"And that is somehow related to his master?" Jacquetta said.

"Our sources say yes."

"Then what?"

"Then he will take you."

"As in... he will kidnap me?"

"On behalf of his employer, to protect said employer."

Jacquetta leaned back in her seat, considering. "My quest, then, is to remain in his dubious clutches long enough to find out the identity of his mysterious employer."

Matilda nodded sharply.

"And not get yourself killed in the process," Red inserted unhelpfully.

Jacquetta picked up the discarded flask from the round table and jiggled it, shaking her head in disappointment when it proved to be completely empty.

She flicked her eyes over to Dominique, who was tugging at her cap. "If I am to break free of his prison, I shall need you to teach me a thing or two about picking locks."

Dominique's hands fell away from her cap, her fingers already itching with eagerness. "It will be my pleasure."

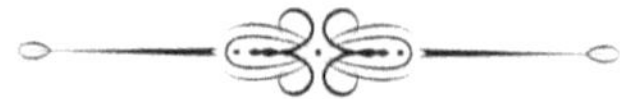

CHAPTER TWO

MISS JACQUETTA LAWSON slumped forward into his arms instantly. Two pressure points applied simultaneously with his thumb and index finger had felled her in seconds.

Grayson suppressed a snort and eased her back into a chair a few steps away.

He'd been sorely tempted to drop the saucy chit onto the thick carpet of Lady Brothwilde's study. But a head injury was not part of his plan. He'd been instructed to bring her to Delaurier whole. Damaged goods were more difficult to barter. And this woman was of particular importance to both Grayson and his master.

Grayson stepped around the young woman's sprawled legs to get a closer look at the gentleman slumped over the leather sofa. An empty glass of brandy was abandoned on the table.

"Amateur," Grayson said under his breath.

The pup had practically been drooling over Jacquetta by the time she led him through the manor's winding halls to the study. She had led him—that had been very clear to Grayson. He'd had very little time to gather intelligence about Jacquetta Lawson, but what he had learned was that she was no wilting wallflower.

Good. He would waste less time reviving her. Smelling salts were in short supply where they were going. Though Grayson did think he'd enjoy tossing a pail of cold water over her.

He gave the hunched young man one last look and then dismissed him entirely.

Lord Andresen had been drinking heavily all evening; it was no surprise that he was unconscious before supper was served. The timing was deuced convenient, though. It spared Grayson from having to make a bigger scene than necessary. It would also provide sufficient cover for his next course of action—removing Jacquetta Lawson from the premises.

First, he needed to be sure she was fully unconscious.

Stepping back to the woman's side, he reached for the wrist nearest to him, draped awkwardly over the arm of the chair. Jacquetta wore elbow-length white silk gloves, like every other respectable debutante in attendance. Unlike every other respectable debutante, she had led a young man away for a private tryst. Grayson did not allow himself to wonder how many other men she'd entertained in such a fashion. It was immaterial to his purpose.

He lifted her wrist, holding it high above her head. He did allow himself a moment to examine the embossed gold armlet she wore an inch above the edge of her glove. It was pretty. Then he dropped her arm. It plunked against the chair unceremoniously.

She was well and truly unconscious.

He doubted she carried any weapons—why would she?—but Grayson ran a quick, professional touch over her bodice and down her legs. Still, she did not move. If she'd been feigning, that would have been the moment he knew. Even a woman with a penchant for secret liaisons would not be able to hold still while a stranger touched her so intimately.

But there was nothing intimate about it, Grayson reminded himself. If she had taken some foolhardy notion to carry a penknife in her stocking, it could mean injury to himself or one of his men. He could not have that.

No weapons. What about a reticule?

Grayson glanced around the study, but saw nothing out of

place. If she had one, she did not bring it into the study with her.

There was nothing else to be done, then.

Grayson bent over, secured his broad hands around her waist, and hoisted Jacquetta over his shoulder like nothing more than a sack of flour.

A heavy sack of flour.

What else was he expecting? He'd had his hands all over her less than a minute before. He knew just how full the curves were beneath that blue gown she was wearing. Had he noticed the wider-than-average hips, or the fullness of her calves? Only insomuch as it was professionally necessary. He did need to calculate how far he could carry her before resting, of course.

Enough dallying.

Grayson covered the space to the door in three long strides. He paused inside, waiting and listening. In the time he'd watched the door from outside, three servants had walked by. None of the guests. There was no pattern to the servants, or at least, not one he'd been able to deduce in the ten minutes he'd watched the door.

Time was not on his side. Eventually, someone would come looking for Jacquetta. He would have to risk being caught. Dispatching a servant would be an unfortunate turn of events, but it might be unavoidable.

Hearing no sound, Grayson nudged the door open. No footsteps, no startled gasps. As good as he was likely to get. He pushed the door the rest of the way open and stepped into the hall, mindful not to bash Jacquetta's head on the door as he eased it closed behind him.

The study was near the back of the house. Jacquetta had done him a favor by choosing this particular room for her rendezvous. He could avoid the partygoers entirely. The main concern was the servants, and a country estate in the middle of a house party was teeming with them.

The hallway he currently strode down connected the two main arteries of the manor. Grayson needed to get the hell out of it. There were doors on either side, leading to various rooms and cellars. Through the door directly ahead of him was the servants' stairwell. He'd gleaned as much from watching.

But the stairwell was not his aim. Much too busy.

As if in answer to his thought, the door began to swing outward.

Grayson bit back the curse on his lips and broke into a jog. He shoved himself and Jacquetta into the door directly to the left of the half-open one a second before the servant behind the door emerged from the stairwell.

The door closed behind him with a thud, but Grayson did not have time to waste wondering if the servant now in the hallway noticed or wondered at it. They were in Lady Brothwilde's morning room, situated on the east side of the manor to take full advantage of the morning sun—and conveniently located on the opposite end of the manor from the curling gravel drive.

Grayson navigated the dark room with ease. The furniture was exactly as the young footman had described. Said footman was now unconscious in a rented room above Exeter's seediest tavern, but he would have no long-term ill effects. A headache when he roused, surely. But the lad would likely attribute that to the excess of spirits rather than the man he'd been drinking with.

A cool April breeze drifted past Grayson's face.

There—in the corner was the window that did not quite close, exactly as the footman had said. It was set to be mended next week. But today, it was Grayson's escape route.

He shifted his weight, tightened his grip around Jacquetta's waist, and used his other hand to lever the window open. It creaked noisily, but did not stick in its frame.

Grayson hefted himself up onto the sill, Jacquetta still over his shoulder. He needed to clear the building, then he could rest in the shadows below the house for a few seconds to catch his breath. Seconds only. It was all he could spare. He was strong and had carried much heavier loads than Jacquetta Lawson. He'd manage fine.

The burning motivation would carry him through. No quest had ever been as important as this one. He would get away with Jacquetta. Grayson would accept no other possibility—not after the torture of the last five years.

He shifted on the sill, preparing to jump, when sounds began to flood in from the hallway.

A woman screamed. A rush of footsteps followed.

Someone had discovered Lord Andresen.

Grayson didn't hesitate. He flung himself the six feet to the ground, clutching Jacquetta to him. He hit the grass and stilled only long enough to ensure she was still firmly situated on his shoulder. Then he sprinted into the night.

JACQUETTA AWOKE TO utter darkness.

Where was she, that they'd managed to so effectively blot out all light? Thane must have taken her very deep into the country. Or was still taking her. For that was the rocking of a carriage or wagon of some kind.

She moved her legs, trying to straighten them out. She was sitting on the floor, wrists and ankles bound. She shifted to the side, expecting a carriage seat, and promptly fell over.

Wagon, then.

But Jacquetta's face did not scrape against the wood of the wagon bed, though her arm did. A shiver snaked down her spine as she realized—there was a hood over her head. That was why it was so dark.

Without realizing it, Grayson Thane had deprived Jacquetta of her most unique gift.

He knew exactly what he was doing, Jacquetta reminded herself. He was a professional, as was she. The first logical thing to do after kidnapping someone—beyond restraining them, which he'd obviously seen to—was to ensure they could not escape. If Jacquetta could not see where she was, she could hardly deduce a route to safety.

Not that she intended to escape. Not yet.

Jacquetta forced herself to think back to the night before at Lady Brothwilde's country party. *Was it last night?* Jacquetta realized she had no actual notion of how much time had passed.

She took a moment to steady herself.

One moment Thane had been standing before her, the next her world had gone dark. He could not have drugged the drink. So it must have been a pressure point, then. Jacquetta had never mastered that technique for rendering someone unconscious herself; she lacked the brute strength to accomplish it in a timely manner.

Jacquetta did a slow perusal of her body. There was no need to rush. She'd be Thane's prisoner for the foreseeable future, and small details might very well be essential to her escape when the time did come.

Her ankles and wrists were bound. Still on her side, Jacquetta wriggled a bit to test the bindings. Rope of some kind, taut and strong, but tied with enough looseness to allow her to move around. But not to run, of course.

Digging an elbow into the rough wood of the wagon bed, she shoved herself up into a sitting position. From the swish of fabric against her legs, Jacquetta could surmise she wore the same gown she'd arrived at Lady Brothwilde's manor in. That was a particular stroke of luck—her mind went to the secrets embedded in her very wardrobe, and her stomach calmed that little bit more.

On cue, Jacquetta's stomach rumbled hungrily. *That* was her best indication of how long she had been Thane's captive. She'd eaten a hearty meal before leaving her hotel in Exeter. She was hungry now, but not ravenous. Nowhere near dizzy. Less than a day, then. Perhaps midday, sometime twelve to eighteen hours after she'd been taken.

Jacquetta wrinkled her nose and reached up to tug at the

hood over her face. Her fingers found the lacing—tied into a tight knot. She bit her lip to keep from growling in annoyance. She'd need a blade to cut it loose. While there was a penknife secreted in the boning of her stays, it would stay hidden until she needed it direly. Suddenly getting herself free of the hood would certainly shatter the illusion of her as the innocent debutante captive.

Despite the hood, Thane's dark eyes flashed in her memory. A simpering debutante would not last a moment in that man's clutches. How much had he seen with those eyes?

Grayson Thane was nothing like the young man she'd watched from afar in her youth. How could he be? He'd been separated from his family for five years. Although her supposed knowledge of the details of that scandal was the bait with which she'd set her snare, the Lady Knights actually knew very little about his activities since leaving London all those years ago.

Jacquetta sifted through the details the Duchess of Guilford had provided her in preparation for this quest.

Thane had been in London fewer than a handful of times over the last five years. But when he did appear, his behaviors followed a predictable pattern. He would arrive in London suddenly. Where from? The Crown's agents had never been able to deduce. Thane would take up a room at a fashionable hotel, stay for a month or two, and then disappear again for months on end—once, they'd lost track of him for an entire year. He never had any contact with his family. He had no known friends or associates.

The agents of the Crown had also never been able to catch Thane doing anything explicitly illegal.

In the darkness of her hood, Jacquetta rolled her eyes.

If the Lady Knights had been tasked with this matter earlier, it would have already been resolved. Thane was not the true target—it was his master who interested Bow Street. But they'd been trying and failing to identify the villain for five years.

Jacquetta would not fail. She'd never failed to achieve her goal on a single quest in the last two and a half years. She certainly would not begin now.

The Lady Knights meant more to her than her own family.

Perhaps that was a bit harsh. They meant *as much* to her as her own family.

Before the Duchess of Guilford slipped that invitation into her reticule at Marie's at-home almost three years ago, Jacquetta had been adrift. Nearing her debut, but nothing like the other debutantes: strikingly beautiful, likely to be named an incomparable, but utterly uninterested in dancing and courtship.

The Lady Knights were her sisters, her home, her destiny. She would not fail in her quest, no matter the cost.

The wagon wheel lodged in a deep divot and lurched mightily, sending Jacquetta tumbling sideways.

She gritted her teeth, her abdominal muscles protesting as she righted herself once again. Perhaps there was something in the wagon she could lodge herself against…

She rejected the thought instantly. While Jacquetta had no notion of when they would stop the wagon, she did not intend to be floundering around trying to explore the inside of the wagon when they did.

She probably ought to be lying on her side sobbing. Jacquetta stifled a groan at the thought.

She doubted she would last long playing the guileless debutante. Thane had kidnapped her mid-tryst. From the way those dark eyes had flashed at her, she doubted they missed much.

Perhaps she would be wise to let some of her spice and verve show through. If anything, it would make maintaining the authenticity of her ruse more sustainable.

She would think on that, Jacquetta decided. The wagon was hobbling along at a steady pace, but certainly not rushed or brisk. Which implied she would have plenty of time to herself to muse. In her dark hood. While her arse got progressively more bruised with every bump in the road.

Her stomach rumbled again.

Hopefully the brigand would feed her soon.

Jacquetta leaned back against the side of the wagon and began to recite the first verse of *Paradise Lost*.

She'd made it through most of Book I when the wagon lurched to an unsteady stop. She did not stop her silent litany, not yet. This might just be another hitch in the road, and she needed to know how much time was passing. She could recite twenty lines in a minute. Forty minutes to finish reciting Book I. Just under an hour for Book II.

The duchess had insisted each of the Lady Knights have a way of tracking the time without a timepiece. *Paradise Lost* had been Jacquetta's own selection. The even rhythm of it made recitation and timing easy.

Jane had chosen a symphony. Of course she had. The youngest lady knight might be quiet, but her mind was sharper than Red's rapier.

At once with joy and fear his heart rebounds…

The words died on Jacquetta's lips as the door at the back of the wagon was flung open.

She kept her body rigidly still, not allowing herself to turn toward the sound. No light leaked through the hood; whatever it was made of, the material was thick and truly obscured her vision.

But his voice… she'd recognize it anywhere.

"Pretending to be asleep is tiresome, Jacquetta."

She bit her lip, considering. "As is the hood, yet you seem to think it necessary."

"It will be removed once we reach our destination."

She did not like talking to a disembodied voice, she decided. Jacquetta could glean Thane's direction—at the threshold of the wagon—and hear the heavy breathing of his companions—two, by her estimation. She could not assess their size, affect, or weapons. But if Thane thought to disorient her, he had another think coming.

Time was on her side.

"I hope that will be soon. I am hungry." Jacquetta's stomach rumbled agreement.

She was being brash, but it was a calculated choice—one she'd made somewhere around line five hundred of *Paradise Lost*. If Thane knew anything about her, he would expect the sass. She, therefore, must deliver.

"Soon enough." Thane sounded vaguely amused. He saw through her attempts to goad him into revealing details of their destination.

But she tried again—not because she expected him to reveal his plans, but because he likely expected her to press him. "Where are you taking me?"

"You will see."

"My father will pay a ransom." He would not. Her father's butler was in the employ of the Duchess of Guilford. Any ransom note would be intercepted and passed along to the Lady Knights.

Thane chuckled, a dry, mirthless sound. "Ransom does not concern me, or my employer. Not yet."

"So you will ransom me when it is most convenient for you? What does this master of yours have up his sleeve?"

"Employer," Thane corrected her, voice tightening slightly.

Interesting. She filed that away in her mind to be examined more closely later.

"Let me go, Thane." She allowed her voice to wobble, just a fraction. She wanted him to think her vulnerable, her bravado flailing.

But there was no quarter in his voice, no sympathy as he said, "I cannot."

Despite her years of training and experience, Jacquetta felt a shard of uneasiness lodge itself into her brain. She determinedly ignored it.

"I knew you were a villain, Thane, but kidnapping a defenseless woman … No wonder your family tossed you out on your arse," she threw out brashly.

One of his companions grunted. The other breathed in sharply through his nose.

"I shall think on that." His voice dripped with icy bitterness so cold, so harsh, that even Jacquetta's seasoned bones tremored within her.

Danger, her instincts flared.

She opened her mouth to soften the words—

Thane slammed the door of the wagon closed with such force that the walls around her shook. She heard a shuffle of retreating footsteps, a horse's soft nicker, and then the wagon lurched into motion once more.

No food, then.

Jacquetta stuck out her tongue at the closed door, though no one could see it.

CHAPTER THREE

"T HE MOUTH ON that one." Rook shook his head, a low whistle slipping from his pursed mouth.

"The chit has a death wish," Grayson ground out, swinging aboard his horse.

"Too bad you have to keep your hands to yourself." Rook winked as he mounted up as well.

Winked—as if this whole endeavor was a jape. Grayson bristled and kicked his horse forward. Rook did not take the hint. He steered his mount alongside Grayson's while the wagon lurched into motion behind them.

Grayson flicked his gaze backward—just long enough to ensure his men had taken up their flanking positions behind the wagon—then turned forward. He ignored the man at his side.

"She's going to make for an interesting voyage," Rook pushed.

Grayson gritted his teeth.

"You'll have to keep a close eye on the men, if you want her to arrive intact. I am happy to volunteer myself as Miss Lawson's personal guard—"

"She does not need a guard," Grayson snapped. He gripped the reins tighter, hating that he'd allowed Rook to bait him.

"You cannot keep a sack over her head indefinitely. The chaps are bound to realize she's a looker eventually," Rook continued, undaunted. The expression on his face said that he had already noticed.

Grayson's gut clenched. Not with jealousy—Christ, no. Rook could have at the chit, if she reciprocated his interest.

No, that clench of unease was fear and protectiveness. Not hope. Never hope. Grayson had stopped allowing himself to hope years ago.

But Jacquetta Lawson must be protected at all costs. She was a valuable prisoner. When she was delivered to Delaurier, Grayson would finally be free.

He did not allow himself to think about that freedom and what he might do with it. Not yet. Once they were truly on their way, with no chance of the chit escaping or being snatched away, perhaps then…

Grayson turned and checked the guard perimeter again.

It was just past midday. He'd have preferred to travel only by night, but he'd surrendered stealth in favor of speed. They would reach their destination just after nightfall, barring any incidents. The only stops would be to feed and water the horses. As for Jacquetta—Grayson was tempted to let her go without.

"We ought to give her a canteen of water at least," Rook said casually, following the direction of Grayson's gaze.

He was looking at the wagon without realizing it.

Grayson straightened immediately and fixed his eyes on the deserted forest road ahead.

"I can give her mine," Rook suggested, a bit more of an edge in his voice.

"Do what you want," Grayson said tightly.

Rook snorted at that. "I always do," he assured Grayson.

"To my never-ending chagrin."

"I would hate for you to become bored in your old age," Rook shot back.

"I am only a year older than you," Grayson reminded him drolly.

"And grumpy as an octogenarian."

Grayson's eyebrows shot up. "And where did you learn that one?"

Rook shrugged. "I read."

Grayson gave the other man a sidelong look but did not comment. Rook *did* read. The man always had a book to hand—to the eternal amusement of their companions. Many of the men did not know much more than their alphabet and how to spell their own names.

"Perhaps Miss Lawson is a bluestocking," Rook mused. "It will be a welcome change to converse with someone other than those muttonheads." He shrugged at the guard of mounted men around them.

"You can talk her ear off, so long as the rest of her remains whole." It would spare Grayson from Rook's antics, at least.

"Ah, but the rest of her appears to be equally compelling."

Grayson could not miss the implication in Rook's voice. There was the tight clenching in his stomach, yet again. Soon, he promised himself. Soon he would be able to relax.

"You knew her… before, yes?" Rook said carefully.

Grayson stiffened, the tension in his stomach gripping his entire body. "She is a debutante. An incomparable. And from the five minutes I spent with her while she was conscious, she's a spoiled, brazen chit. You'd do well to keep your distance, Rook."

Grayson listened to Rook's slow, steady exhale beside him. But he'd known the man for five long years. This was far from the end of it.

"And where shall you keep her, when we arrive?" Rook said a few minutes later.

The barest hint of a smile tugged at the corner of Grayson's mouth. "I have a few ideas," he said wickedly enough that Rook hooted with laughter.

THE BASTARD NEVER fed her.

Jacquetta needn't have bothered with reciting verses of epic poetry. Her hunger alone would have been enough to tell her how long had passed since she'd been unceremoniously shoved into the back of a wagon. Twenty-four hours. A full day. Or very near to it. Jacquetta had no doubt that if the odious hood over her head was removed, she would be met with the dark of night.

At least someone had seen fit to give her a canteen of water. At some point in the afternoon, the wagon had stopped for a few minutes. She'd braced herself for another encounter with Thane, but the footsteps that came to the back of the wagon were lighter, the breathing relaxed rather than ragged.

"Drink, my lady," was all the man said as he shoved the canteen into her still-bound hands and then closed the wagon door behind him. But Jacquetta thought she heard a trace of humor on those words, few as they were.

She did not bother correcting him that she was a "miss" rather than a "lady." It hardly mattered how her captors addressed her. Perhaps if they thought her truly a lady, they would be inclined to treat her better.

It took a fair bit of maneuvering to get the mouth of the canteen beneath her hood. The knots at the base of the hood were very secure. But there was enough slack to get the canteen under the edge and her mouth down—though not nearly enough to get the blasted fabric up over her head entirely.

Then she'd fallen back on her shoulder and dumped half the canteen's contents all over herself while attempting to get a drink… In that moment, at least, Jacquetta had been thankful for the dark to hide her embarrassment.

She recited verse after verse of *Paradise Lost*, keeping track of her benchmarks throughout the poem to determine how much time had passed. She'd tried listening to the sounds around her as they moved down the road—she could only assume it was a road, based on the moderately smooth wagon ride—but after a while, even her sharp senses dulled to the monotony.

A sharp yell roused Jacquetta from her delirium.

Christ, where was she?

Even as she internally chastised herself for nodding off, she felt the words of the poem sliding off her lips. She took a slow, deep breath. Thank the Lord for the rigors of her training. She had not actually fallen asleep.

The yell was the harbinger of a cacophony of noise.

Jacquetta's eyes flew from side to side, tracking noises even though she could not see them with the blasted hood. She was sure it was dark outside, and she was in a wagon. But maybe the wagon had cracks she might peer through…

It did not matter, she admonished herself. *Listen.*

Another yell—this one drunken. Not the first voice, which had been a greeting.

"Pay up what ye owe, or I'll toss ye in the water!"

"I'll not let ye filch—"

A tavern brawl, from the sounds of it. Not one that catered to the nobility, either. But if they were in a carriage town, the two would be more intermingled. If they were in a larger city, it would speak to different neighborhoods.

The wagon rumbled down the street, the sound beneath the wheels shifting. Cobblestones, rather than dirt. So, a larger city, then. Where could they be? Jacquetta summoned an image of a map to her mind, creating a radius of where she could be based on how long they had been traveling.

One of the tavern brawlers had mentioned water. Had they reached the Lake Country already? Perhaps they'd headed toward Dover, if they intended to take her across the channel.

Jacquetta dismissed that idea. Grayson Thane always followed a predictable pattern: arrive in England, loiter for a month or two, then disappear. He'd only been spotted a week ago. Ergo, he still had several weeks before he would disappear, presumably overseas.

The River Avon was a possibility. It ran through Bath.

Jacquetta shifted, pressing her ear to the side of the wagon.

Through her hood, she could feel the cracks between the wood slats. So, it was a worn or poorly constructed conveyance. Hence, the importance of the hood. Otherwise, she would have been able to note too many details about her surroundings.

A spark of interest lit in the back of her mind—Thane was thorough and clever, she'd give him that. But she was cleverer. She was a lady knight.

The wagon jerked to the right and Jacquetta had to throw herself sideways to avoid toppling over entirely. She'd just settled herself when the wagon lurched to a stop and she was thrown sideways once again.

Her shoulder hit something hard on the floor. Had that been there the whole time? She would have sworn she'd explored every inch of the wagon. But she had no time to investigate. Around her, horses were neighing and man after man hit the ground as they dismounted. Jacquetta tried to count each heavy thump. Five, six, seven—were all of these men escorting her?— eight, nine, ten, eleven.

An icy chill slid down her spine. It was far too many men for her to fight her way out, though that had never been her intention. Her plan was to wait, listen, play the part of chagrined, worried captive, and eventually plot a clever escape.

But eleven men… twelve, with Thane, she realized as his feet hit the ground at the same moment that his voice rang out.

"Secure the cargo," he ordered someone.

Was she the cargo? Jacquetta bristled. So much for the "my lady" of earlier in the day.

But the door of her wagon did not open. Instead, the men started moving around, and she heard the scraping of something heavy. The sound repeated again and again, interspersed with the sound of men grunting. They were unloading something, she realized. Had there been another wagon traveling with them? Jacquetta hadn't heard it, which made her uneasy. Either she'd missed it, or they'd joined up with it now.

Where was the cargo being unloaded to?

She didn't have another moment to wonder. Thane's unmistakable steps approached the wagon, and a few seconds later, the door was thrown open with a loud creak.

"We've arrived," Thane said gruffly.

"Where, precisely?" Jacquetta said primly, letting no hint of fear show in her voice.

"You shall find out soon enough." He sounded vaguely irritated. "Let's go."

She did not move.

"Go where?" she insisted.

"Out."

"Out of?"

"Get out of the damn carriage," Thane spat. The irritation in his voice was no longer vague.

There was a slight shuffling of feet. "If you take my hand, my lady, I will help you down." It was the same voice that had offered her the canteen. It was tighter than before. Probably because Thane was there with his black-hearted glare, Jacquetta guessed.

Still, she did not move.

"Enough of this," Thane snarled.

Jacquetta felt Thane shove the other man aside, and the carriage rocked as he did. She shifted back, but, bound at her wrists and ankles, she was too slow. Thane climbed into the wagon and touched his fingers to her neck. Jacquetta's last thought before she succumbed to darkness was that the next time he got that close to her, she'd shove her dagger between his ribs.

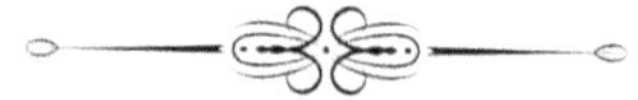

CHAPTER FOUR

THE COOL SPRING mist on her face was pleasant. It had been an unseasonably warm spring in London, but this was perfection. Jacquetta felt it bead in her hair, the droplets an enjoyable trickle as they slid down her neck.

But Exeter had been cooler than London. Someone had put a cloak around her shoulders before depositing her in the wagon. The wagon…

Jacquetta jolted awake for the second time in as many days. The bright white sky assaulted her eyes violently. Jacquetta slammed them shut.

Sky. She'd seen the sky.

Which meant she no longer wore the hood. She could feel the cool mist on her face. Not cool, cold. In her haze of dreams, it had summoned the spring mists of London. But now, it was chill. A shiver shook her. Perhaps they were indeed in the Lake Country, shrouded in cold mist even in late April.

Then the ground swayed.

Not the ground, Jacquetta realized as the crash of waves hit her ears. The deck.

She was aboard a ship.

Jesus, Mary, and Joseph, save me.

Her head was spinning. She was going to be ill. Not from the sway of the ship, but from terror.

Anything but a ship.

The mind is its own place, and in it self
Can make a Heav'n of Hell, a Hell of Heav'n.

Jacquetta bit her lip in irritation. Epic poetry would be of no help in her current situation.

She must get a hold of her terror.

You cannot think clearly if you are consumed by fear, the Duchess of Guilford's voice echoed in her mind. *You need not dismiss your fear, only master it for as long as is necessary to complete your quest.*

She was on a bloody ship. How the hell was she to master her fear when there was water in every damned direction?

Jacquetta could not bring herself to open her eyes. Not yet.

She forced herself to summon up the breathing exercises Jane had taught her. Calm, cool, collected Jane, who was never ruffled by anything. She wouldn't have flinched an inch, no matter where she woke up.

She also was not the one selected for this quest, a small voice in Jacquetta's head reminded her. The Duchess of Guilford always chose the right lady knight for the quest.

She could do this.

Jacquetta started at her toes. She wore the same dainty silk slippers she'd been wearing at Lady Brothwilde's party. She would have preferred sturdier walking boots, but it would have ruined her illusion as a frivolous debutante.

Eyes still closed, she wiggled her toes. Her stockings were dry.

If her slippers and stockings were still dry, it meant the powders secreted in the cushioning of the heels were still dry as well. In the left heel, the same powder she'd used to render Lord Andresen unconscious in Lady Brothwilde's study. In the right heel... well, that powder was decidedly less temporary. She had used it just once before. And she would use it again if necessary.

Jacquetta shivered slightly.

Her legs shook—they were unbound!

Jacquetta's attention went immediately to her hands, and she lifted them hopefully.

That was where her good fortune ended, apparently. Her hands were still shackled. Though it was no longer the tight burn of rope against her wrists, but the cold kiss of metal.

He'd chained her. The bloody arse had chained her to—

"You have finally deigned to wake up, I see."

Jacquetta's eyes flew open. She blinked against the brightness. For a moment, she was so blinded by her anger she almost forgot her fear.

Then a gull squawked overhead.

She fisted her hands so tightly her nails cut into her palms. She did not allow her eyes to close again, just as she did not allow the fear to shine in them. If Thane knew of her weakness, he would surely exploit it. She may be his prisoner, but she would not give him the upper hand.

She fixed Grayson Thane with a stare as cold as the mist that had awoken her moments before.

"Perhaps if I had been allowed a natural sleep, I would have roused earlier," she bit out.

He shrugged nonchalantly. At his side, a half step behind, a middle-height man with fair hair offered her a half-smile.

Jacquetta ignored him.

"If you are more amenable to my orders, I will not have to resort to harsher methods." The chill in Thane's voice signaled danger, but Jacquetta silenced the alarm bells in her mind.

"To think, you were once considered a gentleman," she spat.

"And if memory serves, you were a promising young thing. It seems we have both proved disappointments to the *ton*," Thane returned.

She bit out a sharp laugh. "I am perfectly satisfied with my status in life. Can you say the same, Thane?"

His dark eyes flashed. So, he was not fully satisfied with his lot. Did that apathy extend to his master, Jacquetta wondered?

"For a young woman completely at my mercy, your tongue

is remarkably sharp." As if in demonstration, he took a step closer, his dark eyes daring her to try to reach for him.

Jacquetta had not yet tested the length of her chain, but she doubted he would have stepped into her range. Unless he completely underestimated her.

"You've stolen me away from my family and my country. What more do I stand to lose?" she said, the words he expected of her, letting the terror on her face show just a bit.

"So much more, Jacquetta," he said coldly. "So much more."

His dark eyes burned into her with cold fire. She tried to hold his gaze, while her gut screamed at her not to submit. But she was playing a role. She tore her eyes away, as if she could not bear it a moment longer.

She used that glance to sweep her eyes over her surroundings.

The ship was massive. Three masts. She was chained to the one at the center—the mainmast. An oceangoing vessel, then.

Fear roiled through her gut. This was not a mere channel crossing.

Jacquetta swallowed hard, bringing her eyes back to Thane. The ship was a flurry of activity around them, but she was able to make out glints of gold paint.

An Indiaman—the only ships so ornately bedecked. One question remained, then—east or west?

She raised her chin defiantly. "Where are you taking me?"

Thane met her eyes easily. "Far away," he said.

"Why? What could I possibly have done?" She let a slight tremor shake her voice.

The towheaded man beside Thane gave her a sympathetic look. Thane was unmoved.

"It does not matter. You are here now," he said.

"So you'll neither tell me why you've taken me, nor where we are bound," she said, voice sharp.

"An apt summary," Thane agreed.

It was Jacquetta's turn to fix him with an icy stare. She

speared him with her eyes with all the intensity she could muster, let the distaste ooze from her very pores.

"Then kindly," she began, "leave me alone."

She did not wait to see what Thane would do or say. She shoved her legs under her, pushed to her feet, and walked in the opposite direction. Her chain would not allow her more than a yard from the mainmast, but it was enough.

She dropped to the deck, folded her hands in her lap, and gave Grayson Thane her back.

Behind her, someone swore wickedly under their breath.

Jacquetta could not be certain, but her intuition told her it was not Thane's fair-haired companion.

"SHE STILL HAS not had a proper meal," Rook said before slurping the last of his soup directly out of the bowl.

Grayson ignored the poor table manners, though he was a tad more conscious as he lifted his spoon to his own mouth. Soon, he would return to polite society. He hoped his manners had not degraded as noticeably as Rook's.

"Bryce took her some bread," Grayson said, buttering his own slice.

"I say again—"

"There is no need. She shall eat once she is brought in," he said with finality.

Rook clearly wanted to argue further. "When will that be?"

A sharp knock sounded at the door of the cabin in answer.

Rook shot out of his chair, nearly upending it. Grayson raised his eyebrows at the man's antics, but did not offer a comment. One hardly needed eyes to see that Rook was already besotted with their prisoner.

More fool him.

"Enter," Grayson commanded.

One side of the heavy wooden double doors opened to reveal Miss Jacquetta Lawson, hair a mess and cold fire in her turquoise eyes.

Metal cuffs kept her hands locked in front of her, but the look she gave him was as forceful as any blow. Pure, undiluted loathing gleamed.

"Welcome, Jacquetta," he said into the empty space between them.

Her face did not soften. There was no protest that he address her more formally, no question about why she'd been brought to this cabin. Only sullen silence and the hateful glint in her otherwise beautiful eyes.

"Ahem," said the man behind Jacquetta, visible just over her shoulder.

"Thank you for escorting our guest, Williamson. You may go." Grayson watched as the sailor did as he was bidden, closing the cabin door with a heavy thud.

Jacquetta continued to stare down at him with merciless concentration.

Across the table, Rook let out one of his long, low whistles.

Of course, it was Rook who made the first move.

"Please, take my seat, my lady," he said, swiping up his bowl and utensils in one fluid movement. He also somehow managed to work in a bow.

Grayson gritted his teeth in annoyance.

Jacquetta did not move, but she shifted her gaze to Rook. "I have been sitting all day. I would rather stand," she said, voice ringing with haughty superiority.

Before Rook could grovel more, Grayson kicked his chair back and stood. "Unless you intend to eat your supper standing up, you should accept Rook's offer."

Her eyes raked over the half-eaten meal on the table. "Am I to eat your scraps, then? I truly am no better than a dog to you, am I, Thane?"

It had been a very long time since someone spoke to him the

way Jacquetta Lawson seemed to think she was entitled to. None of his men would have dared. Even Rook, who loved to push at his boundaries, knew which lines ought not be crossed. But Jacquetta? She clearly did not give a damn. It made her either incredibly brave or incredibly stupid. Grayson wondered which it would ultimately be.

Another sharp knock sounded over Jacquetta's shoulder. She jumped right out of her skin, Grayson noted with no little satisfaction.

He nodded to Rook, who went to the door immediately. Jacquetta stepped out of his path, but did not try to move any farther into the room.

"Your supper," Grayson said drily as Rook accepted a tray of food and took it to the table, setting it directly across from Grayson's unfinished meal.

No hint of sheepishness danced across Jacquetta's face.

"Please sit, my lady. You must be famished," Rook beseeched her, pulling out the chair he'd vacated earlier.

Her bright eyes darted between Grayson, Rook, and the bowl of steaming soup. Her nostrils flared as the scent of warm bread hit her; that was the moment Grayson knew he had won.

Despite the hunger that surely consumed her, Jacquetta took careful, ladylike steps to the table and sat daintily in the proffered seat. She reached for the cloth napkin and set it in her lap, a model of gentility despite her haggard appearance.

"I cannot eat with my hands bound," she said matter-of-factly, but not to Grayson. No, she was ignoring him entirely. She addressed her statement to Rook.

The poor man could offer her nothing. He could only turn his questioning eyes to Grayson, who was still standing on the other side of the table.

Lord save him, if she could charm all of his men as easily as Rook. The chit hadn't spared a kind word for anyone, and already Rook was in her thrall.

Grayson took four long steps to his desk and yanked open the top drawer. He tossed the key to Rook. "Unlock her."

Rook shot him a grateful glance, which quickly turned sour when he saw Jacquetta rubbing at her sore wrists the instant they were unshackled.

"That will be all, Rook," Grayson said pointedly.

As always, Rook looked poised to argue. But he held it in check, instead turning to Jacquetta.

"I am Rook, my lady. The first mate. Please let me know if I may be of service in any way," he said, bowing deeply.

Her eyes widened slightly, but she only inclined her head.

Forced to accept that and nothing more, Rook made for the door.

"Rook." Grayson's voice froze him with his hand on the handle. "Key."

The look Rook gave him spoke clearly enough, but he tossed the key in Grayson's direction. Grayson caught it as the door closed behind the other man. He slipped it into his pocket and stepped back around the table.

He could feel Jacquetta's eyes upon him, carefully watching every move he made. Grayson dropped into his seat, but did not pick up his spoon. Instead, he reached for the open bottle of wine and filled the glass Rook had set before Jacquetta.

She did not move.

"Drink," he commanded.

"I do not drink claret," she said through pursed lips, blue-green eyes still fixed upon him.

"You will not like the sailors' grog," Grayson advised, lifting his own wine glass to his lips.

Still she did not move.

Except her hands, Grayson realized. She was rotating her wrists slowly in her lap, testing her freedom. A small stab of remorse prickled in his gut. Perhaps the shackles were an extreme precaution. But she was a precious prisoner—the most important cargo his ship had ever carried.

Jacquetta's stomach rumbled loudly. Still she did not move.

She was as stubborn as any man of his acquaintance, Grayson could freely admit.

"Eat," he ordered her.

"How do I know you have not poisoned the soup? Will I eat only to wake in a few hours chained to the mainmast once again?" she snapped, voice ringing with accusation.

"You do not," Grayson said.

He would not waste his energy trying to persuade her. Eventually, she would be hungry enough to eat. Until then, no food would go to waste. Someone on the ship would take her ration, if only the goat sharing the hen coop.

"You're a bastard," Jacquetta bit out.

Grayson shrugged. "I have been called much worse."

"Give me time and I shall come up with more inventive descriptors," she shot back.

"We will be at sea for weeks. I cannot wait to hear what you conjure up."

Her countenance shifted. "Weeks? Not months?"

"Months are made of weeks," he pointed out, enjoying the way her eyes flashed.

"Bastard."

Grayson clucked his tongue. "Not creative at all. Perhaps I should return you to your station at the mainmast. A few days with the sailors will give you a litany of new words to try out on your viper's tongue."

"Your men cannot surprise me. I have heard it all."

Had she? Where? "Not in the salons of London."

Jacquetta's face went completely blank. Intentionally blank. She had secrets. Interesting.

"You do not know me," she said, eyes fierce even as she kept her face otherwise unchanged.

"Nor do I have any desire to," Grayson said coolly. "You are a business transaction."

She did not bristle at that as he'd expected her to. Shockingly, she reached for her spoon instead. He watched closely as she dipped it into her bowl and raised it to her lush coral lips. She took a dainty sip, then a larger one. The pleasure that rippled over her face was tangible—and set Grayson wondering what her face would look like when—

He shoved that thought down, mortified at its very existence. He'd been too long without female company, that was all. He'd hardly been in London long enough to check into a hotel, let alone seek female entertainment. Jacquetta Lawson, with her quivering debutante's lips and status as an incomparable of the *beau monde*—she was most definitely not his preferred flavor.

"Are these the captain's quarters?" Jacquetta asked casually between bites, interrupting Grayson's internal denials.

He cleared his throat and took another sip of wine. "These are my quarters."

"You are the captain?" she said as she reached for her wine glass, sniffing and wrinkling her nose at it. She pulled a face, but took a sip nonetheless.

"I am in charge," he said. "That is all you need to know."

"Pfft," Jacquetta said. But for once in their brief acquaintance, she did not argue or attempt to rile him. She was too busy eating.

Grayson regarded her carefully. He'd been watching her from the quarterdeck for most of the day, of course, but she'd worn the cloak they'd given her draped over her shoulders. Now, Jacquetta wore nothing but her gown, looking much the worse for two days of abuse. The cerulean silk had torn just below the bust, revealing a hint of the white petticoat beneath. The neckline was decorated with elaborate beading, but it had snagged on something, and several rows of iridescent blue beads were missing. Her golden blonde hair was half up, half down, bedraggled strands curling around her bosom.

But even a mess, she was absolutely beautiful. Grayson would have been lying to himself if he supposed anything else. Her turquoise eyes were framed in heavy, dark lashes. An ample bosom pushed against her bodice. He could see her arms now that those silly white silk gloves were disposed of—miles of smooth, golden-hued skin that had him thinking of sunset on sandy beaches.

Christ, I need a woman.

"You are staring, Lord Grayson."

His attention sharpened instantly. "Thane will do."

"Fine. You are staring, Thane," Jacquetta sniped.

"So?"

She looked ready to launch her spoon at him. "It is rude," she said instead.

"What gave you the notion I was anything but?" Grayson said, shifting forward in his seat.

"You do possess manners, however deep they may be buried." She gave him a knowing look, full of challenge.

How did she know he'd just been reflecting on the state of his manners mere minutes ago…?

Jacquetta did not give him time to contemplate. She set aside her spoon, soup finished, and pinned him with a direct gaze.

"You will not tell me where you are taking me or why. Will you tell me what you have planned for me next, now that you've fed me like a pig for slaughter?" she demanded.

She wanted another argument. Grayson could see it in those blazing eyes. Either she truly could not control her temper or she was hoping to bait him into revealing the details she sought.

It was a credible effort, truly. But Grayson had tangled with far more dangerous opponents than Miss Jacquetta Lawson— Delaurier among them.

"Sleep," he said, holding her gaze, undaunted.

She blinked slowly, as if she had misheard him. "Sleep?"

"I thought you might prefer a bed to a wagon."

Jacquetta's eyes darted over his shoulder to the large platform bed positioned below the row of windows.

"Do not get your hopes up," Grayson scoffed mirthlessly.

Her eyes narrowed. "I would rather sleep by the latrines than in that bed with you."

That did earn a real smile from him. "The head."

She shook her head. "The head, what?"

"On a ship, it is called the head. Not a latrine," Grayson clarified. "While I am sure my men would find that endlessly entertaining, I cannot have you distracting them. You will sleep here."

Jacquetta's eyes darted around the room as she assessed the possibilities.

"Why not throw me in a cell and be done with it?" she asked, her voice a hair softer than it had been.

"Because I need you where I can keep watch and assure myself of your welfare," he said truthfully.

"You ought to have thought of my welfare *before* you kidnapped me," she snapped, anger returned in full force.

Grayson raised his hands, palms up, a mock gesture of surrender. "I am simply doing as I am told, Jacquetta."

Her eyes narrowed. "I will not share your bed," she repeated bitterly.

"No, you shall not," he agreed, getting to his feet.

He strode across the cabin and pulled back the curtain that covered half the wall, revealing the narrow berth built there.

"Rook has kindly surrendered his usual bunk for your use."

Jacquetta shifted in her seat so she could see the bed. With a sharp nod, she got to her feet and crossed the cabin.

Grayson towered above it, but her smaller stature allowed her to fold herself into the berth with relative ease. She scooted into the bunk, ducking her head, then lay back. He could have sworn she let out a little moan as her head hit the pillow... but it must have been his imagination, for a second later she said:

"Do you plan to hover all evening?"

Grayson pushed off the top of the bunk and strode back to the dining table, swiping up the shackles.

"We must attend to one last item," he said, as if it were a matter of politeness rather than bondage. Grayson enjoyed the way her turquoise eyes flashed a darker blue.

But Jacquetta managed to keep her temper in check as she

said, "Are those truly necessary? It is a ship. Where am I going to go?"

He scoffed openly. "If I leave you unbound, what is to prevent you from smothering me in my sleep?"

Her face was mutinous, but she held out her wrists. "You may as well put me in the brig," she grumbled.

"I am still considering it," Grayson said evenly as he snapped the locks into place.

The piercing look she gave him promised a deluge of haughty set-downs. But Jacquetta swallowed them. She lay back on the berth and rolled to her side to face the wall, dismissing him as effectively as she had that morning.

Grayson felt the low chuckle rumbling out of his chest. Where had that come from? He had not truly laughed in ages. He rubbed at his chest as he moved toward his desk, where his logbook awaited him.

He sat down and flicked the book open. Across the room, Jacquetta was still as a statue.

"Goodnight, Jack," Grayson murmured.

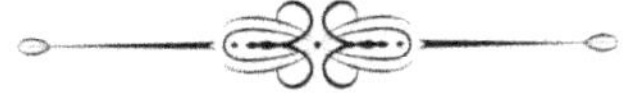

CHAPTER FIVE

ON HER SECOND day at sea, Jacquetta was content to lie in the bunk under the ruse of brooding and quietly observe Thane's rhythms and routines. He did not speak to her, she did not speak to him, and that situation seemed perfect to them both.

On her third day, she selected a book from the shelf built into the wall at the end of her bunk and pretended to read quietly while she watched for any details she may have missed the day before.

On her fourth day, she actually started reading out of utter boredom.

On the fifth day, she picked the lock on her shackles and ransacked Thane's cabin.

She would have liked to ransack it, at least. In reality, she picked through it with mind-numbing slowness. Pick up a book, flip through the pages, return it to exactly where it had been before—mindful not to disturb the dust. She went through the entire bookshelf behind the desk in that manner, finding nothing interesting. Not a single note slipped from between the pages, and there was no hollowed-out core hiding valuables.

Jacquetta straightened, rubbing a cramp out of her back—courtesy of her thorough perusal of the bottom shelf.

"Where do you hide your secrets, Thane?" she mused aloud, eyes sliding over the cabin.

The captain's quarters were large and well-furnished, with personal touches everywhere. Despite what Thane tried not to tell her, it was clear that this was his home. The spines of the books were cracked from use; the aftershave in the top drawer of the desk was his. Whatever services he provided to his master, the majority of his life was spent aboard this ship.

Jacquetta turned back to the desk. She'd searched it first, but it had been rather hasty—by her tortoise-like standards, at least. Perhaps she ought to have another look.

Behind her, the clock positioned on the shelves near Thane's bed chimed noisily. Three o'clock. He would be back before four. She did not have much time.

Her days of brooding and reading, while boring, had been informative.

Thane was a creature of habit. Seven o'clock, a man named Bryce delivered his breakfast. By the way Thane sprang out of bed, Jacquetta knew he was usually awake earlier still. Eight o'clock, he was shaved, breakfasted, and dressed for the day. He left without a word to her. Ten o'clock he returned to the cabin and held meetings in hushed tones with his crew. She recognized Rook, the first mate. The two other men who appeared were not introduced to her.

After luncheon, Thane departed the cabin for the longest stretch of time. Between one o'clock and four o'clock, he was busy with whatever demands the crew made out on the deck. Or below decks. Jacquetta had no idea how he spent his time outside of the cabin. It was a problem she would have to remedy eventually. But for now, combing through the cabin was occupation enough.

Her gaze wandered over his enormous platform bed—she'd avoided searching that area just yet—to the wall of windows behind it. The sea lapped at the ship, and a churning wake trailed behind the massive vessel. Jacquetta swallowed hard and looked away. She would have to leave the cabin and look out over that endless sea soon... but not yet. It would take her a few days to thoroughly go over every inch of Thane's quarters.

Sulking in her bunk served another purpose as well. Let Thane think her broken, resigned to her lot. He would relax his guard and be easier to manipulate.

Thus far he'd proved immovable. How was she supposed to get information out of a man who patently ignored her? *Relax,* Jacquetta told herself. Time was on her side. Wherever they were going, Thane had told her it would take weeks, possibly months to get there.

She was aboard an Indiaman. Jacquetta could not stifle her cringe. If it was an East Indiaman, the voyage would last months and months. But they would likely put in for supplies somewhere along the African coast. Was Africa their destination, then? If it was a West Indiaman, their final port could be anywhere from Cuba to Barbados. The only comfort was that if they were westward bound, the trip would be considerably shorter—a mere seven or eight weeks, perhaps.

A sign she'd seen once at Falmouth came to her mind. Lisbon—fourteen days. Jamaica—fifty-two days.

Fifty days or five hundred days. It did not matter if she did not discover the information she'd been sent to find.

The desk again, she decided, easing open the top drawer. There was a mess of quills and inkpots and a few crumpled sheets of paper. Perhaps there was a false bottom that she had missed—

Heavy footfalls sounded outside the door, followed immediately by animated voices. *Shit.* It wasn't Thane, but that mattered little. If she was discovered out of her shackles, her ruse was over and he'd throw her in the brig for certain.

Jacquetta raced for her bunk. The handle on the door was moving; whoever was coming in had unlocked it. She threw herself onto the narrow berth, dragging the manacles with her as she rolled onto her side to face the wall.

The door opened fully, and not one, but two men came stomping in. Jacquetta didn't have time to process the who or why of it. She slid the metal cuffs around her wrists, but she couldn't click them into place. They were so damnably loud; the two men would surely notice.

She forced a huge, hacking cough up from her chest. Curling her whole body around the motion, she used the sound and movement to cover the clack of the cuffs as they locked into place.

"Are you well, my lady?" Rook asked, taking a tentative step toward the bed.

Jacquetta let out a long, calming breath to steady herself. Then she saw the sparkling hairpin on the bedsheet. Damn it all. She'd forgotten to put it back into her hair.

The pins she'd borrowed from Dominique were innocuous enough when pinned into her coiffure, but a criminal with a half-experienced eye would see it for what it was—a lock-picking device.

Jacquetta coughed again, praying the same trick would work twice. She swiped up the pin and shoved it down the bosom of her tattered gown as her body contracted with the cough. It stabbed painfully at her breast, but she ignored it. Rook was at her bedside now.

"My lady, please, we must send for the surgeon—"

"No, no, I am quite well," Jacquetta said, her voice wavering as she gasped for air. The fake cough had worked too well. She rolled to her back and then her other side, to face the two men. Rook and Bryce.

Slowly, she swung her legs out and moved so she was sitting on the edge of the bunk, blinking up awkwardly into Rook's face. "I must have swallowed wrong. The food does not agree with me."

Bryce looked pained at that, ducking his head.

She felt a pang of alarm and looked to Rook in question.

"Mr. Bryce is the kitchen helper, my lady," he said quietly, giving her a sympathetic wrinkle of his nose.

Jacquetta relaxed slightly. Nothing serious, then. Bruised egos she could manage.

"My humble apologies, Mr. Bryce," she said, bowing her own head. "Everything you have prepared has been delicious. Worthy of any London salon. It is only… My nerves are quite frayed. I have never been held captive before"—a blatant lie—"and I am afraid I suffer from a rather nervous stomach." Another lie. She was quite adept at it. She was a spy, after all.

"My thanks, my lady," Bryce mumbled, pinking considerably.

Jacquetta glanced sideways. The look on Rook's face was something between approval and outright adoration. Perhaps a tad too close to the latter for her preferences. But she could use this, she reminded herself. Rook was the only one she'd seen question Thane. If she had the first mate's ear… Yes, that was decidedly appealing.

"You have been most kind to me, Mr. Rook," Jacquetta said as she smiled up at him. She shifted her arms subtly to cover the tear along the bustline of her gown and press her bosom upward.

"You are our guest, my lady." He gulped.

"Guest," she scoffed, unable to stop herself. "At least you two seem determined to treat me as such."

She flicked her eyes to Bryce and gave him a small smile. The poor man turned furiously red and wilted; clearly, attempting to seduce him would just embarrass them both. Best focus her attentions on Rook, then.

"But I am not a lady, you must know." Jacquetta darted her tongue out over her lower lip.

A smile curled Rook's mouth. He was a good-looking man who smiled easily. She doubted he had any trouble attaining female company when in port. He was more than welcome to turn that boyish charm upon her; she was wise enough not to fall for it.

"Among us poor men here, you may as well be the queen," Rook said, bowing for emphasis.

Jacquetta rewarded him with a chuckle that she knew caused her breasts to wobble delightfully. He did a very good job hiding his reaction, but she did not miss the way his hand tightened on the edge of the bunk.

"I know that I can depend upon you to treat me as such," Jacquetta said breathily. She twirled a finger through a stray lock of golden hair. "I think of your kindness every night as I lie in your bed, Rook."

Four things happened simultaneously—so fast Jacquetta could do nothing but rock back on the bed and grab for something to keep her from falling over.

A strangled croak tore from Bryce's throat—clearly he had heard her words and was duly scandalized by them. Rook took a step forward, his hand half extended as if he meant to touch her. The doors of the cabin slammed open, and Grayson Thane swept into the room. And fourth, the ship rocked mightily on the waves and knocked them all off-kilter.

"Jacquetta I expect to find sprawled on the floor," Thane said. "But Bryce and Rook, I expect you to have your sea legs firmly under you."

No one was quite sprawled on the floor, but it was obvious that the sudden movement of the ship had taken all of them unawares. Despite her roiling stomach and her determined effort not to look toward the wall of windows, Jacquetta felt a surge of pride. She'd been diverting enough that the two experienced sailors had been unable to master themselves.

Thane crossed his arms and stared at the two men expectantly. "Why are you here?"

Bryce flinched. Rook straightened his coat before answering. "Bryce wanted to see if Miss Lawson had any special requests for her supper, being as she has a delicate stomach."

Thane snorted mirthlessly. "Delicate stomach?" He raised his eyebrows at Jacquetta, who was still perched on the edge of the bunk behind Rook.

She stood with as much dignity as her shackles would allow and raised her chin defiantly.

Thane rolled his eyes. "Serve her whatever you like. But get out. I have a meeting with the quartermaster and the boatswain, and you two have other duties."

Bryce and Rook did not argue, to Jacquetta's surprise. Not Bryce, she amended. The poor young man could hardly stand to displease her, a pretty captive, let alone his intimidating captain. But Rook she'd expected a bit more of a show from. She would need to lean more thoroughly into her seduction.

The doors of the cabin closed once again, and Jacquetta flicked her hair over her shoulder, prepared for another afternoon of thoroughly ignoring Grayson Thane.

"You are more ruthless than I ever supposed."

Her spine stiffened. "Whatever do you mean?"

"You do not return Rook's regards," he said as he strode over to the platform that housed his bed.

Jacquetta leaned against the shelves beside her own bed and tried to appear as if she wasn't carefully watching his every step.

"I find Mr. Rook to be a most interesting and kind gentleman," she said with sincerity. Although she was an adept liar, she'd always found it helped to stay as close to the truth as possible.

Thane tugged a wooden box from its spot on the bottom shelf and flipped open the hinged lid. "He is both of those things. You, however…" He shot her a doubtful look over her shoulder.

Jacquetta bristled. "You can hardly judge my disposition. You are my kidnapper," she reminded him, lacing her voice with venom.

He flicked through the contents of the box. "One would think that would mean you would be eager to ingratiate yourself to me, Jack, since I am in complete control of your comfort and wellbeing."

She frowned, disliking the feeling in her stomach. "That is not my name," she growled.

"And yet it pleases me to call you by it." Thane snapped the box shut and shoved it back into its place. He stood up and looked her way, appearing vaguely amused.

Jacquetta resisted the urge to launch one of the books at her bedside at his face. She did not know if her shackles would give her enough range, and the effect would certainly be ruined if the chain yanked her arms back mid-throw.

"I do not care what pleases you, Thane," she said, letting her eyes convey the rage her actions could not.

Thane cocked his head to the side, as if considering her words. He held a folded sheet of paper in his hand, and Jacquetta would have given her small toe to know what it was.

"Then perhaps you are more concerned with what displeases me, *Jack*," he said. A half-smile pulled at his lips as she stiffened. "If you are inclined to amorous pursuits with Rook, I will not stop you. He will not make unwanted advances, but if you are amenable, I will not stand in the way."

Her mouth dropped open. "How—"

Thane stepped forward, holding up his empty hand to stop her from speaking. "Do not forget that when I found you, you were wrapped in young Lord Andresen's arms."

Jacquetta bit her lip. She had no answer for that. This muddle was of her own making.

"As I said, take your pleasure with Rook, if you are so inclined. He may even have some fantasies regarding the shackles. Or perhaps you do." His gaze turned positively wicked at that. But instead of revulsion, Jacquetta found herself pressing her legs together instinctively. "But do not string him along. He is not a puppy like those buffoons in London. He is a good man."

"I am surprised you know how to recognize one." She crossed her arms over her body, hating the clang of the shackles.

Thane took another step forward, so he stood at the top of the platform. He rested one hand on the railing that divided the sleeping space from the rest of the cabin. "I will have your promise, Jacquetta."

His voice was serious. But there was something else in it that compelled her—protectiveness? He had stated this was his job, and yet… this might be true affection he was showing for his first mate. Or, at least, the closest thing to it a heartless mercenary like

Grayson Thane could muster.

It surprised her enough that Jacquetta heard herself saying, "I will seek nothing more than friendship with Mr. Rook."

Even as she said it, she berated herself internally. It was a foolish thing to promise. Rook may very well be the key to her work here. But Jacquetta also knew that she would not go back on her word, now that she'd given it.

Christ. This quest was a complete and utter disaster.

Thane flashed a grin, revealing his slash of straight white teeth. "Good girl," he said softly.

She ignored the rush of warmth between her legs. She could not be attracted to Grayson Thane. First, he was an arrogant arse of a man. Second, she could not afford to compromise her quest. Getting herself physically involved would no doubt lead to emotional involvement, which would be…

… a way for her to figure out who his master was.

Jacquetta blinked in surprise at her own thought.

If he trusted her enough to let her warm his bed, he might let information slip. She'd done it a dozen times—kissed a man, let him paw at her, until his mind was fuzzy and his tongue loose. She would surely get free rein of the cabin, and possibly the entire ship. She could search at her leisure. And she could get rid of these damn shackles.

It would not be that difficult. He already thought her promiscuous, if his comments about Lord Andresen and Rook were any indication.

She decided. Jacquetta nodded her head sharply. Thane had no reaction at all—because he was not looking at her. She'd been wool-gathering like an insipid idiot.

He, meanwhile, had decided their conversation was over and gone to sit at his desk. He was now thoroughly ignoring her, as had become his evening habit.

Jacquetta forced a gulp of air into her lungs. Best start the way she meant to go on, and all of that. She glanced down at her bosom—she was wearing the same clothes she'd been taken in from Lady Brothwilde's estate. Her dress was torn and dirty; her hair had seen nothing better than her fingers by way of combing. But she was uncommonly pretty. At least she was wearing blue— it would make her eyes stand out.

Jacquetta lifted the book she'd been reading off the edge of her bunk and replaced it on the bookshelf. She sighed loudly as she ran her fingers over the spines of the others, appearing to assess the possibilities.

She pulled out one book, flicked through the pages, then replaced it. Then another.

"If you are unhappy with the selection, you may ask Rook. I am sure he has more stashed away somewhere aboard."

Jacquetta was so surprised at *what* he'd said that she almost forgot that the entire point of her actions was to get him to say it. She turned sharply, tossing her golden mane over her shoulder so her bosom was on full display.

"Rook? Did you not just extract a promise that I would let him alone?" She stepped across the floor, though there was still the dining table between them, and touched her fingertips to the neckline of her gown while her mouth formed a surprised little O.

Grayson tucked the paper he'd taken from the box inside his jacket and sat back to regard her. "Borrowing a book is not the same as lifting your skirt for him," he said without looking up.

"I never—"

"You are a beautiful woman, Jack, and you know it. So does everyone else who lays eyes on you."

Seduction—forgotten.

What did he mean by that statement? He found her beautiful? That was annoyance burning through her, not appreciation. Did he mean that he saw through her attempts to catch his eye? He'd hardly given her a glance. He was smart, but he could not read her damn mind.

"I would thank you, but I sense that was not a compliment," Jacquetta said.

"An observation," Thane agreed.

She took a steadying breath. "You think I am beautiful."

His dark eyes narrowed.

"An observation of my own," she said, slowly dragging her teeth over her lower lip.

Thane did not respond, but he looked at her with intense ferocity. Jacquetta held herself steady.

"I would be able to entertain myself more easily if I was unshackled," she said.

His eyes glinted with challenge. "Reading does not require your shackles be removed."

"I could draw." She shrugged. Drawing was an activity most proper young women of the *ton* were supposed to find diverting. "I could mend my clothes," she added, more practically. Though there was nothing practical about the way she swept her hand down her bodice and over her curvaceous body—that was entirely contrived.

Thane kicked back his chair and slowly walked around the table until he was just a yard away from her. "And stab me with a needle the first chance you have?"

Jacquetta dragged her eyes over him in open appraisal. "You shall have to trust me," she said softly.

Emotion flickered over Thane's face, but it was too quick for her to read it. Then there was a sharp knock at the door.

"Enter."

Jacquetta shrank back against the bunk. The door opened and a young man entered. She held in her gasp, but only barely. The lad looked no more than fifteen years old. Down the right side of his face, a wicked scar completely mangled his youthful countenance.

She bit her lip, determined not to make a scene. What could have happened to him at such a young age? Her eyes flew to Thane. His face was hard. Surely, he had not...

"Thank you, Hamish," Thane said kindly. "Put the tub just there." He pointed to the opposite end of Jacquetta's berth. The boy did as he bade, obedient, as all of Thane's men were. But there was no fear in his face or the way he moved his body, and Jacquetta let out a breath of relief at that.

Then she realized what exactly he was carrying.

She could only stare as the boy put the copper wooden tub down, bowed to them both, and quietly left the cabin.

"Is that a bath?" Jacquetta whispered, all of her training melting away in an instant in the face of the small tub of steaming water.

"The closest thing you'll get to it on a ship."

She heard the grin in Thane's voice. Heard it. She spun around so quickly, determined to see what such a thing actually looked like, that she bumped into him.

Suddenly, she was pressed against him from hip to neck. He was hard—his muscles were hard. Every inch of his chest was tight, firm muscle beneath the thin shirt he wore. He did not bother with a waistcoat. Only a shirt and tailcoat—the former of which was unbuttoned and loose around his waist. In short, she was acutely aware of every inch of Thane's hard body pressed against hers.

This was a seduction, she reminded herself.

So instead of pulling away, Jacquetta inhaled slowly so her bosom moved against his chest. Ever so slight, but ever so effective. She watched his eyes as she softly said, "Thank you."

Thane's eyes widened and his nostrils flared. He took a large step backward, distinctly away from her. He would not make this easy, she realized. While he was more than willing to give her to Rook if she so desired, he was determined not to become entangled himself. But why? If his first mate could sample the goods, why couldn't he? Thane was a conundrum. But she would unravel him, as she had countless men before him.

Jacquetta lifted her hands, holding them out between them. She also used the motion to press her ample bust upward.

"I cannot bathe with shackles on," she said. She did not let herself beg, but she tried to keep the bitterness out of it. Now was not the time to be adversarial.

Not breaking her gaze, Thane slowly reached into his pocket and withdrew the key. "You shall remain chained at night. I still do not trust you not to try to murder me while I sleep."

"I hardly think it would do me much good, being surrounded by a ship full of your men," she said, but without her usual sharpness.

He quirked an eyebrow. "You might still decide to take your chances with Rook."

Her spine stiffened. "I have given my word on that matter."

He looked poised to argue, but apparently thought better of it. "The door to the cabin will remain locked at all times, even when I am in the room," he said, but he was already reaching for her wrists.

He inserted the key, and a second later the metal contraption clanged to the floor. Jacquetta tried very hard not to let her relief show, but from the expression on Thane's face, she knew she was not entirely successful. She followed his gaze over her shoulder and turned back to the steaming tub.

Behind her, Thane moved away, opening a drawer at the bottom of the bookcase that adjoined her bunk. He turned back to her, arms full of linens. "Wash, Jacquetta."

She nodded her thanks and took the bundle from his hands. She flicked her gaze up to his, letting her thick eyelashes flutter in the way she knew men so liked. "Are you going to stay and watch, Thane?"

His dark eyes narrowed on hers. For a moment, it seemed like he might say yes, just to see what reaction it elicited from her. But then he was ducking his head and backing away, moving past her and toward the doors of the cabin.

"There is clothing in that same drawer. If you can find something that fits, you are welcome to it. I will ensure that you are not disturbed."

Jacquetta did not get the chance to ask about what lady loves had left behind the clothing—the door was already closing behind Thane and a key turning in the lock. In truth, she did not care.

She was unshackled, given the freedom of the cabin, a steaming tub of water was before her, and there was the promise of clean clothing. Her circumstances had improved so considerably over the last hour that she dared not question her good fortune.

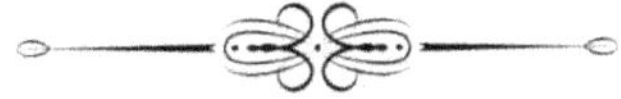

CHAPTER SIX

THE LOCK CLICKED into place and Grayson's hand dropped heavily to his side. His forehead hit the closed door with a quiet thump.

His cock was throbbing.

Damn, the little minx.

She was too clever by half, damn irresistible—and worst of all, she knew it. He'd found her in a man's embrace, Grayson reminded herself. He'd caught her toying all too sweetly with Rook. Was it any surprise that she was now turning her womanly wiles upon him? In short, no. He ought to have expected it and planned accordingly.

Why the hell hadn't he put her in a cell? There were some in the hold, though they were rarely used. Hell, there was even a cabin not in use. He could have his men clear it in a day.

But then she would be out of sight.

"Exactly," Grayson said quietly as he pushed himself away from the locked door.

Behind him, he heard approaching voices—and he recalled why a separate cabin was not a good idea. There were a hundred lonely men on this ship and one lovely female.

While most of the men under his command were biddable enough, desperate to do as he said and not extend their own indentures, there were a few he did not trust implicitly, men who enjoyed the brutal tasks assigned to them a bit too much. Their faces flashed in Grayson's mind—Ball, Griffiths, Payne. He did not want Jacquetta to even lay eyes upon these men, let alone chance them visiting her in a cell or private cabin.

In his quarters, she was safe. Not a man aboard the *Agamemnon* would dare to enter Grayson's cabin uninvited.

The owners of the approaching voices rounded the back of the staircase that led from above down to the quarterdeck. In the more sheltered alcove that housed the entrance to his quarters, Grayson could pick out their voices easily. But still, he did not turn immediately. He gave himself another ten seconds to get a hold of himself. He would not allow Jacquetta to turn him into an addled fool in front of his men.

The quartermaster and boatswain's voices died off as they spotted Grayson. His time was up.

Grayson swung around to meet the two men, summoning his characteristic swagger.

"Late, as usual," he said, looking straight at his gruff boatswain. The man's rough appearance matched his manner, but there was no one else as qualified to care for the ship and her stores.

The boatswain grunted. "Blame him." He cocked a thumb at the quartermaster at his side.

By contrast, the quartermaster was neatly dressed. His hair was combed and plaited back into a club at the nape of his neck. His tailcoat was clean despite being threadbare in places, and there was not a single button missing.

"Ahem," the quartermaster said politely. "I was seeing to a matter between Mr. Payne and Mr. Chapman."

The slight grimace around the quartermaster's mouth snagged Grayson's attention. Payne was notorious for causing trouble. Grayson had attempted to have him assigned to serve on shore rather than on aboard the *Agamemnon*, but Payne was Delaurier's favorite pet of late.

Better not to ask, Grayson decided. The quartermaster was

responsible for arbitrating disputes between the crew members. He would not appreciate Grayson meddling when it was not necessary.

"We are here now," the quartermaster said. "Shall we commence our meeting?" He nodded toward the door behind Grayson, at the key still in the lock.

Panic flooded Grayson's veins.

"We cannot," he said gruffly.

The quartermaster raised his bushy eyebrows, glancing thoughtfully between Grayson and the closed door. His companion was not half as wise.

"I'm chafed. I want some damn tea." The boatswain pushed past his peer, reaching for the door.

Grayson moved so quickly that neither man had any chance to react. In less time than it took to draw a breath, he had the boatswain pinned against the back of the staircase that led down to the quarterdeck.

Grayson had one knee shoved between the man's legs, precariously close to his male parts. The opposite arm was pressed brutally over his neck. A twitch and he could smash the man's windpipe. Another errant word, and Grayson would drive a dagger between his ribs.

"What the hell is wrong with you, Thane?" the boatswain managed to get out between gasping breaths.

"You do not enter my quarters uninvited," Grayson growled.

"Uninvited? You called this blasted meeting!"

He nudged the tip of his dagger at a button on the boatswain's coat.

"Fuck—"

"Keep your filthy mouth shut," Grayson demanded.

"Ahem," the quiet quartermaster said behind them. "If you do not release Mr. Burton, you will be taking on even more duties for this voyage, Thane," he pointed out calmly.

Grayson did not loosen his grip. Rage was coursing through him, hot and overpowering. He'd promised Jacquetta that no one would disturb her.

"Delaurier would also be displeased," the quartermaster added quietly. "Mr. Burton still has many years of service remaining."

And you do not. The quartermaster's unspoken words rang clearly in Grayson's head. If he disabled the boatswain, Delaurier would likely add the man's years to Grayson's own term. The term that was mere weeks away from completion.

Slowly, Grayson eased his knee back down and then released his hold on the man's neck. The boatswain glared, but held his tongue as he rubbed at his throat.

"Miss Lawson is locked inside my quarters. Let us not forget, she is the most valuable piece of cargo currently aboard this ship," Grayson said stonily. "And unlike our usual cargo, she has ears," he added.

Before the boatswain could make another salty retort, the quartermaster clapped his hands together smartly. "I have plenty of room in my cabin. We can hold our discussion there," he said.

Grayson inclined his head in agreement. He would not move until the boatswain did.

"This is bollocks," the man grumbled under his breath, but he turned and followed the quartermaster.

Grayson remained a moment longer, willing his nerves to steady and his breathing to return to a regular cadence.

Where the hell had that rush of emotion come from?

For all that the boatswain was gruff and argumentative, he was a capable and loyal man. Beyond his grumbling, he'd never caused Grayson a whit of trouble. And yet Grayson hadn't hesitated to assault him the moment he took a step toward Jacquetta.

Grayson did not care a jot for Jacquetta—only for what she meant to him. Freedom. Get to Barbados, drop the chit at Delaurier's feet, and Grayson would be free.

If he had to intimidate every member of his crew to get her there safely, then, dammit, he would.

***

IT WAS THE most luxurious bath of Jacquetta's young life.

True, the tub was really no more than a laundry basin half-full of warm water. Anything bigger and the young man would not have been able to carry it.

There was no submerging or delightful wallowing in the heated depths, fair enough.

But after days in the same clothes without more than a cloth dampened with cold water from the canteen to freshen her underarms and private regions, a sponge bath with warm water was nothing short of heaven.

As promised, no one disturbed her. Jacquetta spent the first five minutes or so of her bath flinching at every sound outside the door. After that, she'd decided she did not care and allowed herself to get fully lost in the warm water and sweet scent of soap.

When she'd finally rubbed herself dry, she looked at the soiled clothing she'd removed, now a pile on the floor of the cabin. She wrinkled her nose, cringing at the thought of putting the clothes back on. They'd need to be washed and mended. She glanced longingly toward the drawer where Thane had indicated clean clothes might await her. With a sigh, Jacquetta stepped back toward the tub of cooling water. Better to wash her clothes now while she was naked, so she did not spoil whatever new clothing was about to be afforded her.

A half-hour later, her own clothing was washed and carefully strung up around her corner of the cabin to dry. She'd worry about mending it later—she'd have to convince Thane to give her a needle, which he would no doubt regard as a weapon. Though, as she glanced around the cabin, she could see more than a few items that could be used as weapons to much greater effect.

A quick flick of her wrist and the half-empty wine bottle would be sharp enough to draw blood. She had not tested the weight of the Grecian-style statue that served as a bookend on the shelf, but Jacquetta would wager it would be enough to render a man unconscious. She snorted to herself as she regarded the half-dozen rifles mounted to the wall of the cabin behind Thane's desk. He must really think her inept, to leave her with such things. They might not be loaded or primed, but one of them bore a wicked-looking bayonet on the end.

Jacquetta dismissed the notion of running Thane through with the blade—tempting as it was—and turned back in search of clothing. Once she'd completed that search, she could resume the one that truly mattered.

She pulled open the drawer Thane had indicated—

"Christ, Thane!" Jacquetta exclaimed.

The drawer was filled to bursting. She sifted through the contents, barely containing her chuckle.

No—she did not contain it at all.

"And I thought I would be the one doing the seducing," Jacquetta murmured to herself with a shake of her head.

There must be enough clothing to dress at least five separate women. And they did not all belong to the same woman. No, there was no way the woman who had owned the burgundy velvet evening gown had fit into the tiny boned corset. An evening gown, on a ship! What sort of women was he entertaining?

Jacquetta shivered. She knew precisely what type—and she chastised herself for the shiver of distaste. Women must make their way in the world however they could. She herself was not so much different—she planned to seduce Thane for his secrets, rather than his coin. Which one was worthier? Jacquetta refused to be the judge of that.

She unearthed a pair of stockings with one small hole in the toe. A chemise that was a bit moth-eaten, but clean. Thankfully, there was a lot of room for error in a chemise. There was no chance she was getting that corset on. It was the only one on offer—it seemed that Thane's lady loves did not find them particularly necessary. Or they'd all been ruined in the course of...

Jacquetta shivered again. From distaste, she assured herself.

She settled on a dressing gown to go over the chemise. There were no nightgowns—what need did one of Thane's bedmates have for one of those? But the chemise would do well enough. She would not do him the courtesy of dressing for dinner. She might be thankful for the bath, but he was still her enemy. Besides, a dressing gown was more suitable for the seduction she had planned.

The dressing gown was a practical choice, perfect for bringing the infuriating man to heel. The choice had nothing to do with the silky softness of the sheer fabric that skimmed over her arms, nor the comforting warmth of the strip of velvet that curled around her neck and all the way down the front panels. She admired the intricate embroidery on the velvet that trailed down the neckline only for its sure effectiveness at drawing Thane's attention where she wanted it to go.

Jacquetta shook away her dreaminess and refocused.

The real question came down to footwear. There was a pair of boots. Too big, but if she wore another layer of stockings, they would be wearable. Her slippers rested on the foot of her bunk. She was loath to separate herself from them... they were too important. They were ill-suited for tromping about on a ship, but she would not be roaming the ship yet, she reminded herself. She had not yet earned Thane's trust enough for that.

Jacquetta decided she would wear the slippers in the cabin for now, and address the question of what to do next when she managed to secure free rein of the ship at large.

Finally fully clothed, she reached for her hair to start combing it out the best she could.

No, Jacquetta chided herself. Thane was away. He would surely return soon for supper. She could not waste this opportunity. And she knew precisely what to do with it—her fingers were itching to get a hold of that wooden box.

She crossed the room quickly, trying not to make too much

of ascending the step that separated Grayson's platform bed and the surrounding shelves from the rest of his quarters. Jacquetta had avoided it during her previous search, but she could afford no squeamishness now. She had a quest to complete.

The dressing gown pooled around her legs as she knelt before the shelves and reached for the wooden box on the lowest level. It was solid and well-built. The polished veneer was worse for the wear, scuffed and gouged in several places. What action had this box seen before it had reached its resting place here on the shelf? Were the contents the same as they had been, or had the box been repurposed?

Jacquetta flicked her finger over the brass clasp and flipped open the lid. There were several sheaves of neatly folded paper—at least two dozen. She summoned the image of Grayson flicking through the folded papers and extracting a specific one. But looking at the contents of the box, she could see no writing or distinguishing characteristics on the outsides of the sheets. He must have been counting, she thought to herself—because when he pulled the selected sheet from the box and unfolded it, he had not returned it. He'd known exactly what he was looking for and where to find it.

Somewhere outside the cabin's doors, she heard footfalls. She paused, flicking the lid closed preemptively. But they faded quickly; someone must've merely passed the cabin on their way to some other destination aboard the ship.

She opened the box again and pulled out the first sheet. It was actually two sheets of paper tri-folded together. Jacquetta read the name at the top: Alastair Agutter. Below it were two other names—Jonathan Agutter and Mary Agutter, followed by an address in Surrey. Below that, a list of what appeared to be dates and then numbers she did not recognize.

She scanned the list twice, trying to make sense of it. When nothing sprang to her mind, she replaced the folded sheaf and pulled the next. The format was identical, though the information slightly different. Nathaniel Bryson—that was the kitchen helper she'd offended. Followed by two names, most likely his parents—John and Elaine Bryson, and an address in the Cotswolds followed by more seemingly obscure numbers and dates.

Jacquetta looked through the remainder of the sheets diligently, finding them nearly identical. The only variances were the dates and the numbers beside them. Coordinates, perhaps? Voyages?

She bit her lower lip. She was not very good with geography. She knew where all the continents were, surely, but looking at the numbers did not give her any sense of where they might correspond geographically. She needed to look at a map.

She replaced the box on the bottom shelf, careful to set it back down exactly where it had rested before without sliding it out and disturbing the fine layer of dust that had accumulated since she'd seen Grayson first look through it.

Then she stood, surveying the room for where maps might be kept.

How could one captain a ship without a map? Jacquetta half expected to find one tacked to the wall. But she'd spent enough time in these quarters over the last week to know no such thing adorned the walls here.

Was it the captain's job to navigate? Was Thane even the captain? He'd bristled when she suggested as much. But clearly, he was the one in command. And she seriously doubted there were any more luxurious cabins aboard the ship—though admittedly, she had not set foot outside these quarters in days.

Her eyes combed over the room. His desk warranted another look, of course. There might be a false bottom to one of the drawers. There were shelves on the wall behind the desk, but she'd been through those thoroughly already. Her bunk took up the opposite corner, and the adjoining bookcase was equally unexciting. There was a trunk on the wall beneath the rifles. It had appeared to hold nothing more than clothes when she first opened it, but it merited further perusal. Shelves lined each side of the platform with the bed, where she now stood. There might even be more compartments secreted below the mattress. That would be a feat to heft off and search; she'd need to choose her moment carefully.

As if drawn by the very thought, Jacquetta found herself drifting toward the large platform bed. Whereas her bunk was a mess of sheets, Thane's was carefully made. When he sprang to his feet each morning, he turned immediately and straightened the sheets and coverlet. Another indication that this ship truly was his home; one did not take that kind of care in an inn or hotel.

Jacquetta slid her fingers beneath the mattress and the wooden platform it rested on, testing the weight. Yes, she would need to ensure Thane was nowhere near the cabin when she hefted it to the side and searched the wood below for any secrets. There would be no explaining away why the mattress was on the floor.

The sheets were so soft... so much softer than those on Rook's bunk. Her bunk.

Another indication that, despite what he said, Thane was the captain of this ship. He slept in finery.

Jacquetta trailed her fingers over the sheets to the coverlet. Silk. Jesus, Mary, and Joseph, the man had fine taste.

She rubbed her fingers over the grain, her eyes drifting shut as she appreciated the quality—

But something snagged her gaze.

Jacquetta had assumed the platform bed abutted the wall of windows directly. But no; here, standing closer, she could see that there was a fair six inches between where the mattress ended and the glass panes began. But it was not empty—there was a wooden panel built in to bridge the space. A perfect hiding place.

Her knee hit the mattress, but she did not notice the softness. She climbed across the bed, only half aware of the fact that she would need to remake it before Grayson came in, if she did not wish to be discovered.

She slid her hand over the wooden surface. Only six inches wide, a seemingly solid panel separating the bed from the windows. It was practical, even. The window would let in the cold. It made absolute sense to have a barrier between the bed and the panes. But it was also incredibly convenient.

The wood along the top was smooth, not a single notch. She knocked her fist against it—hollow. There was a space inside the panel. Jacquetta reached around the side, the narrow area between the bed and the window, feeling where her eyes could not see.

Nothing, nothing—there!

Her fingernail caught against a slight notch in the fabric. She felt around, searching for the release. She traced the groove until she finally found the small notch. Jacquetta slid her finger in, applied a bit of pressure—and the secret compartment sprang free.

She could not see well over the edge of the bed, but she felt around true enough. Her fingers curled around a small leather pocketbook. She rocked back on her haunches, pulling the thing into her lap to examine it.

It was small, could easily fit inside a reticule for a jaunt around Hyde Park. The small notebook was bound in black leather, and on the front, a gold-embossed image of a bird was etched. Not any bird, she realized as she examined it more closely. A phoenix.

A metal clasp held the book closed. For a moment, Jacquetta worried it might be a lock. She'd left her hairpins over on her bunk. But it was nothing more than an intricate clasp. A few seconds later, she had it open before her.

She skimmed the first page. Then the second. The third. She flipped the pages until she was in the middle. The book was nearly three-quarters full.

But what she saw on the page was utterly indiscernible.

She flipped back to the first page.

1812. A year. Easy enough.

7.6. A date, then? Perhaps. But the format was not quite right.

Below that, another number—730. What did that mean? It

could not be a date. A quantity? But of what? And why hide it?

The numbers were formatted differently than those in the papers she'd found in the wooden box, though they were in the same hand. Thane's hand, she suspected. Jacquetta resolved to force him to write something the next time they were together so she could verify.

Which would be in mere moments. Behind her, a key turned in the lock.

She threw herself forward, shoving the book back into its hiding place and slamming the secret compartment shut with a loud snap just as the door of the cabin sprang open.

Jacquetta hardly had time to spin on the bed, propelling herself forward before Bryson appeared, a tray of food in his arms, with Rook and Thane over his shoulder.

All three men stared at her, though their expressions could not have been more different. Bryson's eyes darted between her and the tray of food; he was no doubt wondering if his offering would please or upset her. Rook's eyes widened noticeably as he took in her bedtime-clad figure atop nothing other than a bed.

But Jacquetta's eyes went to Thane, who regarded her with an amused smirk.

It was to him she looked as she said steadily, "I was searching for a comb to attend to my hair."

Rook's eyes raked over her, and he clearly appreciated the way her unrestrained mane clung to her shoulders and breasts. Bryson moved to set the tray on the dining table. Only Thane raised an eyebrow in question.

"There is one in the drawer with the clothing," he commented drily.

Jacquetta forced an awkward swallow down. "How silly of me to have overlooked it."

"Indeed," he returned.

Their eyes met, the challenge between them filling the room.

Bryson quivered, but Rook stepped forward to meet it.

"Bryson and I have seen to your meal specially, my lady," he said, offering a bow.

Jacquetta pulled her eyes away from Thane, giving the other two men a sweet smile. "Thank you, fine sirs. I am most excited to partake."

A dark, mirthless chuckle rent the air. "Good. Then we shall leave you to it." Thane turned for the door, dismissing her completely.

Bryson followed, not the type to disobey his master. Rook lingered a moment more, glancing between the food on the table and Jacquetta's scantily clad form. Outside the cabin, Thane cleared his throat expectantly. Even Rook could not resist the implied summons. He bowed his head to her respectfully once again, and then ducked out behind the others.

The door shut with a slam and the key turned in the lock.

Once again, Jacquetta was alone. And all thoughts of seducing Grayson Thane had completely deserted her.

CHAPTER SEVEN

"Jesus, Mary, and Joseph! Ow!"

Jacquetta tried to catch herself, but it was no use. She was disoriented, her forehead radiating pain from where she'd smacked it against the top of her bunk. She grabbed for the edge of the bunk but only managed to twist herself further until she was tangled in her bedsheets and falling to the floor with an almighty thump.

The wind was completely knocked out of her, her shoulder blade ached where it had hit the wooden floor of the cabin, and she could not see a thing because there was a bedsheet wrapped around her neck.

No wonder her seduction of Thane had gone nowhere. She was sure she resembled nothing so much in that moment as a pile of laundry. She shifted, trying to disentangle herself, and groaned uncomfortably.

A complaining pile of laundry, she amended.

Was the dratted man even in the cabin?

"You have all the charm of a meowling cat, Jack."

Of course he was. No chance of his being out on the deck to miss her fit of clumsiness.

Jacquetta yanked mercilessly at the bedsheets, not caring if she tore them, only that she got herself free so she could wipe that infuriating smirk off Thane's face.

From the way his voice carried across the quarters, she knew he must be at his desk, and it was there she directed her furious gaze as soon as she emerged, intending to pin him to the wall with the strength of her disdain—

He was not even looking at her!

"What the hell was that?" she demanded, ignoring the fact that her skirts were around her knees and her hair in her face. The plait she'd managed earlier had come loose in wavy strands, surely only made worse by her thrashing.

"A cannon," Thane said absently, still not looking at her.

Jacquetta's heart stopped. "Are we under attack?"

"No."

"What a comfort you are." But she *was* comforted. If they were truly in danger of being sunk into the great blue abyss, he surely would not be standing in his cabin calmly perusing paperwork.

"We've been forced to take on several new powder monkeys. The master gunner is taking them through the motions of practicing," Thane explained, bordering on boredom. He stood over the desk, one hand braced on the corner as he examined a scroll wide enough to cover most of the space.

A plethora of questions flooded Jacquetta's mind. Forced to take on new crew—by whom? When? Why? Practicing for what?

"Do you expect us to need to defend ourselves?" she asked, voicing what seemed the most pressing of her questions.

That did earn her a glance.

Thane's dark eyes slid over the table between them to where she still sat on the floor. He'd certainly noticed the way her calves were on display. His gaze stroked every inch of bare leg before settling on her face. Suddenly, Jacquetta was feeling better about the viability of her plan.

"Enjoying yourself?" she quipped.

Thane straightened immediately, his eyes shuttering. But Jacquetta had seen the glint of desire there, and now he was aware of it as well.

"I would rather the greenhorns have a spot of practice before my life depends upon it," he said, answering her question.

After untangling the last of the bedsheets and pushing them to the side, she flicked her skirts back down to cover her legs. A glimpse was tantalizing; revealing too much too soon would label her a tart. In fairness, it seemed Thane had already assigned her that label. But it felt the right thing to do, so Jacquetta decided to trust her instincts. They'd never failed her before where a man and his cock were concerned.

Thane was making a concerted effort to ignore her, eyes fixed on the layers of parchment covering his desk. They were huge, curling at the edges—maps, Jacquetta realized.

She contained the surge of excitement. If she managed the next few moments correctly, she might very well find out where they were bound for. She may find out where else Thane's master was active, other routes and ports of interest… It was an effort to keep her face blank.

Jacquetta grasped the edge of the bunk and pulled herself to her feet, making a show of brushing herself off and adding in a few disgruntled noises. Silence reigned behind her. She took the time to loosen her hair and carefully re-braid it so that it hung neatly over her shoulder. If she went out on deck, it would surely become a flyaway mess. But she had no reason to think today would be the day Thane granted her that heretofore forbidden freedom.

Before she turned, she glanced down at the gown she wore. It was her own—the ball gown she'd been wearing when Thane kidnapped her from Lady Brothwilde's study. She'd managed to mend the rip below the bosom, although there was nothing to be done about the missing beading at the neckline, short of removing it altogether. Jacquetta wiggled her toes in her slippers, reassured by their presence.

Her bosom was on clear display and her hair was in good order. She pinched her cheeks to ensure they were rosy and then began her approach.

This time Jacquetta did not bother toying with the bookcase. She cut a clear path across the room, around the large dining table to where Thane hovered over his desk. The rifles on the wall behind him glinted as if they'd been freshly polished. When had he done that? She'd been in these quarters for days. Unless he'd done it while she slept. Did insomnia trouble Thane?

Jacquetta paused a foot from the desk, letting its wide surface separate them. She crossed her arms over her body—meant to seem as if she was unconsciously protecting herself, but having the side effect of thrusting her bosom upward.

"Maps," she said softly, as if realizing for the first time what lay in front of Thane.

He did not respond—not even a wrinkle of his dark brow.

"Captain, navigator, kidnapper. What other roles do you fill?" she pushed, trying to elicit a response.

He did not look up at her as he spoke. "I am whatever I need to be. We are without a sailing master on this voyage, which means the navigation has fallen to me."

She thrust her chin out pugnaciously, though Thane still was not looking up to see it. "In so much of a hurry to kidnap me that you left him behind?"

"He disobeyed my employer. He was dispatched."

Ice slid through Jacquetta's veins. She'd suspected as much; they all had. It was why this quest had been given to the Lady Knights—the danger was very real. But his cold, unfeeling words unnerved her more than she cared to admit.

"You killed him," she said before she could stop herself.

Still, Thane showed no reaction. "I did not do the deed myself."

But he felt responsible for it, Jacquetta could read easily enough. Responsible because he'd ordered the killing? Or responsible because he could do nothing to prevent it? The answer would tell her more about the man than anything she'd uncovered thus far. Too bad she could not ask it yet.

"Where are we going?" she asked instead. Perhaps this time

he would answer her.

"Take a look and see for yourself."

The invitation was far too gentile. Her senses immediately flared.

But she played his game, stepping forward to peer at the maps spread before him.

She sighed heavily, pursing her lips in annoyance. An action that she knew, from practicing in front of a mirror, made her mouth look utterly kissable.

"This map shows the entire ocean," she griped. "We could be going anywhere from Africa, to the West Indies, to the Americas."

Thane stood up and fixed her with a discerning gaze. "Do not play coy, Jack. We both know this map narrows down the possibilities considerably."

He saw through her, at least in part. Fine, she'd let some of her sharp mind show. "We are aboard an Indiaman, or at least a ship that once was an Indiaman. I doubt you or your crew are putting it to such… legal purposes."

Thane clucked his tongue. "And?"

Jacquetta bristled. That was not contrived. The man rankled her to no end.

"It is unlikely we are bound for Africa. The ship is three-masted, made for crossing oceans. If you're hoping to fool other ships at a distance, then you would keep to the routes an Indiaman would take." There. She had not meant to reveal her thought process, but since he seemed to already know what she'd deduced from looking at the map, there was no point in feigning idiocy.

Thane's eyebrows rose and he nodded slightly, a mocking facsimile of being impressed. "So where are we bound, Jack?" Without waiting for her answer, he stepped back and shrugged off his tailcoat, tossing it over the wooden chair behind him.

Why was the cabin so hot, all of a sudden?

That must be why he was removing his coat. Jacquetta

wished she could ditch a few layers of her own clothing.

Thane turned back to her, his gaze expectant. But she was distracted by the triangle of muscled chest visible through the parted neck of his linen shirt.

He had not shucked his coat because of the heat. Thane had created the heat when he disposed of his jacket. That was a blush climbing her bosom. Jacquetta did not have to glance down to recognize the sensation.

She had to get back control of the situation. She uncrossed her arms, reaching up to toy with the end of her braid. She flicked the tail over her palm, then between her fingers, then down over her bosom.

Thane's eyes followed the movements of her hands. He was making no attempt to hide his interest now. But rather than the dark desire she'd seen gleaming earlier, she saw his mouth curl into that infernal smirk. He looked amused rather than aroused.

"Enjoying yourself?" Thane parroted.

Jacquetta's hand fell away from her braid and fisted at her side.

"There are hundreds of islands in the West Indies. But it would be completely out of character for you to find some scrap of kindness and tell me which one," she bit out.

"Barbados."

She blinked. "Barbados?" she repeated.

"You asked, I have answered." Oh yes, he was very amused. The smirk was near to a smile—the least joyful and most irritatingly superior expression she'd seen upon his face yet.

"Why tell me now?" Jacquetta asked. She knew she ought to accept the information and move the conversation along, but she could not help herself.

Thane shrugged, his wide shoulders straining against the linen of his shirt. "As you and Rook pointed out, there is nowhere for you to go."

"Does that mean I'm to be allowed out of the cabin as well?"

His eyebrows shot up. Damn. She'd pushed too quickly.

"For someone who is terrified of the sea, you are surprisingly eager to be on deck."

Jacquetta rocked back on her heels, her hand going to the backs of one of the dining chairs behind her. "How did you know?"

She was met with a dark chuckle. "You are not subtle," Thane said. "Your head never turns in that direction"—he nodded toward the wall of windows—"and while I flatter myself that it is because you are too tempted to think of yourself in my bed, the more obvious reason is that you are afraid."

Jacquetta bit her lip. It was utterly disarming to have the man she was supposed to be picking apart able to so succinctly pinpoint one of her greatest weaknesses.

"It must be a special sort of torture, to be trapped at sea," Thane continued. The curves of his mouth suggested he very much enjoyed torturing her.

"Go to hell." She spun around, forgetting the maps and any attempts at seduction. But her temper got the better of her. "Lord Grayson Thane, cossetted son of a duke turned rogue pirate, must be fearless," she spat.

His eyes darkened instantly. They were so unfathomably black that Jacquetta shivered.

"The things that scare me would turn your pert pink lips white with terror."

The timbre of his voice, dark and ominous, ought to have sent another shiver of unease rolling through her. But it was Thane's description of her mouth that surfaced in her mind. He might feign detachment, but he was noticing her. He was attracted to her.

She would use it and every other morsel he let slip to punish him for this moment, and every other second of humiliation that had come before.

Jacquetta shoved the chair aside and started to storm around the table, back for the privacy of her bunk. But Thane caught her arm and spun her sharply.

He towered over her, dark eyebrows framing his equally dark eyes. The strands of long black hair that had come loose from the club at the back of his neck were wild about his face. The heat that burned in his eyes was terrifying. A less experienced woman would have been cowed. Her heart did tremble. But she allowed none of that trepidation to show in her face.

"I have spent a thousand days staring down my worst fears."

730.

The pages of the phoenix journal flashed in Jacquetta's mind.

His grip on her arm tightened. "Watch your words carefully, Jack. You might not like the response you earn." A threat, a promise, a warning.

A thousand days.

Before she could process what it might mean, an almighty boom rocked the boat and threw both of them to the ground.

CHAPTER EIGHT

"Jesus—"

"Are you injured?"

"What?"

"Are you injured?" Grayson demanded, pulling Jacquetta to her feet. His shoulder throbbed from where it had hit the floor, taking the weight of both their bodies. But it was not broken or dislocated.

She grabbed the table for support, heaving a breath. "I am fine," she said, her voice shaking. "Was that the cannon again?"

But Grayson only heard the question peripherally. He was already shoving the key into the lock and throwing open the door of the cabin. He could not hear whether Jacquetta followed him; the yelling and chaos on deck was too overwhelming. But it hardly mattered—he had to get to the orlop deck.

All aboard the main deck, men were running frantically. Grayson sprinted for the hatch, and men peeled away to allow him to pass. He recognized the top of the surgeon's head a second before he disappeared below decks.

Grayson skidded to a stop and swung himself onto the ladder, hitting the orlop deck seconds after the other man.

The majority of the *Agamemnon*'s gun ports were on the orlop deck, interspersed between the other cabins that provided various functions—the galley, the surgery, and so on. From the bottom ladder he could see straight through from the first set of crew quarters to the rows of cannon beyond.

Except that Grayson should not have been able to see the cannon from where he stood. There ought to have been a wall. Just as he should not be able to see the damn ocean.

There were men sprawled everywhere. Whoever had been at leisure in their hammocks was dumped on the ground, but those injuries would be minor. Grayson clambered over the half-risen forms, right through the hole between the crew quarters and the gun deck.

The sight before him was gruesome.

Blood and limbs and gore were scattered everywhere. Grayson did not have time to hate that he was numb to the destruction and death filling the air. But he did put that numbness to use.

The surgeon had already beaten a line to the master gunner, who was unconscious on the deck. Grayson swept his gaze over the scene, discerning more or less what had happened. A misfire of the cannon had sent the massive iron rolling backward, crashing into another cannon and sending it careening through the wall that separated the gun deck from the crew quarters. The misfire itself had blown the hole into the portside of the ship.

Men were moaning. Boys, Grayson amended. The powder monkeys, all but one new to the *Agamemnon*, had taken the worst of it.

A pair of booted feet extended from between the two cannons that had inflicted the damage. Grayson tensed, knowing what he would find.

But he had to see. He placed a hand on a wailing lad's shoulder and murmured a promise to see to him in a moment, then maneuvered himself toward the cannons.

Grayson forced himself to look at the young man's face. At least, what remained of it. The entire upper half of his body had been crushed between the heavy cannons. Even so, Grayson found his wrist and searched for a pulse.

"He is dead."

The calm voice cut through the darkness.

Grayson jerked to his feet. "This is no place for you, Jack," he said. He did not have time for this. He needed to assign men to help the surgeon, get a crew of uninjured men to patch up the damned hole in his ship—

Jacquetta ignored him outright.

She spun away, kneeling beside the first man she found. Before Grayson realized what she was doing, she was hiking up her skirt and ripping a strip of cloth from her petticoat.

"Hold still," she commanded the young man with all the confidence of a weathered sea captain. She wound the strip around his wound, binding it. "That will need to be stitched. Clear out and wait in the surgery," she ordered him. Then she was on her feet and moving on to the next bloodied man, not even glancing over her shoulder to see if she was obeyed.

Jacquetta went to the surgeon's side, scrambling to brace the master gunner against her shoulder while the surgeon tried to straighten an obviously broken leg. More men were flooding in to help. Grayson could not hear what was said, but he watched Jacquetta and the surgeon exchange words. Whatever they said, they'd reached some tacit agreement. She held the man's hands behind his back while the surgeon snapped his leg back into place. The gunner swooned, but Jacquetta held fast.

"Orders, sir." One of the mates slid to a stop before Grayson. Behind him, more men were massing. Whatever Jacquetta was about, Grayson had no more time to think of it.

WHEN THANE FINALLY took a moment to pause, the sun had dipped below the horizon and the last few minutes of gray light lingered in the sky. One of the powder boys was dead. Three other men were under direct supervision of the surgeon. A half-dozen with lesser injuries were being tended to by Jacquetta.

Grayson stopped beside where the surgeon sat, rummaging through his case of medicaments. He dragged a hand through his hair. "Report."

The surgeon straightened, the grim expression on his face telling Grayson as much as his words would. "If these two last the night, they've a decent chance." He nodded to the man on the other side of the surgery, laid out on the floor. A fellow crewman crouched beside him. "St. Vincent will not last the hour."

Grayson nodded, his stomach clenching. He'd lost men be-fore—many times. But it did not ease the ache.

"What of the others?" he forced himself to ask.

"Your Miss Lawson has seen to them quite ably."

A strangled growl wrenched through his throat. "She is not *my* Miss Lawson."

Somehow, the surgeon had the energy to look amused. "Our Miss Lawson, then," he amended. "She's imperturbable, that one. I've seen grown men swoon at the sight of this sort of carnage. But she's has not flinched for a moment."

She is not what she seems, Grayson thought. Despite what he told himself to try to quell the raging desire in his loins, Jacquetta was not the spoiled, simpering debutante he'd expected when he received word from Delaurier to take her.

Her temper and mind were sharp as knives, and despite her fear of the ocean around them, she'd rallied and cared for his men with the self-possession of the finest sailors Grayson had ever encountered. If she was not another filmy, empty-headed *ton* miss, then what was she? Who was Jacquetta Lawson?

"Hush now, you are perfectly fine," a quiet female voice scolded, floating in from behind him.

"I've a half-dozen stitches in my arm!" a burly voice bit back.

"And Mr. Killigan has a full dozen. But I've heard nary a whimper from him," Jacquetta quipped.

Grayson eased himself back, leaning against a thick pole that held the ends of several hammocks so he could get a view at the scene. Jacquetta stood beside a swinging hammock, checking the dressing on a sailor who was easily thrice her size.

"Killigan's a mother—"

Jacquetta clucked her tongue, cutting the man off sharply. "Spare me your filthy tongue, Mr. Jacoby, and lie still. If you're a good boy, I might let you have a nip of my brandy."

Where had she acquired brandy? And why? Burton, the boatswain, was in charge of provisions; Grayson could not envision her charming spirits out of the gruff man who only a few days before had been huffing at her existence aboard the ship.

Jacoby started to swear again, but swallowed it down with one look from Jacquetta. She rewarded him with her pretty smile and a flick of her eyes toward the flask tied at her hip. Perhaps Grayson could see her charming the grumpy boatswain.

He watched as she rebandaged Jacoby's wound and then did exactly as she'd promised, producing a tiny cup and giving him a swig of amber-colored spirit. As Jacoby's eyes closed with appreciation, Grayson drifted back toward the ladder, silently descending to the lower deck.

Here, things had quieted. Sailors stood at their posts, but there were no crewmen taking their leisure on the cool deck beneath the full moon. Grayson drifted toward the rail, staring out at the endless abyss of the dark sea.

Above, the stars twinkled merrily, and the full moon glinted off the blue-green sea. In the flick of a wave, Grayson saw the color of Jacquetta's eyes.

He should not allow himself to get so riled up by the ocean-eyed chit.

Of course her eyes were the color of the ocean he loved. It was fate's way of mocking him, Grayson had no doubt.

Jacquetta represented his final voyage, his last task before he discharged his debt to Delaurier and was finally free. After which he would return to England and never set foot on a ship ever again.

He could admit to himself that he would miss the spray of

this ocean mist on his face and the gentle rocking of the ship beneath his feet. But to be free of Delaurier meant staying the hell away from the devil. So a future on land it would be.

The swish of skirts alerted him to Jacquetta's arrival. That and the thrumming of desire in his body that seemed to stir to life whenever she was near. He'd told himself she wasn't his preferred flavor? That he was not attracted to an insipid debutante?

Jacquetta Lawson was most definitely not that. And Grayson Thane was most definitely attracted to her.

But what to do about it? He'd given Rook his blessing, but it felt different where he himself was concerned. The stakes were infinitely higher.

"I am surprised you did not scurry directly back to the cabin," he said as she came to stand beside him at the rail.

"I am enjoying my freedom. I do not know if I will retain it come the morrow." Jacquetta took a deep breath for emphasis.

Grayson kept a tight hold on the rail, trying not to notice the way her bosom rose as she breathed in and out, savoring the sea air. "The surgeon is perfectly capable of attending to the remaining injuries."

Her eyes were closed, he realized.

"You have a peculiar way of saying 'thank you,'" she said, still not opening them.

In the darkness, Grayson felt his dark chuckle roll out of his chest. Jacquetta's eyes popped open, sweeping over to examine him in the pale moonlight. He was surprised himself that he could laugh at all, especially after the horrors they'd seen today—what unique power did Jacquetta have over him?

Grayson cleared his throat, coughed, tried to clear it again. "Thank you for your care of my men, Jack," he finally managed hoarsely.

He half expected her to prod him for more flowery prose, but she nodded her chin sharply in acknowledgment and turned back toward the dark expanse of the sea.

"It is less terrifying like this," she admitted. "When I cannot see the waves crashing or the endlessness of the horizon, it could be any other night, anywhere. It could *almost* be peaceful."

Silence stretched between them. She continued to stare out at the sea, but Grayson found himself watching her from the corner of his eye. He hoped she could not tell just how closely.

After several long minutes, she sighed softly and turned to him. Her eyes were a deep jade in the moonlight, her golden blonde hair turned silvery. She was a sea siren, pulled straight from the depths to tempt him.

Jacquetta lifted her hand from the rail. She reached out, hesitated, drew her hand back, then extended it again, finally settling it on his arm.

Grayson had not returned to his cabin to retrieve his tailcoat, and his shirt was rolled up to the elbows. Her fingertips grazed the bare skin of his arm, and despite the cool night, he was flooded with heat.

"When I reach for the door handle tomorrow morning, shall I find it locked?" Jacquetta asked, moving her gaze from where their skin touched to look directly into his eyes.

He did not know whether it was the stress of the last few hours or the way she seemed to glow in the moonlight. Later, he would not be able to account for what he did then.

Her hand on his arm was not enough. He had to know what her touch truly felt like. Grayson swept his arm around her waist, pulling her against him, and claimed her mouth.

It was as hot and welcoming as he'd been imagining. The seam of her mouth parted and her tongue curled around his in a silent but urgent invitation. Grayson groaned against her, tightening the grip on her waist. She fitted against him perfectly, her soft form curved against the hard planes of his body.

But she was muscular and well-formed herself, he realized as he slid his hands down from her waist to cup her bottom. He could feel the shifting muscles there as she thrust herself brazenly against his hips.

He'd thought her a typical debutante? Nothing could be further from the truth. She was a potent sea siren, risen from the ocean to claim his body and his sanity. The longer he spent in her arms, the more gladly Grayson would surrender both.

He had initiated the embrace, but Jacquetta was an equal, fierce participant. She tangled her fingers in his long hair, tugging at the roots none too gently. He growled and kissed the side of her mouth, nipping at her bottom lip. His mouth cut a hot path along her chin and down her throat. She caught his earlobe between her teeth as he did.

The lust threatened to consume him. He would take her here on the deck, regardless of the men scattered around them. The men who were watching.

A low, feral growl unfurled from inside him.

Grayson forced himself to set her down and away from him. The cool night air rushed in between their bodies in a meager attempt to cool the ardor between them. He forced some semblance of reason into his mind and held on to it.

He was the captain of this ship. His men could not see his acting like a lust-crazed adolescent. He needed to remain in full control of himself and his crew. Most of the men were concerned with serving their terms with the littlest amount of fuss or notice. But there were a few among the crew who would like nothing more than to challenge his authority and convince Delaurier to give them command of this ship. Or take it by force. Either possibility spelt disaster.

Jacquetta let out a strangled little sound, forcing his attention back to her.

Standing in the moonlight, lips swollen from the intensity of his kiss and panting slightly, Grayson did not know how he'd managed to get distracted from her in the first place. He wanted to sweep her up into his arms and carry her back to his bed.

Instead, he swallowed hard and inclined his head. They were no longer touching, and he decided that was for the better. For the moment, at least. "The men will thank you themselves, I am sure. But as their captain, I thank you as well."

Jacquetta pouted slightly. "Admitting you are the captain now, are you?"

Grayson merely raised an eyebrow.

She scoffed silently, glanced back out toward the dark sea, then to him. "I will retire now." The look she gave him was full of question.

"I shall remain here for a while yet. It will be a bastion to the men. They would never admit it, but they are shaken by the afternoon's events."

Jacquetta nodded, wrapping her arms around her against the chill wind. "Goodnight."

"Goodnight, Jack."

Grayson watched her go, admiring the swing of her hips beneath the ball gown she'd completely ruined in her brave care of his crew. Somewhere behind him, he detected Rook's mocking chuckle.

Bastion to the men, his ass. If he followed her now, he'd have her in his bed in ten seconds flat. Or on the dining table. Or his desk.

Grayson groaned and headed to the galley in search of a bucket of cold water.

CHAPTER NINE

THE DOOR WAS not locked when Jacquetta reached for it the next morning.

She'd slept late, rolling over and covering her head with her blanket when the knock on the cabin door announced the arrival of breakfast. Bryson usually left her a tray on the dining table, which she'd consume after Grayson disappeared for his morning activities. But today she did not rise even after the door closed behind him.

A glance at the clock across the cabin alerted Jacquetta that she had less than an hour before Grayson returned for his luncheon and afternoon counsels. Though his usual routine might be interrupted by the events of the day before.

She shivered in her bunk despite her ample bedsheets and blankets.

She'd never seen anything so gruesome. At least, not in person. The depictions in *Merriman's Medical* were excruciatingly detailed. But seeing it on the page and seeing it before her eyes was completely different. She'd studied the pages of the medical text for days during her initial training, committing the inner workings of the human body to memory, noting the treatments for everything from a severed limb to a head injury.

Most of her quests involved secrecy and stealth. If there was blood to be let, Red and her rapier usually saw to that. Yet, as

Jacquetta shivered recalling the bloody mess, a surge of pride went through her. She had not swooned or faltered when confronted with a new challenge. She'd risen to meet it, just as she'd been trained to do. She was a lady knight. She was capable.

Which, of course, brought her thoughts to the other major event of the previous day—the kiss Grayson had stolen from her in the moonlight.

Not precisely stolen, Jacquetta amended. She'd been more than willing, and not simply in service of her quest.

No, when Grayson Thane had pulled her into his arms and claimed her lips, it was the purely female part of her that responded, not the lady knight. She wanted what he was offering—every delicious bit of it. That unnerved her more than anything.

She was a virgin.

Jacquetta laughed to herself as she stared at the underside of the wooden panel that loomed over her bunk.

It was a miracle, really, that she was after all this time. Before being knighted, she'd never had a private conversation with a man who was not directly related to her. Afterward... well, she was an incomparable. A diamond of the first water. Gorgeous.

When her queen—through the duchess, of course—asked her to use those external gifts to serve her country? Jacquetta had not hesitated. She'd seduced married men and dandies alike. For the most part, it had been shockingly easy. Men were simple creatures. A flick of the skirt, a well-timed drag of her tongue over her bottom lip, and they fell at her feet.

Grayson was not so different.

Except that he was different in every way.

He too was drawn in by her beauty, of course. Jacquetta had seen him watching her with lust in his eyes. And just like all the men who had come before, seducing him was part of her quest.

But she'd never *wanted* before.

When she kissed Lord Andresen in Lady Brothwilde's study she had been calmly detached, kissing and touching in a coordinated dance meant to systematically untangle his defenses. But with Grayson, all of that care disappeared. The sensations surging through her, the languid heat that overtook her limbs and pooled between her legs—those were new. And so utterly delectable. No wonder men were so easily taken advantage of when filled with desire; Jacquetta was a professional in every sense, and yet when Grayson kissed her, she struggled to find a coherent thought.

It had been easy to stop herself with all her other targets. She'd never given in to their urging touches, had always stopped things well before they reached the point of no return. But with Grayson, for the first time, Jacquetta wanted to know what came next. She wanted to feel every sensation and give in to every urge he ignited in her body.

She chewed on that as she dressed and sipped on the tea from her breakfast tray. She chewed on the dry meat, making a face but forcing it down. They were well in the middle of the ocean now, four weeks into their voyage. Based on the sign she remembered seeing at Falmouth all those years ago, she could estimate that Barbados was an approximately seven-week journey. Which meant that whoever on the ship was in charge of rations would be carefully watching their stores. So, dried meat for breakfast it would be.

She could avoid it no longer.

Jacquetta wiped her hands on her napkin, tossed it to the table, and reached for the door handle.

It opened.

No resistance, no squeaking of hinges.

The door of the cabin swung open and a cool sea breeze swept in.

Jacquetta immediately retreated inside.

A minute later, she emerged onto the deck wrapped in a shawl, the wind already whipping her hair free of the knot she'd arranged at the base of her neck. But the smile that she felt spreading over her face could not be contained.

She was *free*.

Still stranded on a ship in the middle of the blasted ocean, still a captive, but her movements were finally unencumbered.

The crash of a wave against the side of the ship broke her reverie with depressing efficiency. Jacquetta forced a deep breath in, counted to three, and then slowly let it out. She was on a ship. But she was safe. She was on a ship. But the crew around her was experienced and capable. She'd seen that for herself the day before.

Another breath in and out, and she managed to look at the ocean. Only for a few seconds, but she did not go running back to Grayson's cabin. It would do for now.

"My lady!" Rook appeared before her, sweeping into a bow low enough to please the Queen of England herself. "We did not expect to see you on deck," he admitted, grinning. Jacquetta suspected that comment was aimed at Grayson, though she did not see the austere captain anywhere.

"I wish to visit the injured sailors," she said, adjusting her shawl. She didn't have a pin or brooch to keep it in place—other than the sharpened ones in her hair, which she would not reveal for something so unimportant as her own chill.

"Of course." Rook's eyes combed the deck fervently. "I will find someone to escort you."

"Can you escort me yourself?" she asked, offering him a smile.

She remembered Grayson's warnings, and had no wish to disobey them. The thought of seducing Rook, after the way Grayson had kissed her on the deck the night before, was utterly laughable. But Rook was a known entity, and he'd already proven himself eager to please. He would be less likely to challenge her when she started asking questions.

Jacquetta did want to visit the injured men she'd tended to yesterday, of course. But she was free outside of the cabin. There was no telling if Grayson might change his mind and closet her inside once again. She could not pass up this opportunity to scour the ship for as much information as possible.

Rook appeared positively devastated. "I cannot," he admitted sadly. "I must attend to my duties here. But Mr.—"

"No, no." Jacquetta waved her hand dismissively. "If I cannot have you, then I shall fend for myself. As you so kindly pointed out before, how much trouble can I get myself into aboard a ship?"

His expression told her he very much wished he could eat his words. He glanced around hopefully, as if an acceptable crewman at his leisure would appear. But all of the sailors Jacquetta could see were busy about their tasks. The injured from yesterday had depleted their numbers further.

Even better. If she did not have to worry about an escort at all, her search would be that much more efficient.

Rook grimaced as he turned back to her, but Jacquetta did not give him time to espouse another option before she jumped in.

"The men are still on below deck?" She nodded toward the hatch behind Rook.

"Orlop deck," he muttered, looking agitated. "Thane would not like—"

"I do not see Thane at present. Do you?" Jacquetta chirped brightly, stepping around him.

The hatch to the orlop deck was already open to let in air for the convalescing men. With a smart twist of her wrist, Jacquetta pulled in her skirt so that no one below would get a view up her dress, and began to climb down.

Rook rubbed his hand over his face worriedly. She winked at him before her head disappeared beneath the main deck and he was out of view.

Her feet landed on the wooden deck with a thump, and Jacquetta took the moment to straighten her clothing while also slyly observing around her. The hatch dropped her more or less in the middle of the ship; the mainmast towering above her partially blocked out the sun that was visible through the square of light above her head.

Her eyes went toward the bow, where the explosion had

ripped a hole in the side of the *Agamemnon*—and done even costlier damage to several of the men. The damage had been efficiently patched up, and no daylight peeked through the newly applied wooden planks. Jacquetta did wonder where the spare wood had come from. Did the ship sail with a stock of it for such repairs? Perhaps she would find the answer today.

Wary of lingering too long and chancing meeting the eye of an over-friendly sailor resting in his hammock, Jacquetta spun and started aft to the sick bay. She would speak with the surgeon, look in on the men she'd tended to yesterday as well as any other injured sailors, then she would excuse herself. Instead of returning to the main deck, she would slip into the hold and see what answers she might find.

But despite the humidity below the main deck, a shiver snaked down Jacquetta's spine. She glanced back over her shoulder, taking a quick survey of the hammocks swinging behind her. No eyes glinted back at her, but Jacquetta could not shake the feeling she was being watched. Determined to keep to her course, she pulled the shawl tighter around her shoulders and sought out the surgeon without allowing herself another backward glance.

GRAYSON WAS DEUCED tired.

He'd had long days before, of course. Most days at sea were long, especially as a captain. Having taken on the role of sailing master as well, he found whatever leisure time he'd had was filled with the laborious job of ensuring they actually arrived in Barbados and not Georgia or Buenos Aires.

If he had any leisure time, Grayson was sure that a certain entrancing blonde tart would have managed to steal it from him anyhow.

Though it was not his usual habit, he supped with the crew in the mess. His presence was needed. He'd made a point throughout the day to have a moment, however small, with each of the members of his crew—even the less desirable ones. The effort of caring had drained him to the last. He did care. He understood exactly what it meant to serve upon this ship; very few were there willingly. Delaurier held sway over them all in one way or another. But most of the time, Grayson insulated himself from feelings. They were too messy, and they got in the way of sound judgment. Sound judgment was what was required to complete a task efficiently, thus reducing time from his sentence and getting him that much closer to freedom.

Grayson nodded at a man up in the rigging, trying to discern who it was in the fading light of early evening. He failed. The man was nothing more than silhouette. But he raised his hand in salute all the same before continuing on.

He was almost back to his cabin. He would allow himself ten minutes to enjoy sparring with Jack. Any more than that and he was liable to give in to his body's baser needs—both physical exhaustion and seemingly uncontrollable lust. But he needed his head relatively clear so he could note down the status of each crewman.

He could picture the wooden box on the lowest shelf beside the bed, where he kept each man's family information and a tally of their voyages. Delaurier required him to report any errors made by the crew, however minor, which could be used to append additional days to their indentures. It wrecked him to do it, but if he reported nothing, Delaurier would extend them all with impunity.

The looming task soured the food in his belly as he reached for the door handle of his cabin. He'd left it unlocked and spent many a spare moment throughout the day wondering what Jacquetta would do with her newfound freedom. He expected some sly, haughty comment that was not really thanks, but he could not wait to hear what she would conjure up—

She was not inside.

Grayson immediately looked to her bunk, expecting to find her huddled there beneath the blankets, thinking he'd missed seeing her there somehow.

But the bed was neatly made, the blankets flat and tucked in at the corners. Her supper tray was on the table, untouched.

Where the hell was she?

The vision of Jacquetta's lithe body flung out over the ocean flashed in his mind. No, she was not that desperate to escape—and she was terrified of the water. Such a thing was suicide, and she knew it. She might not have been pleased at the fact that he'd taken liberties, but she was hardly some addled debutante ready to throw herself into the great blue ocean over her jeopardized reputation.

Grayson abandoned his quarters as quickly as he'd entered them, not bothering with the lock and completely forgetting the task he'd set himself for the evening. *She must be visiting the injured men.* He crossed the main deck in several long strides, gracefully swinging his body down through the hatch and catching the ladder to the orlop deck halfway down.

Several men's heads popped up toward the bow, where most of the crew's hammocks were strung. Grayson spun on his heel and made for the sick bay. The surgeon was exactly where he expected, sitting on his stool in the corner noting things down in the little medical journal he kept. Grayson had once caught him sketching a particularly nasty arm break sustained from a fall from the rigging. After that, he'd never dared another peek.

"Ahem," Grayson said from the doorway.

The surgeon glanced up from his book, not bothering to bow or salute. He satisfied himself with a subtle flick of his eyes downward.

"Back so soon, captain?" he said as he began scratching away at the page once more.

"Is Miss Lawson still with the men?" Grayson jerked his head back out toward where the hammocks hung. There were, of course, several men around the sick bay. But the damage inflicted yesterday was beyond what the small cabin could handle; many of the healthy crewman had been forced to sling their hammocks down in the hold to make room to care for the injured in the regular crew quarters.

The surgeon paused. "Miss Lawson has not been with us for some hours," he said slowly, head cocked to one side.

Grayson's stomach clenched. "Indeed." He forced himself to sound casual, though he doubted the surgeon was fooled. "Did she mention where she intended to spend her afternoon?"

"She returned to the main deck after..." The surgeon paused, brow wrinkling slightly. "No, I did not actually see her climb back up the ladder. I was busy in here." He nodded toward the unconscious sailor nearest to Grayson. "And when I returned to check on the less injured men, she had already departed. But she must have returned to the main deck. Where else could she have gone?"

"Where else, indeed." Grayson kept his movements easy, though his instincts were screaming at him to start searching— quickly and thoroughly.

He tapped the doorframe in salutation and then stepped back onto the orlop deck, swinging his gaze over to the maze of hammocks. For a moment, he listened very carefully. She could not be in one of those—if she was in one against her will, she'd be caterwauling and wresting her body around like the hellcat she was. If she was conscious.

He dismissed that thought. It oughtn't have bothered him, given the number of times he himself had had occasion to render her unconscious. But the protective urge surged through him nonetheless.

If she'd joined one of the sailors willingly...

That thought had him gripping the ladder so hard the wood groaned beneath his hand.

Wherever the hell she was, he needed to find her. Immediately.

THE SHIP SWAYED mightily, sending Jacquetta stumbling sideways and grabbing on to a crate to keep herself upright. She was not made for the sea. In fact, if she never set foot on another oceangoing vessel for the remainder of her natural life, she would be so incredibly blessed. She refused to remember that another sea voyage stood between her and merry ole England.

She put a fist to her stomach, willing her innards to calm. They'd been threatening to rise out of her for the last hour. No one had told her that the deeper she went into the ship, the more intense the rocking would become. To be fair, she'd told no one of her intentions to search the hold. Or the other parts of the ship she'd managed to scour that day.

She did not even know the proper names for all of the compartments she'd weaved her way through. Many of them had been locked; for today, she'd allowed them to remain so—though her fingers itched for the sharp lock-picking pins in her hair. Dominique's careful instructions floated through her mind, about how to select the correct pin for a given lock and how to minimize the sound of the latch springing free.

She would need to devise another excuse for getting at those locked doors, especially given that she'd learned precious little from her other explorations. The very scary gun room, as she'd dubbed it in her mind, ought to be a lady knight's daydream. For Jane, who was proficient and deadly accurate with every type of firearm Jacquetta had ever seen her with, it probably was. While Jacquetta was able to identify the weapons, she was more worried about how she would manage to escape when the crew was armed to the teeth.

The men taking apart the weapons and oiling them until they gleamed did not make her feel much better. At least they accepted that she'd lost her way, even if they stared at her bosom a bit too much for her to be entirely comfortable. The one named

Payne in particular set her teeth on edge.

She'd found a storeroom filled with extra sail and rope, and the locker that housed the anchor cable, now neatly coiled as the ship cut through the waves.

The most interesting had been the hold. First, it was massive. Jacquetta had not truly appreciated how large the ship was. She'd seen Indiamen in port before, but always from afar. Even aboard one, she'd been confined to the top two decks and never realized how vast the ship's hull truly was.

It did not take long for her to figure out what the main enterprise of Thane and his crew was. They were smugglers.

Crate after crate of goods—the ones she'd heard being loaded when she was trapped inside her wagon immediately after her kidnapping—filled the hold. Some were stacked taller than she was, which did not seem a prudent choice, given the way the ship shifted and swayed beneath her feet. But then, who was she to question the wisdom of the mighty Grayson Thane, *ton* outcast, pirate lord, and smuggler extraordinaire?

The ship swayed heavily again, leaving Jacquetta clinging to the crate beside her. She dimly noted the numbers and letters painted on the side. Some were neat, some were scrawled, some were nearly unreadable. But she'd looked at each of them, committing them to memory, trying to match them up with the box of numbers and secret black phoenix notebook. So far, she had not recognized anything. The first chance she had alone in the cabin, she would look through those pages again and see if she'd missed some nuance.

Several loud thumps sounded above her head, followed by voices. Still holding the side of the crate, Jacquetta edged around toward the side of the ship, where she would not be so easily visible by those coming down the hatch from the orlop deck.

Her instincts proved true. Less than a minute later, a pair of feet appeared, followed by a body and head. Three more sailors climbed down behind the first.

They each bore a hammock slung over their shoulder, bearing the contraptions as if they weren't made of layer upon layer of heavy, knotted robe. Jacquetta had seen the sailors rolling in and out of them in the crew quarters a deck above with ease, though she could not imagine managing such a thing herself.

The group lingered by the hatch, guffawing and talking loudly. The faintly alcoholic scent of grog floated across the hold to where she hid behind the crates. Why were they down in the hold? All Jacquetta had seen here were crates of goods.

But in the low light thrown by an oil lamp one of them had brought down, Jacquetta watched the first sailor begin to string up his hammock. Then the next.

Jesus, Mary, and Joseph save her.

They were settling in—and damn close to the hatch where she would need to make her escape. The light leaking in from the main deck two levels above was heavily diffused, but Jacquetta knew it must be evening. Supper would be delivered to Grayson's cabin soon, and he would expect her to be there to share it.

But if she made for the ladder now…

Jacquetta shook her head, suppressing the heavy sigh in her chest. If she moved now she would be discovered, and have to explain why she was in the hold at all. She'd rather deal with Grayson's ire than his suspicion.

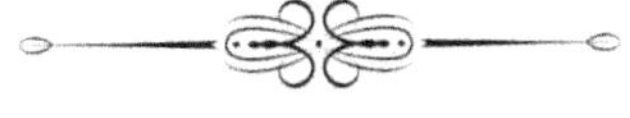

CHAPTER TEN

*L*ONG IS THE *way and hard, that out of Hell leads up to Light.*

She'd been hiding in the hold for three-quarters of an hour. The sailors showed no sign of weariness. Quite the opposite, to Jacquetta's chagrin.

One of them had produced a flask of strong-smelling liquor that burned her nostrils even at a distance. With each round the flask made around the little troop, the more rancorous they became. They even lapsed into song for a time, the words bawdy enough to pinken even the experienced Jacquetta's ears.

Her only comfort was that with the introduction of the liquor, the men's antics would only last so long before they would succumb to drunken stupor and fall back flaccid in their hammocks.

The bloke farthest from her had already dipped back into the shadows more than once. Each time he straightened himself and rejoined the group, his eyes were heavier. She could not see the rest of the men clearly—they mostly had their backs to her. They were all vaguely familiar, though she could not think of their names. Now, if she'd seen a labeled portrait, they'd have been seared into her mind for all eternity.

Two of the men peeled off, whether to relieve themselves or to search out more liquor, Jacquetta could not surmise from the drunken mumbling. But they did not come in her direction, so she allowed herself to relax.

There—the man farthest from her was gone again, fallen back into his hammock. She counted out the minutes, waiting to see if he would return. When four full minutes had passed, she decided he was a goner. One down—three to go.

She shifted on her feet, trying to relieve the strain in her muscles from standing at attention in one place for so long. She even let her head lean to the side, resting it against the hard, vertical panels of the crate. It was nothing compared to the pillow on her bunk two levels above, but even the small action was a relief.

Jacquetta resisted the urge to let her eyes close and instead forced herself back to Milton.

If thence he scape into what ever world,

Or unknown Region, what remains him less

Then unknown dangers and as hard escape.

The stink of the liquor was getting stronger. Had one of the dolts spilled it?

Jacquetta wrinkled her nose, unable to pinpoint exactly what it was. Not rum, but something akin to it. An illicit version made in a home still, probably. She vaguely wondered if there were barrels of it stashed somewhere aboard the *Agamemnon*—it would be part and parcel of the smuggling operation.

The ship chose that moment to move beneath her, sending a wave of rolling, putrid scent to fill her nostrils at the same time that her stomach turned inside of her. Jacquetta bit her lip to keep from groaning aloud and swung her arm around to her mouth—

A beefy hand closed around her wrist, holding her arm out and away from her body.

It took Jacquetta only as long as it did her attacker to twist her arm and bend it behind her forcefully for her to realize what had happened.

One of the men who'd left the group had stumbled upon her. But who—

He leaned forward, just enough of his face illuminated by the lamp on the other side of the hold for her to identify him—Payne.

His hulking form had looked familiar when it came down the stairs, but from behind she had not recognized the leering man whom she'd last seen hunched over a rifle in the armory.

"You have mistaken yourself, sir. I am no stowaway, but a guest upon this ship. Release me," she said in her haughtiest voice.

Payne laughed silently, his mouth tugging up at once side to reveal a row of straight teeth. He might have been handsome, if it weren't for the cruel twist of his lips. And his gaze… the way he raked his eyes over her body and face… His were the eyes she'd felt upon her earlier, when she first landed below deck.

Jacquetta repressed the shiver that tingled in her spine and tried again. "Release me. I am under the protection of—"

"No one," he said sharply. His eyes settled on hers, but she found that even more unnerving than when he'd been ogling her body. "You are a prisoner," he reminded her, tightening his hold on her arm. "And just now, you are a prisoner who has slipped her chains." He stepped closer to her, pinning her to the wall; her arm was behind her and her options were quickly narrowing.

She swallowed but kept her chin firm and stubborn. "Then you had best return me before the master realizes I am missing and punishes you for it."

Payne threw back his head and laughed. "Thane's not my master," he gurgled, an unhinged glint dancing in his eyes.

Her stomach tightened. If Payne was truly unstable… reason would not work. She would have to free herself.

First, she needed to keep him talking—distracted, so she could reach a weapon.

"If not Thane, then who?"

His eyes narrowed. "Chatty chit. Best we put that mouth to other uses."

He lowered his head, and the scent of the liquor on his breath was overwhelming. Jacquetta did shiver this time, turning her head to the side in unfeigned revulsion.

"Find me offensive, do you?" His damp breath licked over her face, but she forced herself to focus. She let her body quake while her mind worked.

"You are out of line," she ground out.

"You didn't seem to mind it so much when Thane had his way with you up on deck." Payne's mouth touched her ear, and she strained away, throwing the arm that was not pinned up defensively. He groped for her hand, but she thrashed her head side to side, evading him for a few precious seconds.

It was long enough—she had two of the knife-sharp hairpins grasped in her fist.

But now both her hands were pinned, in addition to the weight of Payne's body against her. Wriggling her hand too much might give her away, but she could try to pass it off as struggling. She could get those pins into position, and when he gave her a fraction of an inch, she would stab him. Damn the repercussions.

"Get off me! I shall scream," she threatened, tugging hard at her arms. Payne was strong as an ox, and the liquor had turned his thick limbs heavy. She'd need to bring up a knee to off-foot him enough to stab him with the pins. It would be a small injury, but she didn't need to kill him.

"Much good may it do you." He leaned in close to her face again. Jacquetta's stomach gave a traitorous roll. "I like to hear a woman scream."

"You sadistic—"

Before she could finish the sentence, all of Payne's weight was suddenly lifted off her. Her hands were free. She nearly dropped the pins in her fist as relief rolled through her. But a second was the only luxury she had before she grasped what was unfurling before her.

It was so damn dark, the only light coming from the other side of the hold. But Grayson's body moved in magnificent, graceful pounces as he swung and dove. He landed hit after hit on Payne, and if he absorbed any of his own, Jacquetta could not make them out.

She'd thought Red skilled in physical combat? Grayson moved with such swift precision it was like watching an exhibition at the Theatre Royal in London. Though considerably bloodier.

She could only assume the shining liquid staining Grayson's fists was blood, though in the dark of the hold it glimmered nearly black.

After all she'd seen the last two days, it hardly registered.

What did become obvious to her was that they were creating a scene. The other four drunken men appeared, but once they saw that it was Grayson pummeling Payne, they kept their distance. Payne was still standing, his big body strong and stalwart despite the beating he was taking. But much longer, and Grayson would do irreparable injury. Jacquetta had no idea what the consequences of *that* would be, but she doubted it would help her own cause. Even though she'd like nothing more than to toss Payne in the black ocean and never look back.

"Ahem," Jacquetta said. "Thane."

Nothing.

Well, very much something, actually. A lot of blood and fisticuffs. But no response.

"Thane."

She watched his head turn her way, but then he was back at it.

A second later, Payne staggered and fell to one knee.

"Thane!" Jacquetta yelled. Grayson's fist paused in midair. "I require you to escort me back to my bunk," she said, her voice quivering. She did not mind it; let the men think her shaken—in truth, she was a bit—but if it would draw Grayson out of the infuriated haze he was mired in, she would show a bit of vulnerability.

He was breathing heavily as he cut a gaze to the bystanders. "Throw him in the hell." No one moved. "If I hear you've given him any type of comforts, I will have you thrown in with him."

Whatever that meant, it got feet moving. Grayson stepped around Payne's hunched form. As he did, Jacquetta heard the downed man hiss. Whether it was in pain or menace, she recoiled.

Grayson must have seen it, because a second later he was at her side, grasping her arm. Instantly, warmth started to spread through her. Where minutes before Payne's touch had felt like a weight dragging her down, Grayson's hand upon her was different entirely. Not quite calming. Whatever was between them was much too complicated for that. But she did not push him away, and nor did he make any move to stop touching her as he nodded toward the ladder.

"You first," he said.

Jacquetta nodded, climbing one ladder, waiting at the top, and then climbing another. The instant they stepped on the main deck, Rook appeared.

"Christ, Thane, what happened?"

"Go verify they've secured Payne in the hell. Get the rest of those men out of the hold. I don't care if they have to sleep up on the deck. I do not want anyone down there for the rest of the night."

If Rook opened his mouth to make his customary argument, Jacquetta did not see it. Grayson's hand was at the small of her back now, guiding her toward his cabin. She was not inclined to refuse.

She opened the door to the cabin herself, not pausing to wait for any gentlemanly niceties. For once, when she heard the lock clicking into place behind her, she felt relief rather than dread.

She made it to her bunk. Sat down. Buried the pins still clasped in her fist in a wrinkle of the bedsheets. She ought to lie back, ought to rest. But she could not. She felt as if a thousand glowworms were dancing in her stomach, her chest, her arms and legs. She could not sit.

Grayson rifled through the sideboard set into the wall, making more noise than a child searching the kitchen for sweets. His carefully honed finesse seemed to have deserted him. But when he stood, he yanked the cork from a bottle, took a deep swig, and then held it out to her.

The scent hit her nostrils, and Jacquetta went weak in the knees.

Cognac.

She hardly realized she'd stridden across the room—but when the cool bottle hit her lips and the rich liquid slid down her throat, she was verging on ecstasy.

Jacquetta paused to gulp down a breath of air then took another long drink. She might have drained the bottle—drunkenness be damned—if it had not been for the sound of Grayson's dark laughter rolling over her.

Slowly, she lowered the bottle. Grayson's eyes were on her. She dragged her tongue out over her lips, not wanting to waste a single glorious drop.

"What do you find so amusing in all of this?" she said, chest heaving. She still had not caught her breath.

He raised one dark brow. "Cognac?"

Jacquetta swallowed, savoring the slight burn in her throat. "It is better than claret."

His eyebrow lowered at the same time that one side of his mouth lifted in that infernal smirk. "For once, we agree."

He held his hand out for the bottle. With a wistful sigh, Jacquetta surrendered it. Grayson's fingers brushed over hers, and again that warmth began to spread through her. This time, there was nothing calming or comforting. Now the warmth turned to heat. And that heat started to sizzle.

She jerked her hand back.

That was what Dominique spoke of when she got that expression of feline wonderment on her face. Jacquetta had never felt it before. But she wanted to again.

Grayson stared at her, his own breath coming in heavy but silent pants. He stuffed the cork back in the top of the bottle and set it behind him on the table without glancing back. His eyes were fixed upon her. But he did not move. He simply stared at her—her eyes, down her face to her mouth, then back to her eyes again.

"Thank you," Jacquetta breathed. "For saving me."

Not that she had truly needed saving. She was completely confident she would have eventually extricated herself from the situation. Had she been afraid? Of course. But not the all-consuming fear she felt when she looked at the ocean. No, the fear she'd felt when Payne attacked her was useful, sharpening her awareness of her body and her mind so she could save herself. But her mind was not on Payne now. It was on the tall, dark, brooding captain before her.

Payne's assault already felt like a distant memory; the only trace left behind was the adrenaline pounding through her. Clouding her judgment. Or perhaps giving her the final push she'd been too hesitant to take.

Seduction *was* her goal.

"You are incredibly self-possessed, given what you just experienced," Grayson commented.

He expected her to be weeping. Disappointment flared in her stomach; perhaps she'd better play out that ruse.

But his voice was gravelly. He was as affected as she. Jacquetta would have wagered that if she glanced downward, she would see the physical confirmation of it. Thank the Lord that no one could see the liquid heat pooling between her legs.

But he might feel it.

That wanton thought sent another rush of heat to her core.

She stepped toward him, catching one hand on the back of a chair to hold herself steady. She was trembling, but not from fear.

"Payne is a monster. And you would have slain him like one," she added. There was no remorse in her voice, no quarter. Jacquetta thought she saw Grayson's body relax, just slightly.

"It was no less than he deserved."

She swayed her hips forward a half step, very close to touching him. Her skirts brushed over the battered leather of his boots with a soft hiss.

Using the edge of the chair to raise herself an inch or so, she tilted her head and positioned her lips an inch from his chin. She was close enough to see each strand of dark stubble. "Then why did you stop?" She breathed against him.

He sucked in a breath. "Unexpected deaths are inconvenient."

She licked her lower lip, her tongue so close to touching him she could almost taste his skin. "I thought you were in charge."

Grayson's hand went to the chair back now as well, gripping it so hard the wood creaked. But Jacquetta kept her eyes trained on his elegantly curved mouth, the sharp line of his jaw, the layers of unshaven beard that she longed to drag her tongue over.

"I am," he growled.

She rose to her toes and caught his lower lip between her teeth. "Prove it."

She was no longer holding on to the chair. No, there was no need. Grayson crushed her against him, wrapping his hands around her waist and pinning her body against his. Jacquetta could feel the hard length of him pressing against her urgently through her skirts. Had the cognac gone to her head, or was he really that large? She thrust her hips forward greedily, eager to know for herself.

She liked the way his body felt against her? Jesus, Mary, and Joseph… *his mouth.*

A wonderful, wicked thing it was.

His tongue curled around hers in a sinful dance—drawing her out, teasing, then surging inside her own mouth with unbridled possessiveness.

The men she'd kissed before? Idiots, prudes. Nothing.

Nothing in her life compared to kissing Grayson Thane like this, with no boundaries between them and adrenaline pulsing in her ears.

Jacquetta buried her hands in his hair at the same moment that he pulled his mouth from hers and began to kiss his way along her jaw. The days' growth of stubble on his chin scraped along the sensitive skin of her throat. She whimpered, tightening her fingers in his hair. It was thick and silky, and the dark strands curled around her fingers like tendrils of sinuous velvet.

Was she standing? She must be, because Grayson's hands were no longer on her waist. They were assaulting her breasts; his thumbnails dragged along her skin from the crease of her arms along the curves of her breast to meet in the center of her chest. He tugged at the gown and chemise, and then a second later it sprang open and her breasts were revealed.

He'd ripped the laces entirely, Jacquetta realized. But she didn't care.

When his mouth closed around one of her nipples, the short beard on his skin scraping while his tongue swirled around the tightened bud, Jacquetta nearly came out of her skin.

The sound must have been too much for him.

Grayson groaned mightily, dragging his mouth away from her breast. Her skin protested at the sudden rush of cool air. But then he pulled her against him again. He spun her around and in one swift movement shoved the chair out of the way and deposited her on the top of the dining table.

He reached for her skirts, moving so quickly that Jacquetta could hardly register what was happening until she felt his hand sliding up her inner thigh. *Yes, oh yes.* If he was half as adept with his hands as he was with his mouth, she wanted him touching her everywhere. She grabbed the edge of her skirt and yanked it away to give him unhindered access.

She tore her mouth away from his, fascinated, wanting to watch him as he touched her.

Grayson stroked his fingertips over the mound of dark blonde curls with such gentle reverence that it took Jacquetta by surprise. Then he paused, nudging his way inside her folds. A deep rumble resonated from his chest as he explored her entrance, coating his fingers in her juices.

She grabbed the edge of the table as he nudged deeper. "Oh, yes," she moaned softly.

It was all the encouragement Grayson needed—he slid one finger inside of her, pulled it back out, and then joined it with another.

Darkness and light flashed before Jacquetta's eyes. She'd touched herself, but this… it had never been like this.

He did not give her even a second to adjust; his fingers moved within her, pumping in and out. Jacquetta could not watch anymore; she was too overcome with feeling. Her head fell back, and Grayson pounced, making love to her collarbone and throat with his mouth while his fingers moved inside of her.

She could feel the climax building—a thousand times more intense than anything she'd ever managed herself. Son of a duke, criminal, pirate lord—she did not care. So long as he kept moving inside of her like that.

"Good girl, give in," Grayson breathed, watching as he urged her over the edge. With the next thrust of his hands, he curved his fingertips up and dragged them over a spot inside of her Jacquetta had not even known existed.

She exploded with pleasure; her hips arched off the table and her cry of ecstasy rang through the cabin. A rush of wetness spilled from her. She ought to have been embarrassed at her own wantonness, but she could not find it in her. Not when she felt this incredible.

She did not even know her body could do these things… let alone that it would feel so magnificent. Her education, both as a woman and a lady knight, had been woefully deficient.

Grayson was still kissing her. He slowly withdrew his hand, wiping it subtly on her skirts. But he did not pull away. He stepped between her legs, a hand on each thigh possessively. He kissed his way up her neck until he found her mouth, which he took with as much heat as before. Jacquetta opened her lips in welcome, ready for whatever he had to offer.

He lingered at her mouth only for a moment before continuing down to her ear and nibbling at the earlobe, sending fresh shivers and warmth tingling through her.

"I had no idea it would be like this," she said against his glorious, dark hair, barely more than a whisper.

Grayson stiffened instantly.

Jacquetta shut her eyes. *Shit.*

He spoke against her throat, his breath still hot. "You have not done this before."

Damn her climax-addled mind.

"Not precisely all of it, no," she admitted. She kept her hand tangled in his hair, toying with the long strands.

"When I found you with Lord Andresen…"

Jacquetta tugged at his hair, trying to get him to look at her. Or at least to kiss her. "I am not completely inexperienced. But I have never done *that*." Her body shivered involuntarily at the ghost of pleasure still on her skin.

Grayson pulled back then, but when she leaned forward to catch his lips, he stepped back. Not entirely out from between her legs, though. She was tempted to wrap her legs around him and drag him back down.

"But you are untouched," he said.

She laughed incredulously. "After that?"

"You know what I mean," Grayson ground out.

"I am still in possession of my maidenhead, yes." She licked her lips, dragging her eyes over him. She was half undressed, but he still wore all of his clothes. It was not fair at all. "But it seemed that was about to be remedied."

He took a long, decisive step back. Toward the door.

"You are not thinking clearly. You have been through something inexplicably horrible. I should not have done… this." He gestured in her direction.

Jacquetta slid to her feet. The desire burning in her veins danced dangerously close to anger. "I asked you for this."

But Grayson was shaking his head.

"Be under no illusions, Thane. I wanted this as much as you." Her voice was steady, if coated in lust. Jacquetta found she did not care.

"I…" Grayson shook his head as if to clear it, but by the expression on his face, she could deduce he was no less addled. "Rest. I will have a fresh tray brought for your supper."

Jacquetta bit her lip and watched his eyes darken with lust in response. "Won't you join me?"

"You are going to kill me, Jack."

"Then it will be an exquisite death."

He raked a hand through his hair, and she could see that he was truly torn—between some sort of insane, previously unseen chivalric notions… and his desire to toss her back on the table and have his way with her.

Unfortunately for her, the former won out.

Grayson shook his head again, and then turned wordlessly toward escape.

The cabin door closed with a thundering shudder. She would have missed the sound of the lock clicking into place had she not been listening specifically for it.

Jacquetta collapsed back on her berth, her gown still in disarray around her.

She was panting so heavily she could not hear a single sound from around the ship—not the distant voices or crashing of waves, only the pounding of her own desire inside of her.

The black phoenix notebook flashed in her mind, its pages as clear as if she held it in her hand. She ought to get up and look at it now, compare it to what she'd seen in the hold. Grayson surely would not be returning anytime soon.

But she could not quite bring herself to stand. Or move at all. She lay in her bunk, savoring the remnants of pleasure and sated desire that weighed down her limbs.

Seducing Grayson Thane, she decided, would be no trouble at all.

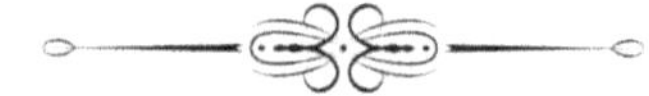

CHAPTER ELEVEN

GRAYSON STOOD ON the deck until it was too dark to think. Only the barest crew were out now, guiding the silent ship through the night. Even the gossip about what had happened was silent, though he knew that by morning, the *Agamemnon* itself would be buzzing.

"Well?"

Rook coughed awkwardly, coming to stand beside him. The mate had been lurking in the shadows near the mainmast for a quarter of an hour, surely debating how to approach him without earning a lashing.

"He's in the hell, and not pleased about it," Rook confirmed.

"Nor am I."

"The men will talk tomorrow." There was a hint of admonishment in Rook's voice.

Grayson let out a dark, mirthless chuckle. "I thought you were Miss Lawson's most stalwart defender, Rook."

The other man was quiet for a few moments. "Certain choices have costs," he eventually said.

Grayson suppressed a sigh. "I know it better than most."

"Aye," Rook agreed. "He's got Delaurier's ear."

"And I have Delaurier's ship," Grayson said sharply. "While it is in my command, I will not have men disobeying me. The order was to leave Jacquetta untouched."

"You did not have to beat him near to death," Rook grumbled.

"Yes, I did," Grayson said evenly. For so, so many reasons.

But his thoughts were not on Payne.

His mind was completely ensnared with the wanton, fierce sea siren waiting for him in his cabin.

Lord, he hoped she hadn't crawled into his bed to wait. If he found her there, naked beneath the sheets… even he did not have enough control for that. Where Jacquetta was concerned, it seemed he had no control at all.

"I am surprised to see you here," Rook said, breaking into his thoughts.

Fuck. Was he as obvious as all that? "Why is that?"

"I would expect you to be wiping away Miss Lawson's tears, naturally."

Not her tears, Grayson thought. The feel of her wetness in his palm, her heat clenching around his fingers, surged through his mind. He almost moaned.

"Miss Lawson is made of sterner stuff than that," Grayson said.

She seemed to be made of steel, the way she was unperturbed by the assault. Or molten ore, the way she began hot and liquid in his hands.

Rook chuckled softly. "Of course she is. I should not have thought otherwise."

Perhaps Jacquetta Lawson was like an itch. She was not the type of woman who usually piqued Grayson's interest. But to deny what was between them at this juncture was outright foolish. He wanted her so badly that his cock threatened to explode out of his trousers at the mere memory of her. And she… she wanted him just as much. He'd felt the evidence of it in his own hands.

But a virgin… Fuck.

She did not act like a damn virgin. That was his mistake, Grayson realized. He'd been so caught up in his own lust that he had not taken the time to truly know the woman. He was blind with his need.

Like the persistent tugging of an itch to be scratched.

He ought to bed her and be done with it.

They would be in Barbados in three weeks or less. At which point he would surrender her to Delaurier, be freed from his indenture, and never see Jacquetta again. It was a natural termination to a hasty dalliance. It was perfect.

That warning in his gut? It was nothing more than the excitement of the night's events and his own lust-addled mind. It would be gone once he'd bedded her.

Another thought had become clear in Grayson's mind while he stared into the abyss trying to cool his ardor: there could be no more leaving Jacquetta to roam the ship unattended. It would be much too easy for something to happen to her—and he would take no chances with the one thing standing between him and his freedom.

But locking her back in the cabin was not viable either. Not if he wanted her to welcome him into her bed. His bed, he mentally corrected himself. Like hell was he going to try to squeeze in that bunk with her.

"Rook."

The man twitched beside him, muscles tensing. Awaiting his command.

"Beginning tomorrow, Miss Lawson will join us on deck each day that the weather allows it."

"If she should wish it…" Rook sounded wary.

"I wish it," Grayson finished. "Assign her to a different duty each day. I don't care if she is merely counting biscuits; she shall have two men with her at all times. But not the same men for more than one day. We do not give anyone the chance to take liberties." Or for her to worm her way into any of his men's good graces. It was not jealousy speaking, Grayson reassured himself, but self-preservation.

"Wouldn't she be safer in the cabin?" Rook asked.

Grayson sighed. "Undoubtedly. But you've met the chit. Would you relish being the one to deliver that news to her?"

Rook squawked.

A half-smile pulled at Grayson's mouth.

But then he remembered what awaited him in his cabin. He blew out a long, slow breath. The course was set. He was ready.

"Goodnight, Rook."

"If you say so." Rook sighed, his mind already distracted with planning his new task.

Grayson felt that pull of laughter that only Jacquetta seemed to ignite bubbling up from him as he strode back to his quarters.

SHE WAS ASLEEP. How could she possibly be asleep?

Grayson felt as if every muscle in his body was coiled, ready to spring into action and take her. His skin tingled with the need to be pressed against hers. His cock… it was making some very insistent demands as well.

But Jacquetta was asleep.

She lay on her back, her blankets pulled up around her shoulders. He could just see the edge of the chemise she'd been wearing beneath her gown; he recognized it from the torn edge visible above the blankets.

"Christ," Grayson said under his breath.

But Jacquetta's chest simply moved up and down in slow, deep, rhythmic sleep.

He stomped to his own bed, selfishly hoping the sound would awaken her. But when he turned, she lay just as before. Not bothering to shuck his clothes, Grayson fell facedown on the bed and tried to ignore the need pulsing through his body.

It was a very long time before he fell asleep.

"The topsail."

"No, that is the mainsail. That is the topsail," Kellerman said patiently, nodding over her shoulder.

Jacquetta smiled sheepishly and nodded. "Mainsail, topsail, foresail," she said, nodding to each in turn.

"Yes," he agreed. "Well done, Miss Lawson."

"Hardly. You've had to correct me at least thrice," she said, still smiling. "Now do I get to climb up into the rigging?"

Kellerman choked on a cough. "My lady, you—"

"Miss," she corrected him for at least the tenth time that day.

"Miss," he acknowledged. "I was told to teach you about the sails and their management."

Jacquetta cocked her head to the side. "What better way to learn than up among the sails themselves?"

"Ordinarily, I would not disagree with you, miss. But given your…" He flinched.

"My gender?" she finished, enjoying the pained expression on Kellerman's face. She did not truly expect him or anyone else to allow her up in the rigging. She was wearing a skirt, for one, not precisely suited to climbing. Secondly, that skirt would give anyone on the deck below quite a display…

But the one man she would not mind showing off for was nowhere to be seen.

"I suppose I shall remain here, then." Jacquetta sighed.

Kellerman was blatantly relieved. "I need to go check the—"

She waved her hand dismissively. He'd minded her well enough for the day. "Off you go. I shall stay here and not get into any sort of mischief." She held up her hand in a mock oath. "You have my word of honor."

The middle-aged sailor's face shone with relief as he swung himself into the rigging and began to climb.

A week of this. For seven days, she'd been passed around the crew, an extra chore that no one really wanted. At least, that was how it had started. But on day two, she was assigned to the galley. After that, she started her morning by greeting the cook and procuring a ration of biscuits. Once she started sharing those with her daily taskmasters, her popularity improved considerably.

And Grayson? She'd not had a private word with him in an entire week.

That was not entirely true, she corrected herself. Last night, he'd told her to stop stealing biscuits. An order that she blatantly ignored.

It was not that he was ignoring her; it was that she had barely seen him at all. Wherever she was on the ship—be it on the quarterdeck, with the surgeon, or standing in the shadow of the mainmast—Grayson was scarce. If he did appear, he was engaged in rapid conversation with one of his men, his steps quick and purposeful.

Did he even see the long glances she sent his way? Jacquetta was starting to feel like an annoying, lovesick dandy. The type she always mocked. Or manipulated.

Had he lost interest in her so quickly? Or was he truly *that* busy?

She had to know. Her quest demanded it—if seduction was not going to work, then she needed to devise an alternate plan. Though the little tasks she'd been set daily were a boon of their own. Biscuits in hand, wearing a low-cut gown and a wide smile, Jacquetta had covertly questioned every sailor assigned to watch over her. She might never be left alone—a method of protection from the likes of Payne, whom she had not seen since the incident in the hold—but she'd learned a fair amount about the ship's operation. Most importantly, she'd learned about the men that crewed it.

Many of them had that same haunted look in their eyes that so often flushed through Grayson's. And she had learned more about the papers in the small wooden box—they did not correspond to shipments in the cargo hold. They were records of the *men* on the ship.

But what all those numbers meant… she needed another look.

Tonight, she decided.

Grayson had not been returning to the cabin for supper. Tonight, as soon as Bryson left the tray, she would have a look.

Tonight, she would not fall asleep.

When Grayson returned to the cabin, she would be awake and she would be waiting.

As if summoned by her thoughts, Grayson appeared from one of the cabins that lined the half-covered corridor near his own. At his side was the quartermaster. One of her minders had pointed out all of the ranking crew members to her on her first day on deck.

Grayson climbed the stairs to the quarterdeck, stopping near the help. The quartermaster followed behind him, short gray hair whipping in the wind, his lips moving in constant speech. He reminded her a bit of an overzealous terrier.

Jacquetta smiled at the comparison. What did that make Grayson?

A wolf, she decided. Naturally.

The wind pulled free a few strands of dark hair from the club secured at his neck, blowing it around his face wildly.

A sea wolf, she amended.

The ship swayed suddenly. Jacquetta grabbed for the rail. How had she drifted so close to it without realizing? She normally kept well away, in the center of the ship. But she knew the answer. She'd been watching Grayson, eager to keep him in her view. As he'd moved, so had she, completely without thinking.

The waves were rough, tossing the ship from side to side. She did not notice so much near the center of the ship, but here at the edge, she nearly lost her footing. The sailors around her hardly seemed to notice, so accustomed were they to the ocean's uneven temperament.

Completely focused on their tasks, they often forgot there was a lady in their midst unless they'd been assigned to mind her for the day. But Kellerman and the other riggers were at their duties.

So no one saw when the wave crashed over the ship and took Jacquetta with it.

IN MORE THAN three years captaining the *Agamemnon*, Grayson had never passed such a hellish week. When they'd sailed from England, they were already under-crewed. With the two deaths and the other injured men in various states of healing, the crew was painfully stretched. All of the sailors were taking extra shifts, their rest cut down to the absolute minimum to allow them to eat and sleep. Grayson himself had taken over additional duties; he'd been up in the rigging, spent time with the constable inventorying their weapons, and even stirred a pot of stew in the galley for five minutes while the cook stepped away.

Today, finally, several of the sailors were deemed fit to return to duty.

Grayson was ready to return to his quarters, sleep for the rest of the day, and then drag Jacquetta into his bed with him and finally give in to the desire that was simmering between them. Once he caught a glance of her on deck, he wagered the order of those priorities would be immediately reversed.

But, of course, then the quartermaster dragged him into his cabin to discuss conflict between the crew. Because with everyone working extra shifts and not getting enough sleep, the brawling had begun. Sailors had to be reassigned to separate them from one another. Grayson was tempted to have them all thrown in the hell—only yesterday vacated by Payne—but then his plans for himself and Jacquetta would be delayed. Again.

The quartermaster trailed behind him as he strode out from the protection of the officer cabins and climbed the stairs to the quarterdeck two at a time. Grayson listened with half an ear, sweeping his gaze over the deck. Rook had assigned her to watch the rigging today...

There.

She stood in the shadow of the mainmast, her pale green muslin skirts whipping around her hips and legs, reminding him exactly how it had felt to stand between those legs, touching her most private, delectable areas. He hadn't tasted her that night, something he'd regretted every moment since. How had it been an entire week and he'd not even managed to steal enough time with her for a kiss?

They were trapped in the middle of the ocean, for the love of God. It should have been simple.

Nothing with Jack is simple.

That was true enough.

The quartermaster was still talking. Grayson moved toward the railing, listening with half an ear, watching Jacquetta with the other, hoping that standing by the side of the ship would hide the massive cockstand she'd given him by simply existing.

As if they were tied together by an invisible thread, she drifted toward the edge of the ship as well. From the corner of his eye, Grayson watched her grip the railing for support. The weather had been tumultuous the last few hours, sending the ship keening unexpectedly to the side. He hardly noticed, but the way she grabbed the rail told him she had not gained her sea legs. Some people never did.

He would tease her about it later, he decided, while he was nibbling on her ear.

"Which should I reassign, sir?"

Grayson suppressed the growl low in his throat and turned an expression of long-suffering annoyance on his quartermaster. "Whomever you think is best."

Bored with the conversation after nearly an hour, he turned back to Jacquetta—

Where was she?

His eyes whipped over the ship, around the deck, but, by the sinking feeling in his stomach, he already knew the answer.

He was shrugging off his tailcoat as he leaned over the railing, frantically searching the waves. For a second he saw nothing but blue water and white spindrift. Then in the next breath, a golden head broke the water.

"Jacquetta!" Grayson bellowed.

He didn't have time to shuck his boots; his jacket was enough. At least that would not weigh him down. He did not waste time running down the stairs to the main deck; he'd reach the water faster from where he was. The thought of the increased pain of impact was nothing.

"Captain?"

"Sir?"

Grayson hardly heard the cacophony of voices as he put one boot on the base of the rail, gripped the top with his opposite hand, and flung himself over the side of the ship in one desperate movement.

He hit the water with such force that not a fraction of air remained in his lungs. Grayson fought the blackness that pulled at the edges of his consciousness and kicked his legs hard, toward the light of the surface. He needed air, quickly. Without it, he'd never reach Jacquetta.

Bursting out of the water, he whipped his head in each direction. "Jacquetta!" he bellowed again, scanning the waves.

From here in the water the crests were much higher than they'd appeared looking down. A single wave could easily swallow either of them.

Fuck, where is she?

His heart had stopped beating. He would not let her die. Could not. If she did not emerge from the water, then neither would he.

"Jack!" he tried again, this time inhaling a breath of water and sputtering violently; the yell dampened in his throat.

There was yelling from the boat. It was distant, like a waking dream. He could not process if they were yelling for him, Jacquetta, or something else.

But one word did.

"Grayson!"

Her voice floated over the water, distorted and devastatingly soft, even though he knew she must be shouting with all her strength.

Grayson threw the entire strength of his formidable body into swimming toward the sound. With each stroke, he scanned in front of him. Still he could not see her. Was he swimming the wrong way?

Fear started to eat away at his strength—not the physical, the mental. He must be losing his mind.

"She's there!" That was Rook.

Grayson paused, letting his feet come underneath him, throwing his gaze toward the ship. Rook was waving his arms and pointing. Grayson followed his direction, chest so tight he wondered if he'd inhaled more seawater than he'd thought. But then a wave crashed and he saw Jacquetta bobbing in the waves no more than ten yards from him.

He covered the distance in seconds, but they felt like years. Her head was above the water, and one arm flailed wildly as if to capture his attention. Even when he reached her, wrapping an arm around her and pulling her tightly against him while his powerful legs kept them both afloat, still Jacquetta waved her arm frantically.

"I have you," he rasped out, catching her arm and dragging it down. "Don't tire yourself out any more." Even with his throat ravaged by the salty seawater, his tone was imbued with command. Jacquetta obeyed, using both arms to cling to him instead.

For a moment, Grayson let himself hold her, treading water, savoring the fact that she was in his arms.

But they could not stay out here. The waves would swallow the pair of them as easily as any individual. Her strength was clearly flagging. He was fine enough for now, but eventually his too would flag.

He glanced over his shoulder, seeing what he knew would be there. The crew was lowering a skiff, which now dangled no more than a few feet above the water.

Grayson took a deep breath. "We have to get back to the ship," he said, keeping that tone of command. If he was too gentle, she might become hysterical.

Jacquetta nodded, panting but otherwise clear-eyed.

"Can you swim?"

She nodded. "Don't let go of me," she said hoarsely.

He gripped her arm so tightly that he was sure there would be bruises upon her creamy skin. But her only response was a flash of relief on her achingly beautiful face.

Giving her a solid shove in the direction of the ship, Grayson kicked hard. She had more strength left that he'd credited her with, though by the time they reached the skiff, she was slowing. She did not resist at all as he palmed her bottom and shoved her up in into the small wooden boat. A second later, muscles screaming protest, he pulled himself over the edge as well.

The moment they were both in, Grayson felt the boat begin to rise.

Her eyes widened as they were lifted feet and feet above the roiling ocean.

He reached for her hand, gripping it tightly. "You are safe," he said.

Jacquetta let out a long, shaking breath. She clutched his hand, and her fingernails dug into this skin. But Grayson did not pull back. He allowed the little pricks of pain to focus him amid the swirling emotions beneath his skin.

By the time they reached the deck, her eyes had returned to their normal size, though her expression was tense and she had begun shivering. The skiff thumped to the deck, and she tried to stand but her wobbly legs betrayed her.

Rook caught her as she swayed.

"I have her!" Grayson growled, springing to his feet and taking her other arm.

Rook jumped backward across the deck a full yard, nearly falling on his arse in the process.

"Hot tea," Grayson barked at no one in particular.

He steered Jacquetta through the crowd on deck, not noticing who stood where or what words they tried to say to him. They moved out of his way, and that was all that mattered.

He kicked open the door to his quarters and pulled Jacquetta through it. After nudging it closed again with a shoulder, he deposited her into one of the dining chairs and sank to his knees before her.

"Are you injured?" he demanded, his eyes raking over her body.

She was soaked through, but there did not appear to be any tears in her gown. No blood.

"I am fine," she said. But her voice shook.

"You are terrified of the ocean," he said. *Obviously, you idiot.*

"I suppose there is no better way to confront one's fears than head-on," she answered, a slightly delirious chuckle rippling through her. She blinked rapidly, forced a few breaths in and out. "You saved me, again."

"Did you expect me to let you drown?" he countered. He was touching her knees, he realized. One hand on each one, his large palms covering her entire knee.

This was good, though. The sparring. It meant she was not about to lapse into hysteria.

The way he could feel every tremble of her body through the thin, wet fabric of her gown, now that was decidedly more complicated—

A sharp knock at the door had him springing back. Grayson opened his mouth to spew a curse, but the door opened and Bryson appeared.

"Tea," he said, holding up a tray.

Grayson strode to the door, relieved him of it, and kicked the door closed. Bryson was timid enough not to make a sound of protest, but Grayson thought her heard Jacquetta snicker. Another encouraging omen.

He poured them each a cup of tea.

"Drink," he ordered her.

For once, she did not disobey him. She took a dainty sip, then a much deeper one. Grayson did the same, watching her over the rim of his teacup. The tea was boiling hot, but his chilled body craved it. Jacquetta was half his size and had been in the water longer than he.

He poured her another cup and shoved it into her hand.

She did take a long draw of the tea, but then she set it aside. "Have any brandy?" she said with a meek attempt at teasing.

Grayson did not laugh.

"I am fine," she insisted. This time she was steadier.

"You are shivering," he countered. "We need to get you out of that wet gown."

Without thinking, Grayson spun her around, and his fingers found the lacings at the back. He reached the bottom, near the base of her spine, but the gown did not slip down her shoulders as it should have. The wet fabric clung to her body. He closed his fingers around the fabric of the shoulders and yanked the garment downward, baring the creamy expanse of skin beneath.

That was when he realized he was undressing her.

As he watched, gooseflesh rose on her neck and shoulders.

Grayson shuddered.

"I beg your pardon…" he said gruffly.

Jacquetta turned her head, so he could see her profile etched against the bright light coming from outside the wall of windows behind her. He watched her tongue nip out over her bottom lip.

"Don't stop," she whispered.

CHAPTER TWELVE

GRAYSON DID NOT move. His hands hovered near her wrists, where he'd dropped the wet fabric of her gown and let it fall to the floor. Jacquetta could practically feel his mind working, his instincts warring with reason. She'd nearly drowned. She had suffered something traumatic—again. They were here, half-clothed, desperate for each other. Again.

Jacquetta needed him to know that she was not a wilting wallflower. She may be shivering, but by now it was as much with pent-up desire as with chill. Well, a significant amount of it was the chill, she admitted to herself. But she could think of precisely how she would like to be warmed up.

She caught one of his hands in hers and held it as she slowly rotated on the spot. She did not have to glance down to know that her wet chemise was completely transparent and clinging to every curve of her body. She could feel her taut nipples rubbing against the fabric, sensitive and burning for his touch.

He was wet too, she remembered. They were both dripping on the expensive rug as if it was nothing. In truth, it was completely inconsequential compared to what was about to happen between them.

"You ought to undress as well. We cannot have the captain of the ship taking a chill," Jacquetta said softly, letting her eyes travel over him.

He already favored close-cut clothing, but with the linen shirt clinging to the hard panes of his body... her mouth started to water. The heat that surged between her legs was a sudden and intense contrast to the chill pebbling over her skin.

She could see Grayson still holding himself in check. Despite the cold, his cock was pushing against the constraints of his trousers. His nipples were tight pinpricks against his wet linen shirt. Though she held his hand, he did not grip hers back or stroke her with the reverence he had that last night they were alone in the cabin, in nearly this very spot.

But it was there in his eyes.

Jacquetta had worried his desire for her had faded?

Foolish. Laughable. The dark burning in his eyes told her everything she needed in that moment. Now she only had to get him to give in, for both of their sakes.

With deliberate care, she used her unencumbered hand to slide the chemise off her shoulder and down her arm. A small tug, and her breast popped free of the wet fabric; her tight pink nipple jutted out proudly. Grayson's other hand fisted tightly at his side.

Jacquetta shook her head, huffing out a small laugh.

"You do not need to fight it," she said. She gave him what she hoped was a meaningful stare, then flicked her eyes downward to their joined hands.

She watched her own movements, hoping he was similarly transfixed, as she lifted their hands to her breast and curved his hand around it. The contrast of his tanned skin against the pale globe was striking. Summoning up all the boldness and desire within her, she guided his index finger and thumb to her nipple.

Whether he moved by instinct or conscious decision, he tightened his fingers around her and pinched lightly. Jacquetta had no control over the whimper that she emitted as glorious sensation shot through her.

Before the next sound of pleasure could pass her throat, his other hand was on her, cupping her other breast, massaging it gently through the wet, clinging fabric.

"We should remove this as well," Grayson said huskily.

"Of course," Jacquetta agreed, attempting solemnity and failing utterly.

She caught the other shoulder of the chemise and tugged it down. She had to wriggle her hips to shimmy out of the garment entirely. He grimaced. She did it again to see what reaction she would get this time.

Grayson did not disappoint. His hands caught her breasts at the same time that his lips captured her mouth.

The heat of his mouth against her in contrast to the coolness of her body was exquisite. But she would not be cold for long. Jacquetta reached for his chest, desperately wanting to touch him as she had not had the chance to the last time they were alone in this cabin.

She touched the icy water of his shirt and jerked her hands back immediately.

A low chuckle rumbled out of his chest against her mouth. "I suppose I ought to even things out," he said, his mouth a breath away from hers.

"It is only fair," Jacquetta agreed, trembling now entirely from the heat surging between her mouth, chest, and the core of desire between her legs. "And necessary, of course. We cannot have you expiring from the *cold*."

She choked on the last word as his shirt felt to the floor and every glorious inch of that chest was finally exposed to her. Her hands itched to touch it all. The large, flat pectorals as wide as her hand... the corded muscles of his arms that she'd felt around her... A shiver of delightful anticipation snaked down her spine.

Grayson's eyes went right to her breasts, which bounced as her shoulders shook.

Then he went further. He hooked his thumbs into the waistband of his trousers, flipped free the fasteners, and slung the dark fabric down to the ground. He bent at the waist for a moment, kicking away his boots as well.

They stood there together in nothing but their stockings.

"We are so very close," Jacquetta said, biting her lip to stop the infernal trembling.

"Close to what, Jack?" Grayson purred, stepping closer.

"Everything," she answered as his hands came around her.

He curved his hand around the nape of her neck and tipped her head back. "You have no business being this beautiful," he said before pressing a kiss to her forehead.

But what might feel childish when kissed by an older relative felt positively sinful when Grayson did it.

"I hope you do not expect me to apologize," she managed to say.

He kissed the corner of her eye next. "We are well acquainted enough for me to expect the complete opposite," he agreed. He lingered at her cheek, his tongue drawing a little whorl before he pulled away.

"Ought I to gloat, perhaps? Preen before the mirror a bit?" she suggested.

Grayson paused, his mouth hovering over hers. His voice sounded strangled as he said, "I would very much like to watch you discover yourself in a mirror. But now... now we haven't the time."

Another delicious shiver snaked through her.

He took her mouth then, and the heat and pressure communicated the primal urgency of the desire thrumming between them.

Jacquetta surrendered herself to it completely, twining her arms around his neck and molding her soft body against his hard planes. Grayson groaned against her mouth then guided her back a few steps. When she stumbled, he scooped her up into his arms and crossed the cabin and up to the platform bed, all while managing to keep kissing her.

Not just a kiss, she amended. An assault.

Even a kiss from Grayson was passionate to the point of breaking her. He began with gentle swipes of his tongue along the inside of her lips. Then, here and there, he would surge deeper, tasting her for a moment before withdrawing to sweeter kisses once more. Just when Jacquetta thought she'd settled into the rhythm of it, that she might be able to think enough to enjoy the hard male body pressed against her, he did not withdraw. He deepened the kiss and stayed, wrapping his tongue around hers in a sensuous, languid dance.

He laid her on the bed, and his own weight bore down upon it as he positioned himself over her. Jacquetta could not ignore the rock-hard length of him, now pressing against her leg with no barrier at all. She arched against him, already reaching for the fullness his fingers had promised days before.

"So greedy," Grayson murmured against her lips.

She wanted to swat him. Or shove his head back down and his hips into place. Instead, he dropped a soft kiss on her mouth and lowered his head. Much lower.

"Grayson." Jacquetta's breath caught in her throat as she watched his dark hair fall forward over her face, brushing across the golden curls of her womanhood.

He paused, tossing his hair back over his head so he could meet her gaze—and smile wickedly.

"Hold on, Jack," he advised before lowering himself back down.

Nothing in the world—her training, her interludes with men, her own explorations—had prepared her for that first swipe of Grayson's tongue over her sex.

Her world exploded into bright light, everything centering to that one spot. His head bobbed up and down, her fingers tangled in his long, dark hair, and the press of his hand on her stomach kept her from arching off the bed entirely.

She was going to climax then and there.

So soon?

The realization hit her a moment before the reality did. She'd been primed, ready for him for days. Weeks. All it took was his mouth touching to her, a few expert swipes of his tongue, and her body gave over completely.

She did hold on, gripping the coverlet so hard she swore her nails tore through it. Grayson did not draw away as her hips bucked wildly. He drove his tongue inside of her, claiming her core with every part of his body.

The instant her pleasure ebbed to a simmer, Jacquetta knew that she wanted him inside of her. Everything else had been a prelude. Now she needed *him*.

"Now. I need you now," she said, shocked at the command in her own voice.

Grayson rewarded her with that low, rolling laugh. He climbed back up her, leaving a trail of scorching, wet kisses from her navel to her chin before he claimed her mouth and closed his hands around her wrists.

Suddenly, they were rolling.

Shocked, Jacquetta found herself positioned above him, her legs planted on either side of his hips and his cock pressed against her mound.

She licked her lips. "I do not understand—"

"Yes, you do." Grayson grinned wickedly.

He reached down and guided himself between her legs. Instinctively, Jacquetta rose slightly. He teased the head of his manhood along her slit, wetting it, she realized. Then he paused, lifting his hips to increase the pressure, and slid himself slightly inside of her.

The expression on his face nearly bowled her over. Jesus, Mary, and Joseph, she was the one making him look like that?

"You are in control, Jack," Grayson said, voice strangled.

He released his cock and reached for her hips, before lowering her so she took another inch of him. Jacquetta sucked in a breath; the sensation was new and invasive and incredible. The urge to thrust her hips down and envelop him washed over her.

Then she understood what he meant. He would let her set the speed, let her explore. He would hold back his own pleasure so she could be assured of enjoying hers.

He belonged to her.

That needful, possessive thought pushed her over the invisible edge she'd been lingering at for weeks.

She sank down on him, inch after glorious inch. She expected her body to protest, waited for that pinch of sharp pain she'd been warned about. But it never came. Perhaps he'd done away with it while making love to her with his hands and mouth. Jacquetta found she did not care. All that mattered was the unending fullness as her body stretched to accommodate him.

She felt the brush of his hair against her golden curls and realized she was fully seated, completely filled. It was wonderful. She felt completed, tender; her flesh tingled inside of her. But what she did not feel was that shooting desire, that flame that he'd ignited when he touched her there before.

As if reading her thoughts, Grayson curled his hand around the nape of her neck and slowly wriggled his hips.

Oh.

Oh, *God.*

Oh, God, *yes.*

She rocked her hips forward, realizing that as she did, not only did his cock slide out and back in, but the friction of their bodies rubbed right at the bundle of nerves seated just above her entrance. When she thrust again, this time Grayson lifted his hips in unison.

Jacquetta flailed around, grabbing for something—anything. He clasped her hand, holding it to his chest in a tight fist, anchoring her.

Whatever wisdom he had would have to be enough for both of them, because she lost herself utterly to sensation. Her eyes were heavy, her awareness turned inward to where their bodies connected. With each rock and thrust, Grayson was deeper inside of her. Her clit ached from the attention but still burned for more. She could not stop. She could not think. She could only be and do and bathe in the hedonistic pleasure of it—of him.

"Christ, Jack, you are magnificent," Grayson said, his words penetrating her fog of pleasure.

One hand still held hers fast; the other was on her hip, digging into the flesh there as he guided her. Through heavy-lidded eyes, Jacquetta fixated upon his face. His expression was a mixture of agony and extreme joy. She rocked forward and pulled off him, and he looked bereft. Then they joined again, and his expression shifted to ecstasy.

She was entranced watching him.

So entranced looking for his climax that she completely missed the building ache toward her own until she was tumbling over the edge.

"I need—Oh God, oh God, Grayson," she said, utterly incoherent.

But Grayson knew. He dragged her mouth down to his and buried his tongue in her mouth, keeping rhythm with the thrust of his cock inside of her. It was too much. Jacquetta exploded in fulfillment, her movements frantic. As the waves of pleasure washed over her, she felt her knees begin to wobble. She was ready to collapse against him.

Grayson tensed beneath her. Jacquetta shoved herself up from the bed, determined to watch his face as he took his pleasure. A second later, his eyes slammed shut and his brows knitted together, then she felt the flood of heat and a roar of completion so loud, she would later lie in bed wondering whether the Queen of England herself had not heard it across the sea.

When his hold on her hip relaxed at last, Jacquetta allowed herself to collapse against him.

Grayson wrapped his arms around her, holding her tight, breathing into her hair. For long minutes, they lay there like that, unable to move.

After what felt an eternity, she rolled off to the side.

"What are you about?" he said, accusation ringing in his voice. He caught her wrist and dragged her back against him, settling her into his side snugly.

"I wasn't going far," she complained, even as she burrowed

deeper into the curve of his arm.

"You won't be going anywhere. You sleep here now."

"Ha," Jacquetta said. "You may be the captain, but you do not give me orders." She bit her lip hard. Minutes before, he'd done just that. And she had *very* happily obeyed them.

To her unending disbelief, he chose not to point that out.

"No more nicking biscuits from the galley," he said instead, walking his fingers up and down her arm.

A small laugh rippled through her. "I am not nicking them," she protested. "They are freely given by the cook."

Grayson hummed in disapproval. "In any case, there is no longer a need."

Jacquetta caught his hand, stilling his fingers. "Oh?"

"You no longer need to bribe the crew. You will be spending your days with me now."

Her heart fluttered wildly in her chest. At the possessiveness in his voice. At the opportunity he was unknowingly presenting to her. And, admittedly, at the thought of being close to him.

But she did not let any of that show, glad her head was nestled in the curve of his shoulder where he could not see her face. "Did it not occur to you that perhaps *I* enjoy the biscuits?"

"Of course you do."

She swatted at his hand. "I shall endeavor not to take offense to that."

"With nothing more than mild success, I am certain."

Jacquetta sat straight up, glaring down at him. "Are you trying to anger me?"

Grayson maintained his place on the bed, tucking both hands behind his head. His dark eyes sparkled.

"You are!" she accused, bringing her fist down at his chest. The damn man! He was baiting her to argue!

Grayson caught her hand deftly. He rotated it, nipping at her wrist before pressing a kiss to the same spot. "I enjoy watching you burn."

Jacquetta swallowed her retort.

"No smart rejoinder, Jack?" He held her gaze as he ran his tongue along the sensitive skin from the edge of her wrist to the tip of her elbow.

"What makes you think I shall burn for you?" she said, unable to tear her eyes away.

"Oh, Jack." He chuckled wickedly. "You already are."

When he kissed her again and her entire body began to heat, Jacquetta knew it was true.

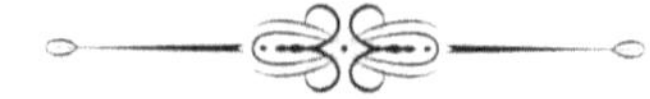

CHAPTER THIRTEEN

GRAYSON COULD NOT, in fact, keep Jacquetta by his side every day. First, it would have drawn too much attention. While it quickly became impossible to hide that there was *something* between them, and the more observant sailors surely guessed what that something was, Grayson was not going to give them extra fuel for the fire.

The *Agamemnon* was a large ship, but not large enough to avoid gossip. For a reason he could not quite name, it was important to Grayson that the men did not think badly of Jacquetta. Which was absurd, given her status aboard the ship.

But as the days went on, even that became less clear. She was a prisoner on the ship. Yet she smiled at the sailors and continued to share her biscuits with them when they did her favors. She was forbidden from going below decks again after the incident with Payne, yet she held court on the deck, reading aloud to the sailors at her leisure, or sometimes singing. She had a beautiful singing voice, low and melodic. Grayson thought it a bit eerie, especially once Rook began teaching her sea shanties and she started singing them in her own haunting, slower-paced rendition.

She'd given over sleeping in the bunk, thankfully. Every night was a new exploration, an explosion of desire and feeling combined. Grayson had taken an occasional companion to his cabin over the years, but always for short voyages to the

Continent or between the islands of the West Indies. Never an entire crossing. He could not imagine sharing his bed or his space with one woman for so long. Yet when Jacquetta drifted to sleep in his arms, exhausted from their lovemaking, he found he did not want to let her go.

That bothered him deeply because, in a few short weeks, they would arrive in Barbados.

He had only days left with her. She drove him absolutely mad. But he could not fathom the emptiness of his cabin without her.

So he would not. He would put it out of his mind. Savor the taste of her, the sharp burn of her tongue that just served to inflame him further.

He fixed his gaze on the horizon, determined to dismiss the worry and refusing to examine his feelings any further.

"Thane!" Kellerman yelled from high in the rigging.

Grayson saw it the same moment the sailor's voice rang out.

On the horizon, bobbing amid the relatively calm morning sea, was a ship.

Possibilities flicked through Grayson's mind even as he reached for the spyglass at his hip. It was too small to be another Indiaman, which simultaneously eliminated a large navy ship. Perhaps a smaller Royal Navy cutter or a packet ship, also bound for the Indies. It was late April, and the hurricane season was very close upon them. If it was a packet ship or merchant vessel, it would be one of the very last of the season. Deuced bad luck to come across them.

He felt Jacquetta appear at his side as he squinted through the spyglass. The sun was reflecting sharply off the water, making visibility difficult.

"What is the hullabaloo about?" she asked. She did not touch him, though part of him expected her to seek comfort by placing a hand on his arm. Which was inane—she was neither the type for public displays nor a wallflower.

"A ship," Grayson said distractedly. He adjusted the spyglass, compensating for the reflection of the sun… *There*. He had it clearly in his sights—and recognized it immediately.

He lowered the spyglass, turning to shout to his crew, when he caught a glimpse of Jacquetta's usually lovely face, now completely stricken.

He watched as a thousand watery deaths flashed before her sea-green eyes. "Pirates?" she whispered.

"Haven't you figured it out by now, Jack? We *are* the pirates."

The words hung between them. Jacquetta's expression hovered between anger and fear, as if she could not decide whether she wanted to go hide in the cabin or slap him with frustration. Rook gave her the opportunity for neither.

"What is it?" the first mate huffed, having run from wherever he'd been to join them on the quarterdeck.

"A packet ship," Grayson said, watching as Jacquetta's eyes turned murderous. Oh yes, she would punish him for this later. He would enjoy every second of it.

Rook seemed oblivious to the undercurrent between them. "This late in the season? They must have been heavily bribed."

"What do you mean by that, Mr. Rook?" Jacquetta interjected, voice wary.

"It is hurricane season."

Her eyes were blazing so brightly that Grayson thought they might actually start to glow. He kept his mouth in its carefully curated smirk.

"Hurricane season?" she repeated, mouth opening and closing like a fish's. "You steal me away from my home, hold me captive, and sail with me across an ocean in the middle of *hurricane season?*"

Grayson wanted to tip her over the edge of the railing and kiss the fire right out of her veins. See if she might bite and how hard, enraged like this. But he could do nothing of the sort. So he met her gaze evenly instead.

"It is the beginning of hurricane season," he said reasonably. "The weather has been quite fair, has it not?"

"You are the most—"

"While I am delighted to hear your expanded repertoire of insults, given the amount of time you've spent with the crew over recent weeks, we do not have time just now." Grayson nodded back toward the horizon. "They will be upon us soon."

The packet ship had already closed half the distance between them, the riggers having let down a considerable amount of sail to slow the *Agamemnon*. There was no reason to run from them; it would only raise suspicions. To all appearances, the ship was a regular West Indiaman making a late but profitable dash to the Indies before waiting out the season.

"What do they want?" Jacquetta asked Rook, pointedly turning away from Grayson.

Rook shrugged nonchalantly. "It could be anything. Short on water, in need of a surgeon."

"Aren't we getting close to port?" she questioned.

"*Close* is relative," Grayson answered for Rook. "We are a much larger ship. We will reach the islands well ahead of a ship like that."

"So why let them close at all?" she challenged.

"To avoid suspicion. Which means, Jacquetta, that it is time for you to return to the cabin." Grayson jerked his head to Rook. "Take her inside."

"You will not!" Jacquetta snapped her arm away from where Rook had reached for it.

"Jack," Grayson sighed. "You know I cannot release you or allow you to speak to the crew. If they see a woman aboard, it will raise unnecessary questions." He tried to appeal to her rational side, though it rarely seemed to prevail. She was governed by feeling and instinct, the same as he was. But they'd passed such a pleasant week. If only he could placate her…

"I will scream," she threatened, backing away from both Grayson and Rook. "I will scream the entire way." She darted her eyes to the ship, judging the distance.

"I could render you unconscious again, but we both know—"

"Do not even dare to think it." Her eyes darted around for a weapon, then, finding none, back to the ship. "If I scream loud and long enough, they will hear me. They are close, now. Their spyglasses are watching this ship as surely as ours are watching them. They will see a commotion."

Ours.

The word sliced through him, shaking awake a part of him that Grayson had thought forever dormant.

"You stay back and you do not say a word."

Jacquetta's chest rose, and an exhilarated smile climbed her face.

Rook spun around to face him, shock written on his face as clear as triumph spoke from Jacquetta's.

"You are my wife," Grayson added.

Her nose wrinkled instantly. *How flattering.*

"An officer's wife might occasionally travel with him. It is the only reasonable explanation for your presence on this ship, and the one I will give to whomever they send across." Grayson stared directly into her eyes, not needing to voice the rest of the order. If she refuted him, there would be a toll.

The triumph in her eyes faded slightly, but she nodded in agreement.

Grayson turned to Rook. "Ready the men. Let's have done with this."

⇻⇉⤙⇇

JACQUETTA SPARED A minute to take a quick inventory of her appearance, even without the use of a mirror. She smoothed her dress and tugged at the top of her chemise so that a respectable inch or so rose above the neckline of her gown. She had no fichu—the women who'd left their clothes for her to scavenge were clearly not inclined to modesty.

She dipped her hands in a bucket of water then hastily scrubbed her face and smoothed back the flyaway hairs that had come loose from the simple chignon she'd fashioned at the crown of her head.

Grayson found her just as the packet ship pulled alongside theirs. He raked an appreciative gaze over her, lingering on her bosom.

"I cannot say that I appreciate the adjustments to your undergarments," he said under his breath as he took her hand and placed it on his arm.

Jacquetta rolled her eyes. "I did not know you were capable of fastening a button," she retorted, nodding toward his neatly buttoned tailcoat.

He leaned in so his breath tickled the shell of her ear. "I am much more proficient at unfastening them."

She shoved down the heat that flushed through her, but she did tighten her grip on his arm. He had much to atone for when she had him alone in the cabin this evening.

Before she could give voice to those threats, Grayson steered her down to the main deck.

The ropes went across, then the plank, and a minute later three men clambered across from the other ship. Beyond the smaller ship bobbing up and down in the water, Jacquetta caught sight of the deck. Crowded—dozens of eyes looking across at them. Not just sailors. Women, children, families.

Her stomach sank.

They needed to get away, and quickly.

Despite the respect that Grayson and the majority of his crew had shown her, the man he worked for was dangerous. Nefarious enough to draw the attention of the Crown. She could not imagine Grayson harming a ship full of innocents. But then… what was she?

She was a lady knight.

Her duty was to the queen and her people.

She would do everything in her power to get the *Agamemnon* away from the packet ship as expeditiously as possible. Even if it meant breaking the one rule Grayson had set for her.

"Welcome aboard the *Agamemnon*," Grayson said magnanimously, stepping forward and offering a bow. "I am Captain David Wright. My wife, Mrs. Wright." He applied a bit of pressure to Jacquetta's hand on her arm, and she sank into a polite curtsey.

The oldest man of the three, short but solidly built, with a completely gray beard, stepped forward and offered his own respectful bow. "Well met, sir. Captain Julius Carpenter of the *Dolphin*. My quartermaster, Mr. Brown, and Reverend Grant, representative of the passengers traveling with us."

Grayson inclined his head respectfully to each man. Jacquetta did the same, keeping her eyes downcast. But that did not prevent her from taking their measure. The quartermaster was the tallest of the three, muscular and imposing. The muscle behind this encounter. The reverend was almost as tall, but thin as a whip. Not much use in a fight. He'd most likely insisted upon accompanying Captain Carpenter on this excursion, if she was reading their postures correctly.

"How may we be of assistance, captain?" Grayson got directly to the heart of things.

Jacquetta released a slow breath, carefully keeping her expression unchanged. Perhaps he wanted this over as quickly as she did. Perhaps she could keep her word to him and not speak at all.

"It is my passengers," Captain Carpenter said. He did not bother to disguise the weariness in his voice.

Jacquetta glanced up at Grayson to see if he'd detected it too, but his face remained impassive.

"We bear an important packet of governmental mail that must be delivered posthaste to Kingston," Carpenter continued. "But my passengers are insistent we divert to the first major port."

Jacquetta's eyes lifted back to the deck, where many interested eyes watched them.

Grayson looked only mildly interested in the predicament. "Does your charter not charge you to deliver the post first and foremost?"

The other captain bristled, his stance tightening and rough gray brows drawing together. "Indeed it does, sir."

"We do not have the provisions nor the cabin space to take on your passengers. Our hold is full," Grayson continued.

Jacquetta kept the startled expression from her face, but only just. It was obvious what Captain Carpenter wanted—to hand off the post to a fellow Englishman. Of course, he had no notion that he would be handing it off to a criminal captaining a ship full of illegal cargo.

Carpenter dragged his eyes away from Grayson, instead fixing the reverend beside him with an icy glare. Tactful, Jacquetta thought, for him to direct his ire at someone other than Grayson. The other captain had already taken Grayson's measure and decided it was best not to take a hard line.

Grayson waited patiently, his face unchanged other than the hint of a smirk he allowed to play at the corner of his lips.

Carpenter finally turned back, his mouth now set in a grim, resigned line. "We can provide financial incentive, if you take on the delivery of the post to Kingston."

To Captain Carpenter, Jacquetta was sure that Grayson's expression remained unchanged. But she detected the subtle shift in his posture and the darkened gleam in his eye that signaled triumph. She tried not to think of where she'd last seen that gleam.

The rush of heat between her legs indicated how utterly she failed at that attempt.

"We are bound for Antigua, I'm afraid. Kingston would be a considerable diversion." Grayson lifted his hand from where it clasped hers to stroke his beard.

"Aye, captain. The men will scream foul—they've been promised a real bed and a woman to warm it," Rook piped up. When had he appeared at Grayson's other side? "They won't take kindly to their voyage being extended."

"Indeed," Grayson agreed, nodding contemplatively.

They'd done this before, Jacquetta realized. They had already decided to accept the post; now they were attempting to squeeze as much profit as possible from Captain Carpenter.

Jacquetta nudged Grayson with her knee. He did not flinch. She tightened her grip on his arm. No response.

Arse.

He was ignoring her?

On his own head be it.

"Surely you could pay the crew an extra wage to compensate them for the inconvenience," Jacquetta said sweetly.

All eyes swung to her, with varying degrees of discernment. Mostly, they seemed to have forgotten she was there and were shocked to discover that Mrs. Wright did, indeed, possess the ability to speak. But Grayson's dark eyes… for a second they were murderous. Then they simmered down to mere annoyance. An acceptable emotion for any husband to direct at his meddling wife.

"It is no less than our duty to the sovereign, is it not? To see this post delivered?" she added.

Grayson's eyes went even darker. Oh, there would be many scores to settle once they were in the privacy of his cabin again. Despite the seriousness of the situation, a delightful shiver of anticipation ran down her spine.

"My dear, you look a bit peaked. Perhaps you ought to retire," Grayson ground out, his annoyance wholly evident and completely unfeigned. "Rook—"

"Nonsense, I am quite well. Perhaps Captain Carpenter might tell me a bit about his ship while you see to the particulars of transferring the aforementioned post." She smiled blindingly at the other captain, who could do nothing but blink between Grayson and his supposed wife, and then offer his arm to her.

Grayson's eyes flashed with dark promises as he allowed her hand to slip from his arm and accept Carpenter's. Jacquetta allowed the other man to lead her toward the edge of the *Agamemnon*, where they could peer down at the smaller packet ship.

But she could feel the burning of Grayson's eyes on her back for the entire interlude. Jacquetta could not say that it bothered her.

GRAYSON DID NOT breathe freely again until the *Dolphin* disappeared behind them on the horizon. He kept the ship at full sail, hoping to put more distance between them throughout the night. It would tire the men, having extra hands to manage through the night, but Grayson did not want another encounter.

Jacquetta had not obeyed his order to stay quiet, but at least she'd kept up the farce he forced upon her.

By the time they were once again alone in his quarters, there had been no time for words of admonishment between them. They were far too busy ripping the clothes from one another's bodies and devouring each other.

Even hours later, after he'd filled his belly with a hearty meal and with his arms around Jacquetta, a singular thought still ate away at him, keeping him from settling.

Jacquetta had been presented with a chance to escape.

But she was still here.

Grayson inched his fingers over the space between them, up her arm and the soft curve of her back. She did not move beneath his hand, sleeping deeply despite his own interminable wakefulness. Her back rose and fell in an even rhythm. The warmth of her skin spread over his fingertips and palms. She was still here.

Why?

The captain of the packet ship had been aboard the *Agamemnon*, two sturdy-looking men beside him. Jacquetta had been unshackled, untethered, and, for a few minutes, unsupervised.

But she had not said a word to the man of her captivity.

Why?

Grayson stared at the ceiling, the utter blackness around them consuming his thoughts.

Perhaps Jacquetta thought him so black-hearted that she supposed he would cut her down rather than allow her to leave with the other captain.

No, she knew she was valuable to him and his master, even if she did not know the true purpose. She'd pushed his limits often enough to be assured of her own bodily safety, at least for the moment.

She was clever. She might have worried that if she pleaded her case to the captain of the packet ship, Grayson and his crew would dispose of the man and leave the other ship to its own devices, ruinous as they might be. She was very focused on the right and wrong of things. Grayson could see her convincing herself that while she might do the right thing by trying to save herself, she would be dooming the captain and his lieutenants in the process, thus committing a grave wrong.

Grayson wished he had left on a lamp. If he focused hard enough, he could just hear the pulsing waves outside the windows that made up most of the rear wall of his quarters. But there was no light in the cabin at all. The utter darkness usually suited him. It allowed him to sink into the depths of his soul and get away from all the shadows that haunted him. But not now. Not today.

Now, he would give anything for a bit of illumination.

Another thought wriggled its way perniciously into his mind.

What if she had chosen to stay because she'd developed an emotional attachment to him? Because she believed he might…

Grayson could not even bring himself to *think* the words.

He rolled onto his side, pulling back his hand as if burned. But a hairsbreadth from breaking contact with her soft skin, he paused. Grayson sucked in a breath. He dragged his fingertips along the curve of her shoulder up into her hair, skimming the silky curls as they spread over the pillow.

If only there was a bit of light, so he could look at her face and see what secrets lurked there, unguarded in her slumber.

Jacquetta had secrets, that much was plain. But what were they? Did they have to do with the nonsense she'd spouted about the rift with his family, and Delaurier's involvement in covering it up? However she'd stumbled across the information, it had led to her kidnapping and subsequent presence aboard the *Agamemnon*. To his bed. To him.

Now that she was here, what new secrets had she gleaned? She knew a fair amount about his crew, though he did not see what use such information would be to a London debutante. No, the more dangerous secrets were the ones about him—about his heart, and her own.

Grayson could not let himself think it. Even in the dark abyss of his quarters, while she slept completely heedless of his turmoil, he could not acknowledge what was taking root inside of him. To do so would mean damning them both.

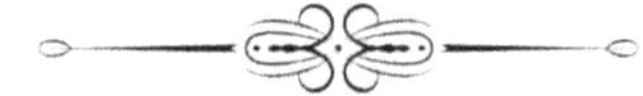

CHAPTER FOURTEEN

A S THEY SAILED into the tropical waters of the Caribbean, the humidity increased and the sky filled with dark clouds. Grayson watched them each day with an impending sense of doom. A storm was waiting for him. There was no avoiding it, no sailing around or changing course. It was coming, as sure and relentless as the waves lapping against the side of his ship.

"Today, then," Rook said with a heavy sigh, appearing at his shoulder.

Grayson nodded wearily. After several days of clouding and clearing, winds and rains that blew up and then settled, they had come to it. On the horizon, a dark storm head had slowly formed throughout the morning. By later afternoon, there was no question of it dissipating or shifting direction. This storm was coming, and they were directly in its path.

"The crew is prepared?" Grayson asked, already knowing the answer.

"Of course, sir. They'd have to be blind to miss that," Rook scoffed, jerking his head toward the looming clouds. As if on command, lightning flashed in the distance, and a minute later the low roll of thunder filled the air.

An hour off, maybe two, Grayson estimated.

There had been a frantic energy in the air all day—the crew had moved about their tasks quickly and efficiently, tightening sails and tying down loose cargo on the deck. Anything could happen during a storm. A shifting crate on the deck could crush a man. An improperly tied jib could knock a sailor overboard.

Despite the fact that most of the men aboard the *Agamemnon* were forced there by servitude to Delaurier, none of them wished for death. All aboard appreciated and understood the gravity of what was coming.

Except one.

Grayson stepped back, turning to scan the deck behind him.

"She's in your quarters."

He bristled at the amusement in Rook's voice and did not bother to utter his thanks as he strode across the main deck to his cabin.

He found Jacquetta perched on the edge of his bed near the window, sewing needle and pile of fabric in hand. He'd found her in this exact position dozens of times over the past weeks, always at work on something. When he questioned why she sat so near to the window when the sea obviously bothered her, she'd shrugged and said it was the best light for mending and altering. But he could see the stubborn set of her shoulders; she was determined to master her fear.

"When you did not appear on deck, I suspected you were still abed," Grayson said, stopping at the edge of the bed and casually folding his arms.

Her turquoise eyes flicked up to him, assessing his body in one quick pass, then returned to her needlework.

"Lying in the bed and sitting upon it are hardly the same," Jacquetta pointed out, setting another stitch.

"Are they?" he asked, moving around the edge of the plat-form and leaning over to get a better look at the garment she held in her lap.

She paused, holding it up for his inspection. Grayson ignored it and nipped at her ear instead.

She hummed in approval, tipping her head to the side to allow him to slick his tongue down the column of her neck.

Grayson applied the slightest bit of pressure, and she lay back against the pillow so he could set his mouth to the swell of her breasts.

Grayson drew a line with his tongue from the center of her chest where her breasts met all the way up to her bottom lip. He planted a mockingly chaste kiss upon her mouth.

"Lying about in bed, as I said," he said softly.

Jacquetta swatted at him, but Grayson was too fast. She tossed aside the garment in her hands and rolled to her stomach, coming to rest on her elbows.

"You are trying to distract me," she declared.

"I am," he agreed, dropping to his knees beside the bed so he could more easily reach her mouth.

"I am perfectly well," she insisted.

He hummed as he twirled a finger in a lock of her golden hair. "Is that why you have hidden in the cabin all day?"

"I can see the clouds just as well from inside as out," Jacquetta said. She did not dart a glance toward the wall of windows, instead keeping her eyes stubbornly pinned to him. "There is a storm coming."

"Yes," Grayson admitted. He dropped the curl and reached back for the chignon at the nape of her neck instead, working his fingers into the tightly curled coiffure.

She tried to capture his hands, but he dodged her adroitly. She huffed in irritation, rolling onto her back again so her hair was pinned beneath her. "How long?"

He leaned over, carefully maneuvering his face so their mouths lined up, and kissed her. It was interesting, facing different directions. Perhaps they would explore it…

She moaned softly against his mouth.

Later. They would explore it later.

He felt her reach up, tangling her fingers in his hair as he'd done with hers moments before. She successfully tugged his long locks free of their leather strap. Then she pulled his head back.

"How long?" she asked again.

Grayson nipped her nose, noting the worry growing in her sparkling eyes. "Two hours. Maybe less."

He watched the nervous swallow as it moved down her delicate throat.

"But we shall be fully occupied until then," he declared, swinging himself around so he was on the bed and they were finally pressed together, face to face and right side up. He fit his legs around hers and determined to chase the worry from her remarkable eyes.

JACQUETTA FORCED HERSELF to keep her eyes closed as Grayson slipped from the bed and dressed in near silence. For such a tall, broad specimen of manhood, he managed to keep his footfalls soft as he crossed the cabin and slipped out the door. There was no click of a lock, unless he'd somehow discovered a way to muffle that as well. Though Jacquetta had no reason to suspect he would lock her inside.

She waited another few moments to reassure herself he was truly gone. She sat up quickly, reaching for the black leather journal she'd shoved between the edge of the mattress and the wall of the ship. She hadn't had time to stuff it back into its hiding place as he came in.

She'd taken to sewing on the edge of the bed nearest the window because it was easy for her to jump between the wooden box of sailors' accounts or the leather notebook and return to the bed, grabbing up her needlework in the process.

Despite examining every page of both sources, she still could not fully make sense of either. Each paper in the wooden box was labeled with a sailor's name and contacts she'd determined were most likely next of kin. It had taken careful questioning, but she'd matched the name of the cook's mother to his entry in the box, and Kellerman's sister to his entry as well. The first column of numbers were dates—voyages, she thought. But the running tally along the other column, some crossed out with new numbers rewritten… those she could not make sense of. There was no pattern to the quantities that were added or subtracted.

Grayson's personal book was similar. Dates, she felt certain. But the other numbers, while formatted more or less the same as the sailors' pages, were nonsensical.

Even so, she took every opportunity alone in the cabin to reach for them and have another look, hoping something would click into place in her mind and suddenly become clear.

Jacquetta leaned over and clicked open the secret compartment where the black phoenix journal lived and slipped it back inside. She could stare at it no longer today. With a sigh, she reached for her needlework again.

She'd cannibalized two gowns to create the one now in her hands. It was pushing the skills of her needlework, but she hoped to have something wearable soon. She had precious few garments to rotate between, and they were all crusted with salt and brine.

Jacquetta set an entire row of stitches before the ship rocked violently to the side, and she stabbed her fingertip with the needle. She shoved it into her mouth, sucking hard to stanch the bleeding.

Sighing, she set the unfinished gown aside. Her back was to the windows, but as her eyes swept over the cabin, she realized how dark it had gotten. It was a wonder she'd been able to see the stitches at all.

The sewing had distracted her—though not nearly as well as Grayson had.

If it was this dark in the cabin, then…

Jacquetta gasped at the sight outside the windows. Her hand fell to her lap, bleeding finger entirely forgotten.

The sky was dark as charcoal, even though it was only late afternoon. She could hardly make out where the thick, swirling clouds ended and the tumultuous water began. They were the same iron gray, and with the rain lashing against the windows, seeing more than a few yards was impossible.

She grabbed the edge of the bed as another wave rocked the boat. Seconds later, another rose right in front of the window, crashing against it violently.

Jacquetta sprinted from the room, grabbing her boots from the foot of her unused bunk by pure instinct. The door to the cabin angrily slammed shut behind her. She tried to rest her back against it so she could tug on her shoes, but another violent roll knocked her to her bottom. She yanked the boots on and clambered to her feet.

She had no notion where she was going, but she sure as hell would not be trapped alone in that cabin.

Jacquetta gripped the underside of the stairwell that led down from the quarterdeck, inching her way forward until she could peer out from beneath it. Her muscles groaned as she struggled to keep herself upright against the heave and pitch of the boat and the slickness of the deck beneath her feet.

The scene on the main deck turned her stomach. It was as bad as that night with the cannon misfire. Maybe worse, with the waves and water involved.

She searched for Grayson, her chest throbbing with terror. Men were yelling, running, slipping. Jacquetta counted heads, marked faces, trying to discern who was where and doing what and if anyone was missing. But it was all a muddle.

Calm, Jane's voice said into her head.

Piss off, Jacquetta's own internal voice screamed back.

What are five things you can see? she heard Jane saying from far away in London as she took tea in the Duchess of Guilford's salon.

I'd rather recite Milton.

But despite herself, she could not think of a single verse of the epic poem.

Fine. I see they've tied down the water barrels. I see there is no one in the rigging. I see three men aft and another three near the bow. I see Rook yelling orders from near the mainmast. I see Grayson doing the same at the helm.

Jesus, Mary, and Joseph. She owed Jane one of those fancy new flintlocks from France when she returned. Not only had Jane's calming technique helped her locate Grayson, it made Jacquetta realize that what appeared to be chaos was actually a coordinated, organized effort.

She needed to be a part of it. Determined and more than a little relieved, she stepped into the rain and began to slowly make her way toward the helm, carefully choosing each step and handhold.

She made it to the ship's waist before Grayson caught sight of her. Jacquetta saw the oath on his lips, though the sound of it was lost to the howling wind.

He turned to the man beside him, barked an order, and a second later was closing the yards between them. She glared at his elegant ease, even when the damn ship was rolling beneath them.

"What the hell are you doing?" he yelled, grabbing her arm.

She snatched it back, anchoring herself to the mainmast to keep from falling. Though she supposed he was as likely to keep her upright as anything.

"I left you asleep in the cabin," he yelled. Yelling, she realized, because that was the only way to be heard. And perhaps he was frustrated at her, just a bit.

"You expected me to sleep through this?" she yelled back. From the confused and mightily put-out expression on his face, she expected he might not have heard her. It did not matter. She leaned in closer to him and yelled again. "How can I help?"

"Get back to the cabin!" he answered immediately.

"No!"

"Jack! I don't have time for this! My men need me!" Grayson grabbed her arm and pulled her away from the mainmast, apparently ready to force her compliance.

Jacquetta closed her hand over his, squeezing tight. He hauled her forward, but she caught his face with her other hand

and held it tight, fisting her fingers in his hair. Rain was sliding down both of their faces, blurring her vision every few seconds. But through the water she could see his eyes—dark, fierce, and a little bit afraid.

Her heart nearly stopped. But she forced out the words nonetheless.

"I cannot be trapped in there." Though she must have yelled for him to hear her, the words felt soft. His grip lightened slightly, but his eyes did not ease. "Let me help. I can go below deck," she said.

His eyes darted toward the hatch to the orlop deck.

"The surgeon," they both yelled at the same time. She could assist the surgeon.

Grayson dropped her arm and grabbed her hand. Together, they fought the several yards across the deck to the hatch. He hauled the heavy wooden hatch open with one arm, refusing to release his hold on her hand with the other. Later, she would be impressed by his brute strength. Now, she swung her legs down the ladder and started down, wasting no time.

She'd started to release Grayson's hand so she could grab the next rung, when he hauled her back up. Before Jacquetta could yell a question, his mouth claimed hers in a searing, searching kiss. A promise—she knew. To find her when this was done. That the storm would not claim them.

Then he tore himself away. She fought back the words on her lips and forced herself down the hatch, already shoving her sleeves up as her feet connected with the deck below her.

CHAPTER FIFTEEN

ALL STORMS MUST end.

This one faded away in the wee hours of the morning, the sizzle of lightning cooling gradually, the sharp rain softening to a drizzle as the winds finally calmed. The air was thick with moisture, and the men were so exhausted that Grayson watched as several of them collapsed where they stood on the deck, leaning against a barrel or wall and simply tipping back their heads and opening their mouths to allow the rainwater to slake their thirst.

Grayson had one thought when he finally surrendered control of the helm to Burton.

Jack.

He knew without going back to verify that she would not be safely tucked up in his bed. If he was still awake then so was she; he only hoped she had not strayed from her assignment in the surgery below.

Gritting his teeth and preparing for the worst, Grayson swung himself down the hatch, careful to close it behind him against the rain that refused to taper off entirely. A few heads popped up from hammocks in the crew quarters, followed by raised hands of greeting. Grayson waved before turning for the surgeon.

He shoved down the memory of the last time his feet had taken this exact route and he found Jacquetta pinned beneath

Payne. The man had been assigned duties in the bowels of the ship and was forced to bunk in the hold by himself, despite that there was now plenty of room for all back on the orlop deck. And Grayson had made it plain that if he so much as breathed in Jacquetta's direction, he would throw the man overboard himself.

Once they reached Barbados, none of it would matter. Grayson would be free and he would never have to work with blackguards like Payne ever again.

The door to the surgery was ajar, and pale golden light spilled out into the corridor.

Grayson nudged it open with his foot, trying not to disturb any patients inside. To his knowledge, there had been only minor injuries. A smashed hand, a twisted ankle, and one sailor who hit his head when he slipped.

Sure enough, Jacquetta sat on the edge of the cot where the sailor with the head injury lay, removing a soiled cloth covered in a poultice of some kind, and adjusting a clean one in its place.

The room was dim, the surgeon nowhere to be seen. Perhaps he'd retired—which hopefully meant Jacquetta was ready to as well.

But a movement in the darkened corner of the small cabin caught his eye.

Grayson's pulse eased when he recognized the young man who stepped forward. Malachi was an Irishman, hardly seventeen years old. He carried a pile of folded clothes, which he held out to Jacquetta as he approached.

The boy usually worked in the kitchens, Grayson recalled. He must have been reassigned for the evening. No one was attempting to cook in a storm like this. Nor did anyone think of eating when being tossed about like that. But he would be needed soon.

Grayson shifted his weight, moving a half step into the room to collect Jacquetta and tell Malachi to go rouse the cook—

Her hand closed around the pile, but instead of stepping back, Malachi lingered. He leaned in near to Jacquetta, whispering something for only her ears, and his thumb swiped along the back of her hand.

The door sprang open with a bang.

Thoughts completely deserted Grayson. He was grabbing Malachi's shoulder, yanking him back. The young man fell to the floor, his youthful body no match for the strength and power thrumming through Grayson.

"What the hell do you think—"

"Grayson, have you taken leave of your senses?"

"Sir, I—"

Grayson ignored Jacquetta, stepping forward so he loomed over Malachi on the floor. "I have made it plain that anyone who laid a hand on Miss Lawson uninvited—"

"I did not!" Malachi protested, hands going up to protect his face.

Grayson realized his hands were curved into fists; he'd lifted them menacingly without realizing it. He forced them down, though nothing could unfurl the tension in them at that moment.

"Do not lie to your captain," he growled, menace etched in every line of his body.

"Grayson, you are out of line," Jacquetta snapped, stepping smartly over Malachi's legs so she stood between them.

"He touched you."

"Did I look like I was in trouble? As if I needed your help?" she bit back, voice low.

"Jack," Grayson warned her.

But she was having none of it.

"Mr. Doyle, fetch the surgeon to watch over our patient," she said over her shoulder, not taking her eyes away from his for a moment.

Grayson stood his ground as Malachi scrambled to his feet and disappeared out of the surgery. Jacquetta's eyes were darker than he'd ever seen them. In the dim night, they were nearly emerald. And the expression they fixed him with was just as sharp and cold as a gemstone.

Once Malachi was gone, Jacquetta jerked her chin toward the

cot where the sailor still lay sleeping. Or unconscious. The injury must have been more severe than Grayson realized. He felt a stab of regret. But then the image of Malachi's familiar touch on Jacquetta set him right back.

"Have you learned nothing since your encounter with Payne? You should never be alone with—"

She held up a hand, her face turning harder than he'd ever seen it. She'd been angry before, but this was something else entirely. "This man has suffered enough. We will not spoil his peace."

His fists tightened further, which ought to have been impossible.

He opened his mouth again, but Jacquetta shook her head sharply. "We will wait for the surgeon."

Grayson wanted to argue, but his duty to the man on the cot kept his tongue in check. Instead, they stood in the flickering lantern light and glared at each other. It could not have been more than two or three minutes before the surgeon's footsteps rang down the corridor, but to Grayson it felt like hours.

"Miss Lawson?" The surgeon swept his eyes over the scene, confusion lining his sleepy face.

"I apologize for waking you, but I must return above deck," she said, trying to sound unbothered. But Grayson could detect the strain in her voice, and from the tightening of the surgeon's brow, he guessed the older man did as well.

The surgeon nodded and moved past them into the room. "Of course—goodnight, captain, Miss Lawson," he murmured as he leaned over the man on the cot.

Grayson reached for Jacquetta to guide her out of the room, but she jerked her arm away.

But the moment the door to the surgery closed behind them, she rounded on him.

"Have you taken leave of your senses?" she asked in a loud whisper that desperately wanted to be a screech.

"Have *you*?" he shot back. "After what happened with Payne, you still manage to find yourself alone with a man?"

"I am more than capable of handling myself with a man." She thrust out her lower lip, the challenge clear.

Grayson had a temper at the best of times. But now, exhausted and jealous and damn possessive… neither of them stood a chance of letting their better judgment reign.

"Do you not realize what you're doing? Letting him touch you like that?" He heard his voice rising, saw the hammocks swaying over her shoulder. He tried to lower his voice.

But Jacquetta felt no such compulsion. "He was handing me clean bandages! We were whispering so we did not disturb your injured crewman!" she exclaimed.

"Jack," Grayson said, seeing the silhouettes of several heads appearing above their hammocks.

"That is not my name!" she yelled. "I am not your plaything! Just because I have deigned to share your bed does not make me your property. I may be your captive, Grayson Thane, but I do not belong to you."

Any care Grayson had for being overheard dissipated. Jealous—pure, green, and unrelenting—was in complete control now.

"Is that it? You invited Malachi's touch? I saw him whispering in your ear. What sweet lover's words did he spout for you?"

"And so what if he was? If I let him?"

You're mine.

But that was not what he said.

"Then you are exactly who I thought you were all along."

The boat swayed, and a sliver of moonlight slipped through the hatch above to illuminate her face. Her eyes burned with fury.

"Bastard," she whispered.

Grayson pretended that it did not feel as if she'd stabbed him directly in the heart with her wicked-looking sewing needle.

He forced out a dark, mirthless chuckle. "Still haven't found anything more creative to call me, Jack?" He clucked his tongue mockingly. "You disappoint me."

Jacquetta's voice was frigid as she said, "Not nearly as much as you have disappointed me."

She turned and reached for the ladder, her shoulder stiffening suddenly. She'd seen the men watching them. For a second Grayson considered offering some sort of reassurance. But his anger and pride held him in place. Another moment passed, and then she climbed up the ladder and slammed the hatch shut behind her with such force that even more faces appeared in the darkness of the crew quarters just beyond. Half his men had no doubt heard their argument—and would report it to the other half come morning.

Fuck.

Grayson turned and strode deeper into the ship, mindless of the darkness. Her words were ringing so loudly in his ears that he could hardly see anyway.

CHAPTER SIXTEEN

"Come."

Jacquetta rolled lazily over onto her side to face him. She hadn't gone back to her bunk; she was not that self-flagellating. His bed was much more comfortable. But she'd wrapped the dressing gown around herself, rather than tumbling in naked, as she had been wont to do for the past few weeks.

"Where?"

Grayson flicked one eyebrow upward, dragging his gaze over her supine form. "Wherever I tell you. You are my captive, if you recall?"

She rolled over and showed him her back. And her rounded derriere. As well as her luxurious golden curls, which she'd freshly washed that morning. Let him appreciate all of it.

"Jack."

"I am perfectly comfortable here."

"If you'd prefer I lock you in the cabin—"

"What?" She shot up in the bed, not caring that the dressing gown fell open to expose the generous curve of her breasts.

Grayson's mouth tightened a fraction, the only outward sign that he'd noticed. Satisfaction thrummed through her.

"The ship is at anchor. There is a small island where we can take on fresh water and collect grass for the goat," Grayson explained. Though it was not really an explanation, Jacquetta thought crossly. It said nothing about why he was there bothering her. "I am going ashore. You are welcome to join me. Or you can stay in bed. In which case, I will lock you in. To protect you from the likes of Payne, of course."

Ah.

Black-hearted bastard.

He knew she detested being confined. He was using this to get his way—to persuade her to come with him when she'd said no more than a few sentences to him over the past two days. Grayson had seemed content to let her stew, leaving her alone in the cabin most of the time. She had used the opportunity to search his quarters for what must have been the hundredth time. When she was on deck, he kept his distance. Which suited her purpose as well. She'd managed to search lower decks again without interruption or discovery. She avoided the hold.

But when he climbed into his bed each night, he did not reach for her. He did not attempt to seduce his way back into her good graces. He merely bade her a polite goodnight and rolled over to face the wall of windows Jacquetta so detested. At least he hadn't tried to retaliate against her anger by forcing her to sleep next to the dark, ominous windows overlooking the sea. She would have retreated to her old bunk then, no matter how comfortable his bed was.

"Come, Jack," Grayson said, his voice softening almost imperceptibly.

But Jacquetta gave no quarter. "I am not a dog or a child to be summoned."

He uncrossed his arms and slid a hand into his pocket. She sat up just in time to catch the key as he tossed it toward the platform bed.

"Lock the doors behind me after I leave," he advised, the tails of his coat spinning behind him as he turned.

Damn him. If she wasn't so irritated at him, she would have admired the graceful lines of his body as he strode away, the wide set of his shoulders...

"Wait."

She knew even before he turned that he would be grinning. One of those rare, rakish smiles that melted her bones like butter.

Jacquetta shoved her legs underneath her and stood, letting the dressing robe fall open to reveal she wore nothing beneath. His smile faded, but at the base of his throat, she could see him struggling to swallow. Unable to resist the temptation to taunt him further, she unfastened the dressing gown fully and shrugged it off her shoulders.

Grayson grabbed the back of a chair.

Heady power thrummed through her veins.

"We only have a few hours," he said. To convince himself or her?

"Then we should not delay," she agreed.

He tore his eyes away from her and glanced in the direction of the bunk built into the wall and the stacked drawers beside it.

"We will be walking. Wear something sturdy," he advised. Then he spun on his heel. "I will wait outside," he said over his shoulder.

Jacquetta did not hold back her rich, throaty laugh at his expense as the door clicked shut behind him.

She emerged less than ten minutes later, as suitably attired for a mysterious outing as she could manage, given her limited selection of clothing. She'd taken one of Grayson's own leather thongs to tie back her mess of golden waves.

When she yanked open the door, Grayson stood with his back to her, arms crossed over his body.

He turned around slowly, raking his gaze over her appreciatively.

Jacquetta quirked a brow. "Do I meet your approval?"

He merely smirked. "Come."

The first chance she had, she was going to slap that word right out of his mouth. But he was already striding out from under the shadowed overhang before his quarters and onto the sunny deck.

She stomped after him, determinedly avoiding the eyes of the crew. She did not need them to—

Land.

Grayson had told her they were at anchor by a small island, but seeing it for herself after so many endless weeks at sea... Jacquetta drifted forward until she could grip the edge of the rail.

She had to get to it—had to run her hands through the sand, smell the damp shade of the leaves overhead. She looked around frantically, trying to find a way—

Grayson's dark chuckle rolled over her. He caught her hand, holding her in place. She did not yank it back, despite her continued irritation with him. He tugged her hand in the direction of a small skiff.

"Shall we go ashore?" he asked, raking his thumbnail over her knuckles.

Jacquetta shivered. "Yes," she breathed.

Grayson nodded toward the assembled men and led her to the skiff. Jacquetta only tangentially watched the process as they climbed aboard the small boat and were lowered to the waves. Four other crewmen sat with them and began rowing for shore the moment the wood touched water.

Two of the men jumped out as they neared the shore, then dragged the skiff the last few yards until it was beached on the edge of the sand. Grayson offered her his hand, but Jacquetta clambered out on her own—simply because she wanted to savor every second of it.

Her boots hit the sand, and she stumbled forward a few feet then fell to her knees. She rolled onto her back and lay on the hot sand, completely ignoring the crew chuckling and nudging.

A minute later—or was it an hour?—a dark head blocked out the sunlight directly above her.

"If you've finished making a spectacle of yourself, I have something to show you."

Jacquetta raised a hand to her brow so she could see him clearer. Grayson was regarding her with no little amusement dancing in his dark eyes. "Is it better than the sand and the beach?" she asked.

He reached for her hand, and this time, she accepted it. "You shall have to judge that for yourself."

With a sigh, she let him pull her to her feet. "Lead on, then."

She followed him up the beach to the tree line. Another skiff had come ashore beside their own, though both were now abandoned as their crews set off on their various tasks.

"Bold, to let so many of your men come ashore after weeks and weeks at sea," she observed. "I wonder they don't make straight for the nearest brothel."

Grayson gave her a look over his shoulder as he led her down a path into the jungle. "The island is uninhabited. They'd have to swim to Barbados to find any sort of human female companionship."

"Meanwhile, you are secreting me away to…"

"To bathe," he said.

"I had a bath this morning."

"I did not."

"Well—"

"Hush, Jack. There may be no people, but there are plenty of wild hogs who would like to eat us for their supper."

Jacquetta grabbed a tree branch for support. Grayson glanced over his shoulder, smirked at her expression, and continued through the jungle.

After a quarter hour of walking, his pace slowed. He paused before a bend in the path to turn back to her. When he did not speak, she stopped in the middle of the path and folded her arms over her chest.

"I am not impressed," she said, glancing around at the verdant jungle surrounding them.

In truth, she was completely bowled over. The green was so much more vibrant than the forests of England. Red and orange flowers bloomed above her head. Over Grayson's shoulder she thought she spotted a pink orchid, the likes of which she'd only seen in Lady Worthington's conservatory. But she would not give him the courtesy of her wonder. Not until she'd heard something resembling an apology.

Grayson matched her brooding pose. "Stop being obstinate, Jack."

Jacquetta's hands curled into fists as she slammed them onto her hips. "Obstinate? You are accusing me of being obstinate?" she cried.

His expression did not shift. "It is time to move on. The crew has," he said. Clearly, he had not seen the sidelong looks they'd given her when she stomped onto the deck an hour before.

"I do not care what the crew thinks," she said.

"You do, otherwise this would not be a point of contention."

She spun to the side, so frustrated that she could not even stand the sight of him.

Grayson, self-centered dolt that he was, continued speaking. "If you did not care what the crew thought, you would not mind that I have publicly warned them off. But given your temper tantrum, I think we both know you care a great deal."

"Temper tantrum?" Jacquetta's voice was a low growl. "You arrogant, rude oaf of a man."

He rolled his eyes and turned away from her. "Perhaps I ought to have left you on the ship," he said under his breath as he rounded the turn in the path.

"You—" She flew after him, prepared to pound her fists on his back or his chest or whatever part of him she could get a hold of.

Instead, she stumbled out of the jungle into a wide clearing.

Her mouth dropped open with wonder, all pretenses momentarily forgotten.

For the space of a few breaths, Jacquetta was thankful her kidnapping had gone so thoroughly awry, if only because it meant she was able to behold this magical scene.

They'd stepped onto a large, flat rock that jutted out into a pool of shimmering turquoise water. There was a pool to her right, ringed with boulders and tree roots, still and inviting. And directly in front of her, a glorious waterfall cascaded over the brown rock outcropping, spilling into the pool and sending waves lapping against the verdant shoreline.

Jacquetta let her eyes drift closed, just for a moment, so she could savor the soft mist from the waterfall as it caressed her skin and listen to the roaring of the water drowning out all the world's other sounds.

It was easily the most beautiful place she'd ever been. Almost worth crossing an ocean and being held captive by the arse of a man beside her.

Grayson's hand touched her elbow. "Am I forgiven?"

Jacquetta's nose wrinkled, but she did not look at him. She stepped closer to the edge, leaning over and dipping her hand into the warm water.

"I do not appreciate being treated like a possession in front of your men, even if I am a captive," she said as she stood, trailing the droplets of water over her sweaty neck and bosom. She glanced up at Grayson through her thick lashes.

"Understood."

"I am my own person."

"I have never doubted it."

"You have no claim to me."

Grayson's face was completely serious as he said, "That, Jack, is where we both know that you are mistaken."

"I have heard no apology," she said stubbornly.

"I will better control my more... possessive tendencies." The look on his face told her that offering was the closest she was ever likely to get.

"It is beautiful," she said, the closest she would get to acknowledging and accepting his offering.

Grayson caught her hand where it fluttered above her bosom and lifted it to his mouth. Slowly, holding her gaze, he dragged his tongue along her fingertips to lick away the fresh water that remained. Jacquetta couldn't suppress the shiver it sent through her.

"Are you brave enough to go in?" he said, nodding over her shoulder toward the glistening pool.

"I am not afraid of all water," she said, stepping away so she could tug at the laces of her boots.

He cocked an eyebrow. "Only the endless abyss of the ocean?"

She wrinkled her nose. "Something like that."

Grayson's brow smoothed and his lips turned up slightly. That smirk of his was devastating. The dark brown of his eyes glinted, softening from the obsidian black they glowed when filled with anger. The shadow of stubble along his jaw was hard to discern from the shadows cast by the jungle trees around them, but imagining the way it would feel scraping against her skin sent a shiver through Jacquetta.

She kicked off her shoes and reached for the laces of the shirt she wore—Grayson's shirt. When she was on deck, she wore it very tightly laced. After her encounter with Payne, she had no desire to draw the eye of any of the less noble crew members, though Grayson had pointed each of them out to her. She could defend herself—would have, against Payne. But it would ruin her deception.

Even with the laces undone, the shirt showed very little of her body. It hung off her, oddly more conservative than most of the gowns she wore back in London. But from the look in Grayson's eyes as she pulled the last knot free, she knew the effect of seeing her taking off his own clothes was tantalizing.

It was for her as well.

Jacquetta did not resent the wet warmth spreading from the apex of her thigh and taking over her body as she slowly pulled the linen shirt up over her head. She reveled in it.

Her breasts were bound in an oversized petticoat she'd cannibalized. Her thoughts shot to the would-be owner of the tiny corset that lived in the bottom drawer beside her abandoned bunk. Jealousy ripped through her, hot as the burning metal of the *Agamemnon*'s cannon a second after being fired.

Grayson was reaching for her, his hand curving to cup her breast. But he paused, brow furrowing. "What is it?"

Jacquetta shook her head to loosen the ill-timed emotion. "It is nothing."

His dark chuckle rolled through her with the smoothness of brandy. "You, Jack, are a terrible liar," he intoned softly, catching her chin with his hand instead of her breast.

If only you knew.

She tried to pull her face away, to step back and get air between them. But Grayson held her chin firmly in his grip. Pulling her closer, he dipped his mouth to hers and brushed his lips roughly against the closed line of her lips. Jacquetta felt herself open for him, completely outside of her own control. But he drew back before she could deepen the kiss.

"Tell me the truth, Jack," he ordered her.

All of the air was sucked from her chest at once.

She did not dare look down to see if her fingers shook as she reached for the fabric binding her breasts. Jacquetta held Grayson's eyes, licking her lower lip with seductive slowness as she pulled the knot free and loosened the fabric. As it fell away, she heard the sharp hiss of breath that he failed to control.

"Your previous mistress must have hardly eaten at all if she managed to fit into the corset she left behind," she said.

His eyes slowly trailed down her face, past her collarbones to take in the generous curves of her breasts. He made no attempt to disguise the hunger in his eyes.

Despite the precariousness of the moment, Jacquetta arched her hips toward him. Grayson caught them and dragged her against him. His rigid length pressed against her. Their lower halves were both entirely too clothed.

"Are you implying you've taken up the position, officially?" Grayson said against her ear.

Jacquetta touched her lips to the column of his neck and started to unbutton his linen shirt. "I'm still your captive, if you recall." She nipped at his earlobe for emphasis.

"Hmm," he said. He stepped back and dragged his shirt over his head, so they were both bare-chested before one another. "Do I detect a hint of jealousy, Jack, for the other women who have shared my cabin?"

Her palm connected with his bare chest in a hard smack that sent him back several paces. Grayson rewarded her with that dark chuckle he'd perfected and, finally, that fleeting grin he bestowed so sparingly. Jacquetta's heart clenched—if his smirk was devastating, his smile was disarming. It threatened to lay her completely bare.

"You shall pay for that comment," she said. She ripped loose the tie that held her skirt in place and shoved it down over her hips.

His mouth fell open as the muslin fell into a pile on the rock at her feet. She basked in his admiration.

"You seem to have forgotten your underthings," he commented, shucking his own boots and stockings.

Jacquetta shrugged daintily, knowing her breasts moved tantalizingly as she did. Grayson was ready to pounce. The pulsing between her legs wanted him to. But not quite yet.

"If you mention your prior lady loves again, I shall toss all remaining traces of them overboard. Then what shall you have as a keepsake? Love letters stashed away, perhaps?" She bent gracefully at the waist, removing one stocking and then the other. When she rose again, she was completely bare before him.

Grayson hooked his thumbs into his trousers and dragged them down. "Ah, but then what shall you wear?"

"I would rather go naked than think of another woman's hands on you," she said ferociously. The truth of that statement rang in the air between them. But Jacquetta was too sexually charged to dissect it. Or too cowardly to.

"There is only you," he said, stalking a step closer. They were both nude now, nothing between them but the mists of the waterfall at Jacquetta's back.

And secrets.

She could not think of it—would not. This moment was hers. Theirs. There was no duty, no quest, no ulterior motive. Only her and Grayson and this ravenous hunger between them.

"Allow me to worship you," he said, now just two feet away from touching her. "I will convince you that you have my utterly devoted, undivided attention."

She took a step closer to the edge of the rock where they stood and glanced over her shoulder, appraising the pool and its depth. The waterfall was at her back, its mists filling the humid air and coating her skin. She could not tell where her own heated, wet hunger for Grayson began amid the sweat and mist. But a ring of rocks and a curving amalgamation of tree roots created a still, languid pool just a few feet below them.

"Jack," Grayson said, voice wary.

She dragged one hand down the front of her body, cupping her breast and then pinching the nipple between her fingertips as she met Grayson's eyes. A low groan tore from his throat.

He lunged for her at the same moment she threw herself over the edge of the rock.

CHAPTER SEVENTEEN

S HE WOULD NOT have even known she'd reached the pool were it not for the weightlessness of her body, buoyed by the turquoise water. The pool was as warm as the air around it, but still she could feel every place where it skimmed against her super-sensitive skin. Jacquetta had hoped the water would cool her ardor, help reorder her mind.

But the crash of Grayson hitting the water a few seconds behind her and the waves emanating from his body reminded her of the inevitability of what was coming.

He closed his hands around her waist and dragged her up. She had enough time to gulp in a breath, and then his mouth was on hers.

"You shall pay for that," he said against her lips in the half-second reprieve he gave her.

He dragged his hands through her hair, pulling her curls into a tight fist, which he used to anchor her mouth against his.

"I thought you wanted us to end up in the water," Jacquetta said as he burned a path down her throat. "Is that not why you brought us here?"

He pinched her nipple, earning a whimper she was both startled and aroused by. God almighty, the man used her own sounds against her.

"I planned to seduce you under the mists of the waterfall.

Slowly." He gripped her bottom and lifted her so his teeth could replace his fingers on her nipple. "Devilishly."

"Show me your worst," she said, arching against him.

The words seemed to unleash something within him. From the first, Grayson's caresses had been a torrent of emotion and sensation that threatened to burn her alive. But now… his lips and teeth and tongue moved over her with such ferocity that Jacquetta thought he might be trying to devour her whole. And she was more than willing to sacrifice herself to the rolling waves of dark desire.

He dipped his tongue into her navel. She gasped at the intrusion, so unexpected and yet so strangely erotic. He nudged her toward the edge of the pool until her feet touched the rocky ground. A few steps more, and then she was standing with the upper half of her body bared to the tantalizing mist and the lower half still submerged.

Grayson dropped to his knees.

He could not possibly…

Oh God. Oh yes, yes he could.

He took a breath and then dragged his tongue over her throbbing center. He nipped at that one spot, finding it easily with his teeth and then his tongue.

She was going to die. It was too much—she was going to climax now, less than a minute after he touched her. Jacquetta tangled her fingers in his dark hair, which was long and free of the cue at the back of his neck. She braced herself for the onslaught of feeling—

But then Grayson was kissing his way across her navel, up over her stomach. She tugged viciously at his hair, yanking his gaze up to hers to display her displeasure. He grinned wickedly, dragging in a long breath.

He held on to her hips to brace himself as he came to stand. When he captured her mouth, he tasted of salty seawater.

No, Jacquetta realized. This was a freshwater pool. She was tasting herself on his lips.

"Grayson," she groaned, thrusting her hips against him. She needed friction, contact, grinding if that was all she could achieve. She needed *him*.

He slid his hands around her bum and lifted her easily. She reached down, catching his rigid length in her hand and holding him in place as he slowly lowered her onto him. Jacquetta threw back her head, eyes closed as she savored every inch of him sliding into her—spearing past her slick folds into the burning center of her core.

He let her slide down his body until he was fully sunk into her depths. Then he caught her mouth, plunging his tongue inside her at the same time that he moved his cock inside her. Jacquetta tightened her legs around his hips and lifted herself; the sensation of her clit rubbing against the tightly curled, dark hairs of his loins while his cock was inside her was absolutely exquisite.

She grabbed a handful of his thick hair to anchor herself. But instead of balking, Grayson tightened his grip on her. "Mine," he breathed raggedly against her mouth.

Jacquetta nipped at his bottom lip, then dragged her tongue along the stubble on his chin until she could nip at the shell of his ear and smell his hair and cologne filling her senses at the same time his rigid cock filled her trembling wetness. "Yours," she said.

Something ignited between the two of them. There was no gentleness, only their own desires to possess, to claim, to wring every bit of pleasure from each other.

Jacquetta levered herself against him with such ferocity that she knew the muscles in her legs would ache the next day. Grayson drove himself inside her again and again, matching her stroke for stroke.

She felt his speed increase. His breathing was ragged and uneven, his control in shreds. So was hers.

"Jack," he pleaded.

"Give yourself to me," she demanded, a shiver racking her as she realized just how slick they were.

"Jack, are you—"

"You are mine. Give yourself to me, Grayson," she said again.

He shuddered against her, and a second later she felt him begin to lose himself as an almighty groan ripped from his throat. The sound pushed Jacquetta over the edge. Her own climax roared through her in time with his, driven by the pleasure he drew from her with each long stroke.

She clung to him as they both slowly relaxed, but her thigh muscles quivered with exertion.

Grayson eased himself back, deeper into the shimmering pool until they were both submerged to their shoulders, letting the water take the weight of their muscles. But Jacquetta continued to cling to him, resting her forehead against his shoulder as both of their breathing slowly returned to normal.

Neither of them commented on the words they'd said in the heat of passion. Whether they were true, where they came from... Jacquetta could not allow herself to examine. From his silence, she deduced he was similarly conflicted.

To her surprise, it was Grayson who finally spoke into the yawning emptiness between them.

"If I'd met you earlier... I would never have been able to leave."

Her heart nearly stopped. But she forced out a soft laugh. "Yes, you would have. I am a simpering debutante, if you recall."

"I can think of many interesting adjectives to describe you, Jack. But simpering is not one of them." He eased her back far enough to look into her eyes.

She wrinkled her nose. "Perhaps not. But debutante I am." She pushed back from him, suddenly needing the space. The pool was not overly large, but she was able to float a few yards away.

Grayson did not follow, seemingly content to lean back and float as well. "Why did you debut so late?"

Jacquetta snorted. "If I'd had my way, I never would have been presented at court at all."

He rolled his eyes.

Lord, but he looked so handsome even when he was feigning

annoyance.

She let her limbs spread around her, let the warm water caress her skin. A slow sigh rolled from her chest. "I knew I would be declared an incomparable. It was all anyone ever told me. I knew I would have men falling all over me, making wagers about who could win the next set or manage to entice me into an unchaperoned tryst on the terrace."

Jacquetta thought Grayson would bring up Lord Andresen, but he merely watched her, dark eyes contemplative.

"I knew it was not what I wanted. My sister Marie was already out, so my mother was sated. I convinced my father that a few years' delay would do no harm. He allowed it." Saying it aloud, she realized how lucky she had been. So often, she bemoaned how adrift she'd felt in her own family, thinking the Lady Knights her true place.

But her father understood her. Not just her taste for brandy but her desire to go her own way.

She felt a pang of remorse—when would she see him next? How many months until she could sit in his study and share a brandy with him?

Grayson nudged her foot with his own. Jacquetta sat up a bit in the water, catching his eye. The soft smile that came to her face as she took him in, dark hair plastered to his head and tan skin gleaming, was unfeigned.

"I have never quite fit. I am beautiful, but I do not revel in the attention of others—neither the adoration of men nor the jealousy of other young women. I am intelligent, but not really a bluestocking. I can sit a horse quite elegantly, but they've never interested me beyond a convenient pastime." She sighed.

"You prefer brandy to claret or ratafia," Grayson added with a rueful smile.

"I have never voiced an opinion about ratafia," she countered, nudging him playfully with her foot.

"Consider it an educated estimation." He caught her ankle and tugged her closer to him. Jacquetta allowed it, floating across the blue lagoon until just a few inches of swirling, crystalline water separated them. "I know what it is, to be out of place," he said softly.

The longing ache in his eyes threatened to break her heart. He was going to unburden himself—to spill his secrets. Here, in the secluded pool away from his men and his ship, free from the outside world, if only for a few hours, he was going to unburden his soul in the same way they'd each unleashed their deepest desires during their lovemaking.

Jacquetta pushed away from him, finding a foothold on the rocks along the edge of the pool. She kicked up water, splashing him playfully and ducking her head. Grayson retaliated, sending a rolling wave of water in her direction. She forced a laugh out, hoping the water would disguise the tears that escaped down her face.

SHE LOOKED LIKE some ancient water goddess, long forgotten by mankind. The turquoise of her eyes perfectly matched the shimmering pool behind her as she pulled herself up onto the rock. Wet and heavy, her fine, sun-bright hair had turned a deep, burnished gold. It clung to her neck and shoulders, with a few long tendrils curling around her breasts.

Grayson's breath caught in his throat as she pulled her mass of wet hair from her body and shook away the excess water. Shining droplets slid down her golden body and her breasts bounced enticingly, begging for his hands to steady them.

A long, unsteady groan shuddered through him. One side of Jacquetta's mouth curled upward in a feline smile.

"It is very beautiful, is it not?" she said, motioning at the tropical tableau surrounding them. But her thickly lashed blue-green gaze remained fixed on him.

"The most beautiful thing I have ever seen," he rasped. It was true. Jacquetta was unparalleled.

She gracefully folded herself into a cross-legged sitting position on the rock. Grayson fought the urge to look down at her sweet folds so boldly on display.

"It is quite the compliment from a man as worldly as Lord Grayson Thane," she murmured, leaning in close enough to brush her lips over the soft shell of his ear.

It was hot and humid all around them, but still the flutter of her breath against his skin set him afire. Grayson could not picture her in a ballroom or at Buckingham Palace. She was too vibrant, too free to ever fit into the neat, tiny boxes society would always try to shove her into.

But Jacquetta was not distracted—or, at least, not by such grim thoughts. No, she was fully engaged in touching him. Her palms caressed his knees while her breasts pressed into his bare chest and her mouth nibbled a line from his ear down to his jaw.

"Where have you been all these years?" she murmured huskily against his mouth.

Grayson stiffened.

Jacquetta stilled as well, her hands poised on his thighs and her mouth hovering near his.

Fuck. He'd ruined it. A moment as close to perfect as they came… Why couldn't he have just kissed her and thought nothing more of it?

Even as he berated himself, Jacquetta was sliding away. Grayson caught her wrist, desperate to keep her close. When he met her remarkable eyes, they were soft and questioning. Deep inside him, something shifted, loosened. He lifted her hand and brushed his lips gently over her knuckles.

"Tell me," she commanded softly. And a command it was—to share himself with her as fully as she had with him. To finally let them be equals in all ways.

Grayson nipped at her knuckles, letting his dark eyes settle onto her cooler ones, letting them soothe her.

"It is not a happy tale," he warned her.

But he wanted to tell her, he realized. Dark and bitter as it was, most likely it would shatter the tentative lifeline between them. But even so, Grayson wanted to tell Jacquetta everything.

He folded his hands, setting hers atop his own—so she could pull away, as she inevitably would. He swallowed hard, the words sticking in his throat. But he managed to force them out.

"I killed a man."

Jacquetta held steady. Of course… she must think he'd killed dozens of them. He'd given her every impression.

"My plan was to join the Royal Navy. My brother married young and, by the time I came of age, already had two young heirs of his own. My father's dukedom was well looked after, so like most second sons, I was left with a choice between the church and soldiering." He flicked his eyes upward in time to see a small smile curve Jacquetta's lush pink lips.

"I cannot imagine you in a church," she said.

"Nor was I well suited for one," he agreed. "Thus, I intended to join the navy. I had always been fascinated with boats. My father preferred for me to buy a commission in the cavalry. As you know, neither of us saw our wishes fulfilled."

Her eyes flicked over his shoulder, as if she could see the *Agamemnon* and her crew waiting through the thick jungle trees.

"My father and I struck a bargain. I would work as common crew on a ship bound for Portugal. He had a friend who owned several ships and was willing to take me on. If after the voyage I was still determined to join the navy, he would stand in my way no longer," he explained.

"Your father sounds very reasonable," Jacquetta said softly.

Grayson nodded, his words catching in his throat once again. "We were very close—my entire family."

He paused, struggling to continue. He had not expected it to hurt so much. He'd never told anyone this story.

Over his hands, Jacquetta stroked her thumb slowly, then again and again, a reassuring reminder that she was still there, that she wanted this story as much as he needed to give it to her—to make her understand.

"I never made it to Portugal. Several of the crewmen took me out the night before we were set to depart. We went to a seedy tavern on the Thames, drinking and gambling until the wee hours. I was sure they intended to get me so stinking drunk I would not be able to see to my duties the next morning—a ritual hazing of sorts. But it never got that far." He stared at her thumb, still moving rhythmically against his skin. "There was an argument. A man in the tavern accused one of my fellow crewmates and me of working together to cheat him of his purse. We weren't, though it hardly mattered in the end."

As if she could sense what was coming next, Jacquetta's stroking stopped and she gripped his hands hard.

"A brawl started. When it ended, my crewmate and I were left standing and the man who accused us was dead. My hands were the ones covered in blood. I killed him."

Silence reigned between them.

She did not speak, but neither did she get up and run away from him. There was a small measure of comfort in that, at least. But Grayson would not look at her eyes. It felt wrong, to look into her beautiful, kind gaze and tell of the horrors of his life these past five years.

"Why did you not go to your family for help?" she finally asked.

"I love my family very deeply." He sighed. "My first instinct was to run to my father and ask for guidance. I was ready to stand trial or turn myself in to the authorities. But then I realized what a scandal it would heap down on my family. They would pay the real price—my brother and sister-in-law, my nephews, my mother. They would be turned away by society, given the cut direct. My two younger sisters would by unmarriable, despite being the daughters of a duke."

Jacquetta was shaking her head. "If you were as close as you say—"

"No. It is *because* we were as close as I say that I could not put them through that, could not force them to pay for my mistakes." Anger rattled through him even all these years later. Anger at his own stupidity. And shame. Such devastating shame. "Even so, alone in the night, I did not see many options. My crewmates abandoned me. I'd become too much trouble. I was ready to surrender myself when Palmer Delaurier appeared."

She stiffened slightly. Had she heard of Delaurier somehow? It was unlikely; Delaurier did not move in society. He hired others—like Grayson—to do it for him. But Grayson knew that he'd infused enough hatred and pain into the word to spike anyone's senses, especially someone as closely attuned to him as Jacquetta had so quickly become. It was a terrifying comfort how she seemed to deduce everything about him with that clever mind of hers.

"Delaurier offered me another solution. He helped me to cover up the man's death, and in exchange, I entered into a term of service working in his smuggling operation."

A garbled choking sound escaped her throat. It was mortifying, yes. Grayson understood that entirely.

Finally, he forced himself to meet her eyes. They were sparkling with wetness, but they held no fear or reproach. Inside of him, Grayson felt the weight he'd carried in his heart for so long begin to lighten.

He found the strength to say, "I have been indentured in Palmer Delaurier's service for one thousand eight hundred and twenty-three days."

She gasped. "Years of service for one night of wrongdoing?"

"I killed a man," he reminded her.

"Maybe. Without a coroner's inquest, you have no way of knowing you were the one who landed the fatal blow," she insisted.

Grayson shook his head. It did not matter. "I am responsible nonetheless. I would pay the price twice over, if it protected my family. I have, in fact."

Jacquetta's throat bobbed. He could see her piecing together the bits he'd given her, but she still asked, "What do you mean by that?"

"My original term of indenture to Delaurier was two years," he answered flatly.

Her eyes widened in horror. "One thousand eight hundred days? That is nearly five years."

"Every time a delivery was late or part of a shipment was lost, my term was extended. I was young and sloppy in the beginning. It cost me dearly."

Jacquetta's golden curls swayed to and fro in front of him. She was shaking her head, trying to make sense of everything he'd said. Still she held his hands. Grayson would never be able to adequately communicate what it meant to him.

He met her eyes, waiting for her to draw back. She stared at him, brow furrowed. A flash of understanding showed on her face, as if she'd just made sense of something. "You could have defected… but you did not. I presume that Delaurier threatened your family?"

Grayson could only nod his acknowledgement.

She finally pulled her hand away from his. But instead of moving away—afraid of him and what feelings for him might mean—she reached up and cupped his cheek.

"Oh, my love," she said softly.

She raked her thumbnail over the stubble on his chin. A second later her mouth was on his, offering a gentleness that until that very moment had never existed between them.

Grayson groaned. He should push her back and take her roughly against the rock, cloaking them both in the safety of those hot and heavy embraces. But he could not. He stroked his hand down her spine and knew that this joining would be different.

I AM A traitor.

As they picked their way back through the tangled jungle, each step watchful, the word repeated a deafening chorus in her mind:

Traitor. Traitor. Traitor.

Grayson had laid himself bare before her. Jacquetta suppressed a shudder as she thought again of everything he had recounted to her. It was horrifying. The things he'd been forced to do to protect his family were unfathomable. Her heart ached for him.

He'd divulged his most damning secrets—she'd urged him to do so!—and she'd given him nothing.

Well, not entirely nothing.

They'd made love again on the rock in the mists of the waterfall before dressing and starting back toward the ship. Alone in that secluded paradise, Grayson had given her his heart and soul. And Jacquetta?

She'd filed the information away. She created memory aids within her mind as he spoke so she could recall dates and names. All so that, when the time came, she could betray him and bring down his master—Winston Delaurier.

Jacquetta had everything she'd come for. She'd fulfilled her quest. And she felt as evil as Delaurier himself.

She'd cheated, lied, and stolen.

She'd killed in the service of her queen. She was prepared to betray someone who trusted her completely.

What made her better? What made her good?

When she finally made it back to London and the round table to make her report to the duchess, she would walk away and continue her life with no repercussions. But Grayson... the life he'd always wanted, the future with his family... It would be impossible. He would never be allowed to return to England without facing prosecution.

Jacquetta's legs failed her, and she stumbled over an exposed tree root. As she scrambled for a vine or branch to steady herself, Grayson caught her arm. He pulled her to her feet, setting her hand against his chest.

"Careful, Jack. You are precious cargo," he said. The smile he gave her was warm and affectionate.

Jacquetta died a bit inside.

She could not keep the misery from her face, watching as Grayson's happiness dimmed. He curled his fingers tightly around hers.

"We shall find a way out of this," he said so quietly that not even the trees around them could hear.

Jacquetta's heart started to fracture. He had no idea just how doomed they truly were.

Grayson turned away and led her down the path. The beach was just visible through the trees. Their respite was over.

Whatever happened next, Jacquetta knew there would be no happy ending for her and Grayson.

CHAPTER EIGHTEEN

BARBADOS APPEARED FOUR days later.

Jacquetta had not believed the sailors when they said that land had a smell. One reported that the goat was feisty, scenting the fresh greens. For hours, she caught the men staring in the direction from which the island was bound to appear, as if they could see it in the distance, when such a thing was impossible.

But as they sailed into Bridgetown, Jacquetta was prepared to revise her judgments. It was not until the ship entered the small harbor that she could hear the distinct clash of human sounds or smell the scent of many bodies in motion. But she recognized it all the same. Perhaps the sailors could too, their senses more finely honed to detect the signs farther out at sea.

She stood gripping the rail tightly as the town got larger and larger. Everything was about to change. She could avoid her quest no longer.

"Pardon, my lady," a familiar voice said behind her.

Jacquetta did not bother forcing a smile to her face as she turned to Rook—she was still a prisoner, after all. But when she saw what he held in his hands, the sides of her mouth drooped in disgust.

"Is that really necessary?" She rubbed at her wrists instinctually. The metal shackles were nowhere in sight, but she knew precisely what that length of rope was for.

"Thane's orders." He winced apologetically.

Jacquetta closed her eyes as she swallowed, trying to steady herself.

She was Grayson's captive. She would be conveyed to Delaurier, unless she managed to escape sometime before she was delivered. She was still mulling that over—her quest was to identify Delaurier and report back. But the parameters of her quest had not included a transatlantic voyage. There was room for interpretation and choice. She had made it all this way; she should try to find out as much as she could about Delaurier.

And if she waited to escape until after Grayson turned her over, he would not be punished for it. His indenture would be completed. He would be free.

She could play this part for a bit longer.

Jacquetta held out her hands, though she did not mask the distaste on her face. "He ought to have come and bound me himself, the damn coward."

Rook only grunted, though from the slight quiver at the corner of his mouth, she knew he agreed.

"Where is he hiding?" she asked, pursing her lips. Jacquetta knew the effect it would have on the ever-loyal Rook.

He glanced over his shoulder, but it told her enough. Thane was not in his quarters, but in one of his meetings with the quartermaster or boatswain. Rook finished tying her hands, and Jacquetta jerked them away immediately, pointing her feet toward the row of officer's cabins.

"He's in a foul mood today, my lady. I would not challenge him, or—"

"Or what? He's like to lock me back in his cabin?" She smiled grimly. "Some threats have ceased to frighten me, Rook."

The look he gave her was full of regret. Jacquetta's heart ached. In every quest she'd undertaken for her queen, she had been steady and sure. But this... the criminals felt like her allies and her quest a chain around her neck. Right and wrong had become too blurred for her to decipher.

She wished she could offer some words of comfort to Rook, but she did not even have them for herself.

So instead, Jacquetta marched up to the quarterdeck to wait for her captor to deign to deal with her.

SHE HAD NO business looking so damn delectable as she sashayed through Bridgetown. She'd been a prisoner for the last seven weeks, for Christ's sake. To anyone with a half-discerning eye, it would look like exactly what it was—a farce.

Jacquetta had not been abused or left to gather grime in some lightless cell in the belly of his ship, like a proper prisoner. She'd slept in his damn bed, eaten his damn food, and, through some miracle work with a needle and thread, managed to fit herself half a trousseau from the odds and ends in that single drawer of women's clothing.

As they strode down the quay toward the town, she wore a white and blue striped gown that he could not recall ever seeing before. Rook offered his hand to help her over a dubious-looking puddle, and Grayson realized that the skirt was actually panels sewn together, rather than striped fabric. When the hell had she found time to fashion herself an entire new skirt? And manage to make it so fit so well that he could see the rounded curve of her derriere through it as she swayed from side to side on Rook's arm?

That was not helping the illusion. Despite the fact that her hands were bound, she held Rook's arm with the grace of any lady in London. Rook, as always, was mooning over her.

"Shit," Grayson said under his breath, and muscled past the handful of sailors between them and himself. He cleared his throat emphatically—*a throat clearing, not a growl*—and grabbed Jacquetta's arm roughly.

"Ahem," she said, managing to infuse the sound with dainty exasperation. "Excuse you, sir."

"My lord," he corrected her gruffly. He dropped his voice as he leaned in and made a show of checking her bindings. "You two must stop appearing so damn chummy."

"She is a lady," Rook said, utterly dismayed.

"She is not a lady, though I know she's enjoyed letting you address her as such," Grayson replied. "She is a 'miss' or a 'madam,' but as the daughter of a viscount, never a 'my lady.'"

Rook's gaze darted to Jacquetta. She offered him an apologetic smile before turning her ire back to Grayson.

"You do not have to be an arse," she bit out.

"I do. You are my prisoner. I have a certain reputation here." He grabbed her hands and pulled her forcefully away from Rook for emphasis.

"Yes, as an arse. I understand that perfectly. Well earned." Jacquetta tried to wrench her hands free, to no avail.

"Don't push me, Jack."

She looked him square in the face and rolled her eyes.

He nodded over her shoulder at Rook. "As I said, *not* a lady."

He tugged her up a handful of stone steps, and then they were on the street. While it was the capital of Barbados, Bridgetown was not a large city by England's standards. Or by the standards of the West Indies, really. The island itself was tiny, most of its commerce coming from sugarcane. The legal commerce, that was.

The island was largely ignored by the colonial government, which was precisely why Delaurier had set up his headquarters there. A handful of well-placed, generous bribes, and he was able to run his smuggling operation with minimal interference. What conflicts could not be solved with money were ended with bloodshed. Grayson was leading Jacquetta right into the heart of it.

"You have been in a temper all day," she said as they walked up the street, which was busy at midmorning. By the time the sun was directly overhead, most would retreat indoors to escape the heat.

"Perhaps this is my true nature." He steered her around a corner. They were almost there.

"Oh, I have no doubt of that," she agreed. "But most of the time you are better at disguising it under some semblance of gentlemanliness."

"We have a part to play," he reminded her. He should not have to remind her.

"And aren't we playing it well?" she said. "You've dragged me onto the high street and scowled the entire time while doing it. Very much a captor aggravated with his haughty prisoner."

Damn her. She was playing along—she'd probably paired herself off with Rook just to ensure his hackles rose. He wanted to smack her bosom and kiss her hot little mouth in equal measures.

"Bridgetown does not have a high street," he said.

"You are an arse."

"You still have not come up with anything more creative."

Grayson stopped abruptly, sending Jacquetta crashing into him. He caught her hands, tied together in front of her, and used the brute strength of his body to keep her upright. Did he haul her against his body for just a second or two before setting her back on her feet? Yes, he did. The sharp intake of breath through her peachy mouth and the way her eyes darkened slightly made it entirely worth it.

"Keep your mouth shut for the next few minutes, Jack. I know it will pain you." He leaned in as if he was about to kiss her, and despite the chagrin etched on her face, Jacquetta's eyes flitted closed.

Grayson pinched her cheek.

She tried to slap his hand, but he caught her wrist in time, dragging her behind him through the door he'd stopped in front of moments earlier.

The inn was dark, even in the midmorning. While most

buildings had their windows thrown open to capture the morning breeze off the sea, here all the windows were shuttered. The floor was... oily. That was perhaps the kindest way to describe it. It made no difference beneath Grayson's booted feet. He glanced down at Jacquetta's feet and winced—she wore those damn slippers she was so fond of.

"Hello, captain." The voice rang through the nearly empty taproom, reaching out to caress him with its velvety tones.

Jacquetta stiffened instantly.

Grayson ignored it, instead pulling his hat from his head and inclining his head toward the one source of light in the room— and the owner of the voice as well.

"Evening, Angela."

A silky-smooth, deep laugh. "It's not even noon yet, by my reckoning."

"Then perhaps you ought to open a window," he said, repeating the same banter he'd exchanged with the woman a hundred times.

"And risk whomever might blow in? Might not be the most honorable of types," Angela said, stepping into the light.

She was as gorgeous as ever. Her tan skin glowed despite the darkness, and her black curls were artfully draped over her shoulders, meant to entice a man. Many times, they had enticed him. But now, nothing. Exactly as he'd supposed.

"I cannot account for that," he said, dropping a hand on the table beside him. When he withdrew it, he left behind a fat purse.

He could feel Jacquetta behind his shoulder, still as death. For once, at least, she was keeping her mouth shut. A small mercy. Though he had no doubt she would have more than a few choice words for him once they were alone again.

Most of them to do with the raven-haired beauty before them, if he had to wager.

"Rooms, Angela."

She reached into the pocket tied to the outside of her skirt and withdrew several keys. "How many?" As she waited for a response, she began to stroke down the shank of each key, as if she was stroking…

Christ. Jack was going to rip his throat out the first chance she had.

"Just one."

Angela's finger froze, and her gaze skipped over Grayson's shoulder to the woman behind him.

Despite that Jacquetta was perfectly capable of handling herself, he shifted in front of her.

She subtly shoved her elbow into his side and pushed her way to stand beside him. "Do you plan to introduce me, *my lord?*"

Grayson grabbed her arm and pulled her back, putting a healthy distance between the two woman who looked like nothing more than spitting jungle cats.

"Mrs. Angela Smith. Her husband is the proprietor of this establishment." Technically. Grayson did not add that her husband had mysteriously disappeared some years ago and Angela had assumed the running—and control of the associated profits. He tipped his head toward Jacquetta. "Miss Lawson is my captive."

Angela's eyes danced at that, making his gut churn.

"I have a cell down below," she purred, jerking her head toward a trapdoor just visible behind the countertop.

Jacquetta bared her teeth. Grayson tightened his hold on her arm.

"She stays with me." That tone had cowed many brawnier, wiser men.

But Angela merely raised a dark eyebrow. "Of course, captain. Follow me."

He ignored the curses that Jacquetta mumbled none too quietly as Angela led them around the back of the building and up a narrow staircase.

The proprietress unlocked the door herself before holding out the key on her palm, a sensuous smile on her face as she waited for Grayson to take it from her hand—and the inevitable physical contact it would require for him to do so.

Jacquetta scoffed loudly and shoved past him, grabbing the key from the other woman's hand with surprising swiftness for someone whose hands were bound together, and stomped past her into the room.

"My thanks," she said over her shoulder, giving the woman her back.

Angela's dark brows rose dangerously, but Grayson already had one angry woman to worry about. He brushed past her and closed the door on a thoroughly affronted woman who would doubtless run downstairs to send a message to Delaurier confirming their arrival.

The door thudded behind him, and Grayson braced himself—now that they were alone, Jacquetta was sure to unleash herself upon him.

But she was quiet. She drifted around the room slowly, running a hand over the small writing desk tucked in the corner and fingering the coverlet, which was not as fine as his own bedding aboard the *Agamemnon* but was at least clean. They could have stayed aboard the ship until he brought her to Delaurier, but Grayson thought she would appreciate at least one night with solid ground beneath her feet. A seafarer Jacquetta would never be.

She stopped at the lone window, looking out at the bay through the rough-hewn glass.

Grayson moved toward the bed, intending to give her space.

No, fuck that.

His time with Jacquetta was limited. He could delay delivering her to Delaurier by a day. But come tomorrow, he would have to surrender her. He had turned over every possibility for weeks. What could he do to protect her? What bargain could he make with Delaurier? How could he work the situation, play a role, to keep her from harm's way?

So far, he had no answer.

But Grayson did know that he would spend every second

between now and then touching her, memorizing the lines of her face and body—before that inevitable parting.

He moved up behind her, waiting for her to flinch or recoil. But she stood still as he wrapped his arms around her waist and pressed his rigid form into her softer one.

"She works for Delaurier, I presume?"

"She is paid a stipend to keep her mouth shut about what happens in her tavern," Grayson confirmed.

Jacquetta gripped the windowsill, her eyes still fixed on the flotilla of boats in the bay. The ropes around her wrists cut into his heart as surely as they did her tender, creamy skin.

He began to reach for the knife in his belt, but forced his hands to the knots instead. They would need the rope again tomorrow.

"How long have you been involved with her?"

Grayson kept his hands moving, tugging at the rope until the knot sprang free. "*Involved* might be a bit generous of a term."

Jacquetta caught his hand, sliding her fingers between his to link them together. She raised their joined hands to her mouth and nipped at his knuckles. "I presumed your connection was purely physical in nature. Though her gaze was rather proprietary for my liking."

He chuckled, leaning in and pressing his mouth to her neck. She sucked in a breath as his teeth grazed her shoulder, followed quickly by a flick of his tongue. She was making a show of indifference, but the way she was dragging her mouth up his hand and around his wrist possessively suggested otherwise.

"If I belong to anyone, it is not her," he said against her ear.

They both paused at that, the weightiness of it filling the air around them. He did not mean Delaurier. They both knew it.

Jacquetta reached up, curving her hand along his chin and locking him into place as she turned her mouth to meet his. For the space of a few seconds she simply held him there as they shared breath. In and out. In and out.

When she touched her lips to his, her kiss was hot and urgent.

Grayson cupped her breast with one hand while sliding the other down her stomach, between her legs, and began rubbing her through her gown. Jacquetta arched against him, sinking into his touch and grinding her hips greedily.

He could not resist the invitation. He tugged up her skirts and dived beneath them, rooting around urgently until he was able to fully cup her quivering mound. She was wet, and the heat of her desire pooled in his hand. He thrust a finger inside her at the same time he slid his tongue inside her mouth and claimed the hot depths there.

Jacquetta moaned, moving her hips in time with his thrusts. She began to ride his hand, and her mouth made needy sounds against his as she took control of the pace. She'd released his head now, had one hand gripping the windowsill and the other holding tightly to his shoulder as she made love to his hand.

"More," she commanded.

"Where?" Grayson chuckled against her, delighting in the way her breasts bounced as she huffed in exasperation. "Here?" He nipped at her collarbone. "Perhaps here?" He slid his free hand inside her bodice and found her nipple, before pinching it tightly enough that she cried out. "Or here?" he purred as he slid a second finger inside her.

He curled his thumb so it touched her center, and she screamed, throwing her head back in ecstasy. Grayson watched her face, determined to burn this magnificent golden creature into his memory forever—how her hair was coming loose in sweaty strands around the nape of her neck, the scent of his own soap upon her skin, and the way her cunny clenched around him as she came, moaning so loudly Grayson wouldn't be surprised if they heard it all the way out on the quay.

Jacquetta's chest heaved and her forehead fell against his shoulder as the waves of her climax washed away. Grayson nudged her head up, reaching for her lips to give her a long, searching kiss. But when she met his mouth, the fire he'd ignited in her burst into flame once more.

She grabbed his shoulders, plastering herself against him and arching her hips into the rock-hard outline of his cock through his snug trousers. Her hands climbed over his body, every motion proprietary. Claiming. He was hers, and she was about to prove it.

She snaked her hands between their bodies, unfastening his trousers and pulling them halfway down with a brutal yank. Her urgency was infectious. There was no time to undress. All that mattered was getting his cock inside of her as quickly as possible.

Grayson slid his hands from her wet center back to cup her bottom and lifted her up to the edge of the windowsill. Hands on the lapels of his coat, she tugged him forward and planted her mouth on his.

Her hand was inside his trousers, closing around the length of him. She pumped him once, flicking her thumb over his throbbing head and eliciting a groan. Grayson felt her lips curve against his in a smile of pure satisfaction.

He thrust into her hand, pushing her back farther. Her skirts were up around his knees. She was guiding him in. The moment his cock touched her dripping entrance, he shoved himself inside of her with one unforgiving stroke. No shallow dips inside of her or teasing; the desire that drove him was primal.

Jacquetta braced herself against the window, a hand going to each side to keep herself from crashing into the glass behind her with the force of his thrusts. For a second Grayson wanted to throw the windows open so the whole world could hear the sounds of their passion, the claiming that they gave to one another.

None of the women who had come before could ever compare. Jacquetta encircled every inch of him, literal and metaphorical, and made him hers.

But the thought faded as quickly as it had surfaced. There was no time. He was already so close, the way her body gripped and squeezed, threatening to push him over the edge. Grayson gritted his teeth, reminding himself to hold on. He flitted a hand down, searching for her love button, wanting her to climax again as well.

Jacquetta caught his hand, dragging it to her mouth and biting the knuckles between her teeth. "Don't stop. Don't slow down," she ordered him. "Take me. I am yours."

Whatever semblance of control he'd maintained deserted him in that moment. Grayson ripped his hand away, grabbing her hips so he could drive into her harder and faster. Jacquetta held his gaze, biting her lip hard. He was so close.

He roared his release, throwing his head back as it overtook him. But she caught his face in her hand and held, forcing him to meet her gaze. He thought he saw a word on her lips. Some part deep in his mind tried to read what it was. But his last coherent thought before he surrendered completely to delightful oblivion was that Jacquetta's eyes were the exact same shade of turquoise as the tropical bay behind her.

THEY DID NOT bother dressing again. Grayson held a sheet around his waist when Angela delivered luncheon, and later supper, to their room. Jacquetta was inclined to think the food might be poisoned; he reassured her that Angela knew well enough not to bite the hand that fed her, even by extension.

They kept each other distracted, making full use of the room—the bed, the writing desk, the floor. Jacquetta tried to banish the thought of Grayson sharing this space with the woman who tended to the taproom below them. She was not jealous, not really. It would have been the epitome of hypocrisy; she had her own storied past, and she was thankful Grayson had not asked about it. She would not have enjoyed lying to him.

But as the daylight faded, she watched his eyes darken. He did not want to turn her over to Delaurier. He might even love her. But he loved his family as well. Failing to deliver her would mean being parted from them for even longer… months surely, years possibly.

They'd finally fallen asleep in a tangle of limbs just as the stars were emerging. Grayson had hardly let go of her all day, seeming to need to touch her. She felt the pull as strongly as he did. But when his breathing finally evened out, his mind exhausted from the war she was sure was being waged inside of him, Jacquetta's refused to quiet.

They'd opened the window to let in the evening breeze, but even so, she was sticky with the heat everywhere their bodies touched. Jacquetta did not care. She needed his arms tight around her stomach, his legs tangled with hers as she tried to sort through the mess in her mind. Without him to anchor her to reality, she might very well drift away into the abyss of despair.

Her eyes floated across the room, which was bathed now in moonlight. The edge of her chemise lifted with the breeze where it was flung over the back of a chair—the chair Jacquetta had held on to for dear life while she straddled Grayson and wrung every last bit of her pleasure from his body. The remnants of their supper were covered beneath the lidded tray, but she could still taste the rose syrup she'd licked off Grayson's chin and throat.

She shivered delightfully at the memories as the ache between her legs built again. She wriggled her hips back against Grayson, feeling his length start to harden instantly even in sleep. Perhaps she would waken him for another—

Then Jacquetta's eyes landed on her slippers discarded on the floor.

When she saw the rug they rested upon, she did not picture how Grayson had laid her back upon it and kneeled between her legs, feasting on her.

She saw the blasted blue satin slippers for exactly what they were—her choices, laid out before her with cruel starkness.

The left slipper promised escape. Grayson's knife was in his belt. She could slip from his arms, run the tip of the blade along the seam, and reveal the crafty little pocket where the powder was secreted. A midnight joining, a glass of wine to slake their thirst, and he would be unconscious. Jacquetta could disappear into the night, stow away aboard a ship bound for another island. She would be free. Grayson would be punished by Delaurier and his sentence would be extended. And she would never see him again.

The right slipper… She shuddered. There was one person she might use that upon—Delaurier himself. Perhaps Payne, if she had the chance. But Grayson—no. She could not harm him if the Queen of England herself stood before her and ordered it done. Of that, Jacquetta was certain.

Or she could leave the slippers exactly as they were, allow herself to be delivered to Delaurier tomorrow, and assume all of the risks associated with that particular choice. She would have more information to deliver back to London—perhaps she could even apprehend Delaurier…

What of her and Grayson then?

Would she be able to love the man who turned her over to a villain such as Delaurier?

That, Jacquetta realized, was irrelevant.

She was already in love with Grayson Thane.

And if he handed her over to Delaurier, she would not stop loving him for the loyalty he felt to his family. She suspected he would only do so with some other plan in his mind, however dangerous to himself it might be, though she could not be certain. There were too many variables—his family and their safety, the torture he himself had endured during the years of his indenture, and, finally, whatever feelings he might bear for her.

Jacquetta did not know if Grayson loved her. She did not know that it mattered. It would not change the course of events. Her decisions were her own, and she would not hold him accountable for feelings he may or may not feel, that he may not even be capable of after all he had suffered.

She stared at the slippers for so long that eventually they were fully bathed in the rays of moonlight spilling through the open window. She watched until they faded into muted darkness once again and the moon began to drop in the sky. When the last of the stars winked out, she rolled over in the bed and twined her arms around Grayson's neck, her decision made.

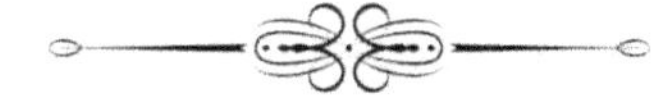

CHAPTER NINETEEN

S HE HAD A penchant for sleeping late, he'd learned during those weeks and weeks closeted together at sea. At first, Grayson had thought it was a way for her to escape the reality of her kidnapping. Eventually he realized it was sheer laziness.

He awoke before dawn. By the time Bryson arrived at his cabin door each morning at seven o'clock, Grayson had usually been awake for an hour or more.

The morning that would determine the course of the rest of his life was no exception.

He did not often think of the day he'd killed the man in London. Most of the time, the crushing guilt that lived permanently in his gut was sufficient reminder. But as Jacquetta slept in his arms, he did think about it. He examined every interaction as best he could remember it: who spoke and what they said, who responded and how. He made himself remember the crunch of the man's bone beneath his knuckles as he punched him.

I deserve this, he told himself—a life of punishment and indenture.

I do not deserve her.

That was the decision made.

But until he had to act on it, he could hold her in his arms for a few hours more.

THEY DRESSED IN the same clothes they'd worn the day before, which were rumpled but mostly clean. They had not worn them much before discarding them on the floor. Jacquetta braided back her hair and then curled it into a knot at the crown of her head. She even went to the trouble of pulling down a few tendrils at each temple to frame her face. Grayson did not comment that appearance would do her no good where she was headed.

When she was finally ready, he retied her hands and led her below into the taproom. Rook and a few others waited for them—their escort out to Delaurier's lair. Delaurier was smart enough to not leave the task of delivering Jacquetta wholly in any one person's hands.

Rook came to his feet slowly, looking morose. He bowed solemnly to Jacquetta. Kellerman and Burton rose beside him, ducking their heads so they would not have to meet her eyes. They were the only ones in the taproom; most residents of Bridgetown knew this was not a place to idly pass time.

Grayson steered Jacquetta to an empty table on the other side of the room, then pulled out a chair and waited for her to sit before he turned back.

"Angela. Breakfast," he barked at the dark-haired woman lurking near the door to the kitchen. She opened her mouth to say something that would irritate the hell out of him, but Grayson cut her off with a sharp look. She disappeared with a flick of her skirts. He turned to his men. "Get out."

"Gray…" Rook said, voice strangled.

"Meet us at the end of the quay, where the road forks. I would like one last breakfast in peace with Miss Lawson." Grayson stared hard at Rook, daring him to argue. But he knew his mate had a soft spot for Jacquetta, and he was depending upon it guiding his friend now. The other crewmen would follow the first mate.

"Fine. A half-hour, nothing more," Rook agreed. "It is luncheon, by the way," he said over his shoulder as he filed out with the other two men.

Angela emerged a few minutes later with a meager offering of bread, meat, hard cheese, and a small selection of tropical fruit. He and Jacquetta ate in near silence, neither wanting to say much with the haughty proprietress looking on, listening to every word.

When Jacquetta stopped nibbling at the fruit, Grayson offered his hand and led her out. Angela huffed a sound of annoyance behind him, but he did not have the ability to process its significance. He was thinking through the next few moments.

They walked a different route than they'd initially taken, going down a narrow alley instead of up to connect with the street that ran along the quay. Jacquetta shot him a questioning look.

"A few more moments of privacy," he said as he steered her on, urging her with his hands on her arm to walk faster.

They broke out into the sunlight a few dozen yards from the steps that led down to the quay. Up the road and around the bend were the crossroads where the others would meet them. Grayson wasted no time checking for onlookers; their brief respite was closing.

They reached the crossroads, where a tall white pole with signs pointed either direction stood. To the right, the road curved around the coast and then up the hills to farmland. They would take an offshoot path from that road to reach Delaurier.

To the left, the road led deeper into the jungle.

But Grayson was unconcerned with either road. He nudged Jacquetta into the shaded shrubbery, less than a yard from the dense forest.

Her golden brow wrinkled worriedly. "What are we—"

"Go northeast for a half-mile. You will reach a small spring; turn north from there and run like hell. You should reach Speightstown before nightfall. It is small, with fewer ships, but I trust you can talk your way aboard something." He shoved a small purse into her hands.

She swallowed hard. Grayson's eyes tracked the movement down her delicate throat.

"What are you doing?" she choked out.

"Letting you escape."

Jacquetta's beautiful mouth dropped open. He recognized the moment she understood what he intended. Her eyes widened until each glowing turquoise iris was surrounded by bright, bewildered white.

"No." She grabbed the post, as if he wouldn't be able to pry her off it if it came to a test of strength.

"This is our only chance. The rest of the crew will be here any moment. They are good men, but I will not ask this of them." No matter how good they were, he doubted the entire crew was enraptured enough of Jacquetta to risk extending their own indentures to save her. Besides, this was his decision. He would be the only one to face Delaurier's wrath.

She shook her head, making golden strands fly around her face. "Do not do this. If you do not hand me over to Delaurier, you will never see your family again."

Grayson caught her hands, bound in rope, and held her still. With his other hand, he caught the side of her face. He leaned in very close, pressing his forehead to hers. He crushed his mouth down on hers one last time, vaguely aware of the sounds from down the road. The rest of their escort was almost there. They had only seconds left. He tried to put every last bit of emotion into that final kiss.

"I can find a way to get away from him," Jacquetta whispered against him, trying to draw out the kiss.

But Grayson eased her away. He refused to let himself notice the anguish on her face or the shining wetness in her unforgettable eyes.

"I will not risk you," he said. Then he brought his dagger down with a swift thrust, cutting through the rope binding her hands. "Go, Jack."

He pushed her back into the tree line.

Behind him, the voices of the crew were louder.

Grayson allowed himself one last glimpse of her turquoise eyes as she melted into the dense blue-green jungle, then he turned to play out the next bit of his farce.

SHE WAS A prize idiot.

Of course he'd let her go.

A man who had sacrificed his own freedom for years to protect the ones he loved would do nothing less for her.

He loved her.

That was one question answered, at least.

But she would never get to tell him.

As she pounded through the forest, the ragged branches and vines tearing at her clothes, emotion bubbled in her chest. She wanted nothing more than to duck underneath one of the broad green leaves and sob until the burning ache in her chest eased. But she could not stop running. If she allowed herself to be caught, all of Grayson's sacrifice would be wasted. If she...

Jacquetta froze, her body unwilling to go another step.

She gazed up through the thick canopy, tilting her head to locate the sun. Then she turned her feet accordingly and starting picking her way through the jungle once again.

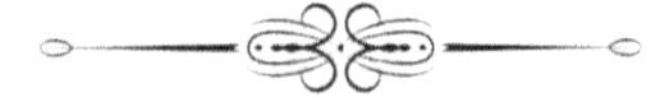

CHAPTER TWENTY

"**W**HAT WILL YOU tell him?"

Grayson stood in the small jungle clearing, staring at the dark, narrow entrance to Delaurier's lair.

"The truth, I suppose."

Rook touched his arm, and Grayson shuddered, jerking away.

"Dare I ask what that is?" Rook asked, voice low even though they appeared to be alone.

Grayson stared into his friend's face, saw the usually jocular lines troubled, pained. Rook had said nothing when he arrived at the crossroads with the other men to find Jacquetta gone. They'd searched the surrounding jungle for nearly an hour, then Grayson sent them back to alert the rest of the crew and begin searching Bridgetown. He could only hope that Jacquetta was far enough away to be aboard a boat by the time the search expanded to the other side of the island.

"She escaped," he said.

Rook sighed heavily, but nodded. "She escaped," he agreed, adjusting his belt and turning toward the cave.

Grayson caught his shoulder. "Go back and help lead the search."

Rook shook his head, as Grayson had known he would. "I should be there with you, to take some of his ire. I am your second."

"Jacquetta was my responsibility," Grayson responded. His responsibility to deliver, his choice to release—all of it came back to him. "I will not let you bear my burden."

"Gray," Rook said, "let—"

"Go back to Bridgetown and take command of the search efforts. Focus on the town—that is where she would go, seeking a way off the island," Grayson said, staring meaningfully at his friend. With Rook in charge and focusing the crew's efforts on Bridgetown itself, Jacquetta would have a better chance of slipping in and out of Speightstown unnoticed.

Rook swallowed hard, but nodded in understanding. Grayson would not accept Rook's sacrifice for his own sake, but he would let his friend do what he could to protect Jacquetta.

"If you do not return to the ship by nightfall, I will come back here and drag you out myself," Rook promised.

"See that you do," Grayson agreed. By then, he would know the cost of losing Jacquetta. Perhaps Rook would help him drink away the agony.

The first mate nodded, gave him one final squeeze on the shoulder, and then disappeared back into the jungle.

Grayson squared his shoulders, forced a deep breath in and out of his lungs, and descended into hell.

The mouth of the cave was narrow but quickly opened up as it sloped downward. The entrance was less than two yards above the level of the ocean at high tide. At low tide—as it was just then—it dipped lower still. Soon the rocks crunching beneath his feet were wet and pools of water sloshed around his boots. The dark walls of the cavern glimmered with damp.

Just when the light from the entrance began to fail him, a torch roughly driven into the cave wall appeared. The flame flickered eerily against the wet rock all around him. Delaurier was here—that was what the torch meant.

Grayson gritted his teeth and continued on. The cavern itself was not deep, and there were several small tunnels that veered away from the main path. But only one of them led to an actual egress—the cave's back entrance, which was guarded at all times when Delaurier was holding court. The path Grayson trod would lead to his throne room.

The incline steepened abruptly, forcing anyone entering to clamber awkwardly over the pile of gravel and wet stones. Grayson willed himself not to slip as he crested the mound and sighted Delaurier himself.

He hated that he had to drag his gaze away from the man to keep his footing, but it would be worse to slip and fall the last few feet, landing in humiliation at Delaurier's feet. But Grayson did dart looks across the dark chamber.

Delaurier reclined in his makeshift throne, a church pew thing that had been stripped from an abandoned parish outside of Bridgetown. It was set atop a pile of stones, with the cavern wall at the back, but still the ocean submerged the bottom few inches when the tide was high. Seaweed and barnacles clung to the feet. Grayson wondered if one day the supports would give way and Delaurier would tumble to his arse. He would pay good money to see it.

But just then, Delaurier was as comfortable as any king or emperor. He did not look surprised to see Grayson alone. Worry began to uncoil in Grayson's stomach.

Finally landing safely on the relatively flat stones at the base of the mound, Grayson stopped. He did not bow; for all that Delaurier saw himself as a king, Grayson would never go so far.

But he did incline his head. "Sir."

"You are late, Thane. I had word your ship arrived yesterday."

"There were unexpected complications."

"Would one of those complications have to do with the fact that you are here… alone?"

Now was the moment.

"Indeed, sir," Grayson said. "I am empty-handed. The woman escaped."

He did not have to feign the bitter disappointment in his

voice. Jacquetta's absence felt like a missing limb. But all Delaurier would see was his frustration at having his term extended.

Delaurier tapped a finger against his temple, appearing nothing more than vaguely bored with the situation. Grayson knew it was an act. Those hands could turn brutal and cruel in the space of a moment.

"How does one escape while at sea?" Delaurier asked.

"She escaped after we landed at Bridgetown," Grayson answered, voice gravelly.

Delaurier picked at a bit of lint on the arm of his gray tailcoat, the material fine and expensive, a sharp contrast to the jagged stone walls of the cavern.

"It is unlike you, Thane, to be so careless with your cargo."

Grayson did not let himself stiffen. "I prefer when the cargo does not talk back."

Delaurier chuckled at that, a rough sound that held no joy. "Your task was to retrieve the chit. I would have thought it particularly important to you, given the falsehoods she was spewing."

It took all of Grayson's self-control to keep the expression on his face unchanged. "Falsehoods, sir?"

Delaurier shrugged. "She claimed to have knowledge of the terms of your estrangement from your family, if you recall?"

"I do."

"Your secrets and mine are one and the same in that particular matter, are they not?" Delaurier said with velvety softness.

Grayson's skin prickled in warning.

"But, of course, it was all a ruse," Delaurier said, straightening and gripping either side of his makeshift throne. The anticipation in his eyes filled Grayson with sickening dread.

"I do not understand." But he had a terrible sense that he was about to.

Delaurier's eyes narrowed to sparkling slits. He flicked his wrist. From the dark corridor to his right, the escape tunnel, feet crunched over the stones. Boots splashed through the shallow water, mingled with a muffled grunt, and then they stepped into the light.

Jack.

He'd set her free only for her to be captured again, caught in Payne's brutal clutches. Grayson did not think of the ramifications of this: that she was captive once more, and that he would be punished by Delaurier regardless—that his sacrifice in letting her go had been for nothing.

No, Grayson could not form those thoughts. His heart might as well have been wrenched from his body and thrown on the wet stones between them.

Delaurier had Jack. Nothing else mattered except getting her free.

But he could let none of that play on his face.

"Where did you find her?" he asked, keeping his voice calm.

"Skulking around in the jungle by the beach. Near the rear entrance to the cavern."

An alarm bell rang in the depths of his mind. How had she ended up there? He'd sent her in the opposite direction. The jungle was dense, but she'd gone wildly off course.

He inclined his head toward Payne. "And your dog found her."

"He's a useful pet," Delaurier confirmed with a wink. "It did, of course, confirm what we already knew about the chit. Payne brought me word as soon as you landed in Bridgetown."

Grayson blinked, the only outward sign that he did not understand what Delaurier was speaking of. But it was enough for Delaurier, whose grin only grew as he continued.

"You ought to keep better watch on your men, Thane, even when you are in port. Someone ought to have alerted you that Payne slipped off."

Grayson shrugged. "I do not concern myself with the men's exploits at shore. I have no desire nor need to track them to every brothel across the islands."

Delaurier nodded as if that was perfectly reasonable, but his smile did not budge. The small bites of food Grayson had eaten at the tavern turned over in his stomach.

"But then perhaps your looseness has been a favor to me," Delaurier mused. "For it allows me to savor the look of surprise on your face."

Grayson had no notion what Delaurier was talking about and could not make himself much care. He was calculating how far he'd get before Delaurier sprang upon him, whether he would be able to get Jacquetta away from Payne unharmed. He thought Rook would take his side to protect her, or at least would not stand in their way as they escaped.

But as he silently hedged and calculated, Delaurier's peal of laughter punctured his mind and made his skin crawl.

"Did you not realize, Thane?" Delaurier's malicious smile reached all the way to his eerily dark eyes. "Miss Lawson is a spy."

All the warmth leached out of Grayson's body. Every tear that had repaired over the last weeks was torn asunder once more. All he could feel was bitter, hollow cold.

In an instant, all the gears inside his mind shifted into place. Like the intricate inner workings of a clock, they all moved as one and he was able to read the face. The careful exploration of his belongings, the way she ingratiated herself with his crew and always seemed to turn up in the oddest places... and her methodical seduction. It had all been a ploy.

Jacquetta was a spy.

She had made an utter fool of him.

"Grayson," she whispered brokenly.

"Who?" He refused to look at her, could not let himself. "Who does she work for?"

Delaurier cocked his head to the side. "That, Thane, is the answer which still eludes me." He flicked a finger in Jacquetta's direction. Payne clawed at her hair brutally, dragging her head back.

A second later, his blade glinted at her throat.

Grayson felt himself lunge for them, but unlike that night below decks on the *Agamemnon*, Payne was ready for him.

Delaurier's wicked laugh cut through the wet, dank air of the cavern. Grayson turned back to face his master, but he did not take his eyes off Jacquetta. He could not—whether from gut-wrenching betrayal or some fractured fragment of what had once been his heart, tearing his gaze away from her was impossible.

"How do you know she is a spy if you do not also know whom she is spying for?" he forced himself to ask, working his jaw uncomfortably.

Delaurier glanced between Grayson and Jacquetta, clearly enjoying the torment in both of their eyes.

"My informant in London told me just before I departed for Barbados that a spy was being placed aboard the *Agamemnon*. I thought it prudent to depart immediately, knowing you would only be a few weeks behind," he said. "But Payne here takes the credit for discovering Miss Lawson's deception."

Grayson gritted his teeth, trying desperately to anchor himself amid the swirling eddies of information and betrayal.

"Why was Payne given this task, aboard my ship?" He did not have to force the anger in his voice. It was rolling off him in bitter waves.

"*My* ship, Thane," Delaurier corrected him sharply. "I worried that perhaps with your term so near to completion, you would not be as motivated to root out the spy in your midst. A concern which, given Payne's reports on you and Miss Lawson's behavior while at sea, was not misplaced."

Grayson felt his throat tighten. He did not know how many more of these blows he could withstand. Jacquetta was gagged, but he was sure the instant it was removed she would say something brazenly awful—

No, he realized.

He did not know Jacquetta at all.

The fear in those mesmerizing turquoise eyes even now was

likely an affectation, a distraction while she plotted an escape with that wickedly clever mind of hers. Disgust roiled through him, and bile formed in his throat.

"Enjoying the cargo does not interfere with my ability to deliver it to you," Grayson said, imbuing his words with a casualness he did not feel.

Delaurier chuckled under his breath. "Then you will not mind if Payne has a taste?"

A second later, Payne's mouth replaced his knife at Jacquetta's throat. She fought him, sinking her elbow deep into his gut despite her bound hands. He sank his teeth into her skin, and she screamed even through the gag.

Grayson was ready to rip Payne apart. One lethal, targeted hit to his neck and the beast would be on his knees. A kick between his ribs followed by his groin and he would be prostrate on the ground.

But Grayson did not move. He forced the lines of his face to stay impassive, and the effort was so great that every muscle in his body ached and screamed in protest. But still he did not move. Everything depended upon his staying still now. Even if Jacquetta never forgave him. He knew he certainly would never forgive her.

She writhed against Payne, fighting him with surprising success for someone so much smaller than he.

"Enough, Payne." Delaurier shifted in his seat, bored with the pointless scuffle. His calculating, dark eyes landed back on Grayson. "You are right, Thane. I have no quarrel with your bedding the chit." Grayson fought back his grimace. "But then you lost her. Your mission is unfulfilled."

Even though Grayson knew what was coming, was in fact counting on it, the words still cut through him with the viciousness of Payne's knife.

"Which means your term is not completed. Seven months for the failed mission. Another seven for losing the tart and forcing me to expend Payne's energy recapturing her."

More than a year.

Grayson would not allow himself to think about it. He still had one last move to make.

"A bargain, then."

Delaurier's eyes snapped to him. Grayson watched in the periphery of his vision as Payne unconsciously loosened his hold on Jacquetta. He must have realized his plaything was about to be snatched away. Silently, Grayson willed Jacquetta not to try something foolish.

"A bargain." Delaurier weighed the words, shifting on his throne so his legs were no longer draped over the arm. "What do you think you have that would interest me, Thane?"

Grayson swallowed hard. He jerked his chin in Payne and Jacquetta's direction. Her eyes were murderous, but he ignored whatever she might be trying to communicate. "Send them out. This is not for their ears."

Delaurier rubbed his chin contemplatively. "Worried for your lady love, even after her betrayal?"

"I do not trust him"—Grayson gnashed his teeth at Payne—"not to try to take my notions for himself. Clearly he will be put in his place on the *Agamemnon*'s next sailing."

Delaurier chuckled darkly. "Payne, take Miss Lawson to the antechamber."

"But—"

Delaurier grabbed a pistol from seemingly thin air and fired it over Payne's shoulder without an ounce of hesitation.

Payne's eyes widened, but he did not argue further. Grayson kept his eyes firmly fixed on Delaurier as Payne dragged Jacquetta out. She was too valuable to be harmed, he reminded himself.

A spy. *Christ.*

Delaurier stashed his pistol and looked at him expectantly. "Entertain me, Thane."

"Give her to me," Grayson said evenly.

Delaurier narrowed his eyes, leaning forward to balance one elbow on his knee. "Why?"

"She is in love with me." At least, he'd thought she was.

"She is a spy. She could very well have been pretending," Delaurier said, his amusement written plainly on his face.

"She could have," Grayson agreed. Then he flashed a wicked, purely male smile. "But she was not."

Delaurier barked a laugh. "Arrogant."

"Confident," Grayson countered. "She is in love with me—and she believes I return her feelings. Give her to me and I will find out whom she is spying for."

"And in exchange…"

"My freedom."

Delaurier leaned back on his throne, his face unreadable.

Grayson was very close to losing control. He'd been playing Delaurier's stupid, dangerous games for years. But he'd never cared about the stakes beyond his own freedom. Jacquetta had betrayed him. It hurt worse than he'd ever contemplated. But seeing her in Delaurier's control, in Payne's meaty, brutal clutches, was worse.

"And what becomes of Miss Lawson once you've finished with her?" Delaurier asked. His eyes bored into Grayson.

One last lie, Grayson told himself, delving to find the strength for it.

He shrugged his shoulders and rocked back on one heel casually. Bored. Uninterested. Self-serving above all else.

"I care not," he said.

Delaurier's eyes gleamed.

Grayson's stomach turned. If he did not get out of the cavern soon, he might very well retch up his last meal.

"You have a bargain, Thane." Delaurier sat up abruptly. "Payne!"

The other man appeared instantly, proof he had not retreated far. But the unfeigned confusion on his face when Delaurier commanded him to release Jacquetta was proof enough that he had not managed to overhear the terms of Grayson's deal with the devil.

Payne's grip slackened, and Grayson seized the opportunity. He grabbed Jacquetta and yanked her across the uneven rock. He tried not to notice the array of purple bruises Payne had already left on her pale arms. He had to get her out.

He slid his arm around her waist, anchoring her at his side. She stiffened but did not try to squirm away.

"Delaurier," Grayson said, inclining his head and bending in a sort of irreverent half-bow.

"Thane. You may go." Delaurier flicked his fingers toward the yawning, dark mouth of the cavern "Good luck," he called, and his ominous, dark chuckle chased them out over the treacherous drifts of stone and seawater.

⟫⟪

GRAYSON LOOSENED THE gag as soon as they cleared the cavern, but he did not pause to speak to her.

"Where is Rook? And the others?" she asked.

"Gone," he barked.

Jacquetta did not push him, though all she wanted was to explain. The unspoken words were burning a hole inside of her, had been since the moment of Delaurier's stunning revelation.

But they were too close. They needed to put distance between themselves and Delaurier before they could speak safely. So she followed Grayson silently, each step etched on her heart.

After nearly an hour of walking—she estimated the time; Milton had no place in her head just then—the lights of Bridgetown appeared out of the darkness. Relief flowed through her when Grayson made not for the tavern they'd bedded in the night before but for the docks.

Late as it was, the quay was mostly deserted. Many ships sat at anchor, but Jacquetta did not know enough to discern their origins or ownership, even after the seven weeks at sea. She did not see the *Agamemnon*, which was both a relief and a bit of a disappointment. She'd come to care for many of the men so unfairly held in service to Delaurier, like Grayson.

Men she had betrayed, like Grayson.

Jacquetta stopped walking. "Grayson."

He froze two yards ahead of her.

They were on a deserted quay, with a tall wall of rocks on one side. On the other, nothing but the ocean and a few empty skiffs swayed in the nighttime breeze. As good a place as any to have it out, she supposed.

He turned slowly, his face unreadable in the darkness. The only sources of light were the glowing torches along the road that abutted the quay, yards and yards away.

Perhaps this was a conversation better had in darkness.

"Who do you work for?" he asked. The hollowness of his voice threatened to cleave her in two.

"Grayson, please—"

"Who? The Foreign Office? The Spanish or the French? Who?" he demanded.

His voice cracked her apart. And though it betrayed everything she'd ever sworn to protect, Jacquetta heard herself say, "Her Majesty, the queen."

"Damn it all, Jack! Enough of your games!" The hurt in his voice gave way to anger.

Fine. Anger she could deal with.

"It is not a game," she said quietly.

"Not a game?" Grayson echoed in disbelief. "This has been nothing but a game to you, Jacquetta. From the moment you stepped aboard my ship."

"I was carted aboard your ship unconscious," she reminded him sharply.

"Another fabrication, another play you orchestrated. Right?"

She did not respond.

"Right?" he demanded, advancing a step toward her.

"Yes," she said with a sad sigh.

"I cannot hear you!"

"Yes! The kidnapping was arranged! We put it out that I was onto the circumstances of your scandal with your family so you would kidnap me and take me to your master. So I could identify Delaurier." She was practically yelling, but it did not matter. There was no one to hear her secrets except the one person they could hurt the most.

"I told you Delaurier's identity and my history days ago. Why are you still here?" His face shone with such a gut-wrenching mixture of betrayal, hope, and longing that Jacquetta wished she had it in herself to lie to him this one last time—to make a clean break, as they said.

But she could give him nothing but the truth.

"I stayed because I fell in love with you," she said. His face crumpled, but she stumbled on, all the words she'd held in spilling out at once. "I love you, but I could not betray my quest. I knew if I went back and gave my report, you would be condemned and never see your family again. I could not do that to you, not after all the suffering Delaurier has put you through."

She took a step forward, expecting Grayson to back away. When he did not, she braved another. Finally, when she was close enough, she reached for his hand.

"I found your notebook. I memorized it. When you released me, I followed the directions toward the caverns and allowed myself to be captured. I thought—" Her voice broke. "I thought if I could bring back Delaurier to London I might be able to bargain for your freedom."

From Grayson's lips fell a dark, mirthless chuckle, the likes of which Jacquetta had not heard since that first night in Lady Brothwilde's study. He pulled his hand away, moving to the edge of the quay. He sat down and allowed his legs to dangle over the water.

"It seems we have both made foolish bargains tonight," he said into the darkness.

Jacquetta slowly lowered herself down beside him. She desperately wanted to touch him. But Grayson had pulled away. She would not force her affections on him. But nor could she leave his side.

She loved him.

And she had one last story left to tell.

"I told you the truth before. When I was seventeen, I was approached by an emissary of the queen. I was recruited to join an elite group of female agents. Spies—but more. Lady Knights. Intelligent and brave, yes. But honorable, graceful, uniquely talented and positioned within society. Joining Her Majesty's round table... it was like jolting awake after years spent in that half-lucid space between sleep and dreams. It was the happiest I have ever been. Until I awoke aboard the *Agamemnon*."

Grayson did not interrupt her, but he also did not respond. He let her sit in silence. Jacquetta wished she could see his face. He was difficult to read at the best of times, but just the familiar planes of his cheeks and curve of his mouth would have been a comfort.

She hardly deserved comfort. Perhaps neither of them did. But all she wanted in that moment was to crawl into his lap, tell him she loved him, and pray for some answer.

Grayson stood up. He did not touch her shoulder in farewell or tell her that he loved her as well.

"It seems you sacrificed your quest for nothing, Jack. After letting you escape for a second time, Delaurier will ensure I never see my family or the shores of England ever again." There was just enough light for Jacquetta to see as he lifted his arm and pointed, just enough of her heart left to break as Grayson said woodenly, "That ship leaves for Jamaica on the morning tide. I suggest you be on it."

Then she was alone again.

CHAPTER TWENTY-ONE

J ACQUETTA SAT ON the quay until the sun rose the next morning.
Grayson had made his feelings clear enough—he would
save her life, but he wanted nothing more to do with her. He
might love her. But if he did, how could he leave her like this?
Alone, again.

When the Duchess of Guilford approached her with that oh-
so-tempting offer, Jacquetta had not hesitated. As a lady knight,
she'd known her first true happiness; she'd made her first true
friends. Their faces flashed through her mind.

Dominique, with her Gallic beauty and courtly manners,
could shapeshift into whatever and whomever her quest required
her to be. But Jacquetta had seen the young woman beneath—the
kind smile, the stubborn brightness. She was a soul who had seen
the worst side of London society and still chose every day to
protect it.

And Ethelreda. Oh, Red. Was there any greater friend than
the one who knew all your weaknesses and flaws but loved you
in spite of them?

The vision of Jane that came next gave her a knowing stare.
Jane, who saw all. Jane, self-possessed to a fault. That first day
aboard the *Agamemnon*, tied to the mast, Jacquetta had mused that
Jane herself would have been better suited for this quest.

Her heart clenched at the thought.

The notion of Jane going toe to toe with Grayson was unthinkable.

He belonged to her, and her alone.

More importantly, Jacquetta belonged to him. Whether he wanted her or not, whether he wanted it or not, her heart was his.

Which made her next decision quite easy, really.

She pushed to her feet just as the dock began to echo with the voices of sailors starting their morning tasks. Up on the street, the heavily accented voice of a street vendor selling fishcakes for breakfast filled the air. Jacquetta's stomach grumbled, but she did not turn in his direction. She did not walk into Bridgetown at all.

Her feet touched the sandy beach. Grayson had disappeared down the jungle path that wound along the island's interior. But it was not the only approach she'd discovered perusing his journal.

SWEAT SLID DOWN his back in rivulets, leaching the moisture from his body with an effectiveness peculiar to the Caribbean.

For the hundredth time that day, Grayson cursed his own stupidity. He'd stomped off into the jungle without a bite of food or canteen of water, desperate only to get away from Jacquetta before either of them could do or say something else utterly devastating.

It was just as well there was nothing in his stomach. He was sure his body would have turned it to bile instantly. Bile and hate and regret coursed through his veins with every pump of his traitorous heart.

Jacquetta was the traitor, he reminded himself as he shoved another vine aside.

She'd rifled through his personal possessions, even finding the secret compartment that held the blasted journal. He would burn it the next chance he had. What use was there keeping track of the days of his indenture after all that had happened? He could never return to England. He could never have Jacquetta.

Why the hell would he want her? his anger sneered.

Because you love her, his heart whispered back.

Grayson swallowed hard. Or tried to. The dry scratchiness of his throat nearly prevented the action. He needed water soon or he would collapse. He could only keep his body moving so long in this endless heat.

He stopped at the next clearing and tried to orient himself. He'd stumbled north, through the crossroads where he'd left Jacquetta the first time. A few minutes ago, he'd spotted the coastline through the trees. Speightstown was not visible. The spring he'd told her about ought to be more or less due east of where he currently stood.

Grayson turned his feet and stalked on, delving into his anger to fuel his steps.

She'd betrayed him—not only by allowing herself to get caught and forcing him to save her and extend his servitude to Delaurier indefinitely. If it had been only that… Well, he understood sacrificing yourself for those you loved.

But the whole voyage from London, those long nights spent making love and exploring every inch of one another's souls… it had all been a lie.

She professed to love him. But it was all a goddamned lie. He could never trust a word from her beautiful mouth.

She would not have come to Delaurier's cavern if she did not love you.

Unless she was interested in her own glory, if she wanted to capture Delaurier and deliver him to London to bolster her own status with her beloved Lady Knights.

Even as the thought passed his mind, Grayson could feel the wrongness of it.

He burst through the trees and nearly walked right into the spring—sparing him from having to dissect that thought for at least a moment.

Grayson fell to his knees at the waterside, dipping his hands into the water and taking a deep drink. Then another and another. He rocked back on his heels, coming to rest on the ground behind him. His eyes traced the ripples of water, the rings sliding outward from the edge and back again in concentric circles of turquoise just a shade different from Jacquetta's eyes.

Eyes he would never see again.

Christ, it hurt.

What hurt the most was that, as Grayson stared into the clear water, he knew in his gut that if he had it to do again, he would not change a thing.

He snorted. Perhaps he would have taken Jacquetta to his bed sooner. He would have spent every single day across the Atlantic worshipping her, body and soul. Even knowing he would have to give her up at the end of it.

Even had he known her identity, known she was a spy from the beginning, he would never have been able to stay away from her entirely. His heart called to her, as hers did to him.

He sat on the edge of the spring, watching the ripples until they faded away entirely. A glance up at the sky through the trees told him it was near midday. Jacquetta's ship was well away by now. Delaurier would be expecting him.

AMONG HIS MANY flaws, Grayson Thane clearly did not know how to estimate a distance.

The dark rock that curved up from the edge of the beach to form the top of the cavern was twenty feet tall, not ten. And there was no way Jacquetta would be able to scale it while wearing her gown.

She cursed him as she stripped away the fabric, already anticipating how much she would miss its protection as her knees and arms scraped against the sharp rockface. Tucking it away underneath a thick plant with venomous-looking red blooms, she contemplated whether to remove her chemise as well.

Even she was not brazen enough to gallivant through the jungle in nothing but her stockings.

She did knot the chemise at her waist so the bottom edge hit her at mid-thigh rather than mid-calf. She also kept her stays, though she adjusted the penknife so that it would be easier to access. There was no longer any need for secrecy.

Jacquetta would defend herself and would rescue the man she loved. She would use every weapon at her disposal and every bit of training—including the deadly poison in her slipper, if the opportunity presented itself. But somehow, she knew whatever happened with Delaurier over the next few hours would be much too quick to allow for the use of such a subtle weapon.

Gritting her teeth, she found her first handhold and started to scale the ominous wall of dark rock.

By the time she hauled herself over the side, sweat dripped from every inch of her body and she was gasping for breath. Gasping quietly. She quite literally could not get the air inside her lungs quickly enough, and was trying to smother the sound as she did. But if she was caught here, everything would go to pieces.

She pulled herself to her hands and knees and carefully picked her way through the undergrowth. A narrow strip of jungle separated the cliff that led down to the beach from the small clearing at the entrance of the cavern. The night before she'd approached from the jungle and then circled around to reach the rear entrance to the cavern.

Today, she would approach from the beach.

But she had to ensure Grayson was inside before she attacked. He may not choose her, but he would help her eliminate Delaurier. Of that, at least, she had no doubt.

She had to move slowly, so as not to rustle the bushes and alert Grayson if he were ahead of her. But after several long minutes of crawling, she spotted the entrance to the clearing. She started to recite *Paradise Lost* reflexively to track the time.

Twenty minutes passed. Then forty. A full hour.

Had she missed him?

She'd assumed he would dally, waiting long enough to give the ship bound for Jamaica enough time to be well and truly gone before going to Delaurier and admitting he'd lost her once again. They both knew Delaurier was unlikely to believe it, and Grayson's punishment would be harsh.

Jacquetta refused to let herself think of it. There was only one way for this day to end—with Delaurier dethroned and Grayson a free man.

A few minutes later, her fortitude was rewarded.

Grayson appeared, not bothering to muffle his footsteps. He walked heavily, tailcoat nowhere to be seen, linen shirt rolled up to his elbows. His dark hair was wild around his shoulders.

Misery was etched in every line of his body. Her heart broke as she watched him. He paused only for a moment before descending to his fate, resigned. He pulled a leather tie from his pocket and tied back his long hair. His face was gaunt; the stubble of the day before shadowed the planes of his face beneath his high, angular cheekbones.

It took all of Jacquetta's strength not to call out to him or run in behind when he disappeared into the darkness.

Patience, the duchess's voice rang in her mind. *Wait for your moment. Choose the battlefield. Only duel when you are assured of a win.*

Jacquetta scoffed as she began the careful descent back down to the beach.

She'd chosen the battlefield. But assured of a win? Hardly.

Once she was safely back on the sand, she retrieved her dress and took a bit of wisdom from Grayson and re-plaited her hair. She did not need it whipping around in her face for this next bit.

Slowly, she crept around to the cavern's rear entrance. Yesterday, it had been guarded by Payne and one other. Two sentinels seemed a reasonable assumption; she hoped it was no more than that.

Relief poured through her when she peeked her head over the jutting black rock. Two men stood on the beach. The tide was out, revealing the tiny opening that led into the cavern.

She took quick stock of the two guards, recognizing neither from the *Agamemnon*. Though there were well over a hundred men who crewed the massive ship, she trusted her infallible memory; neither of these men had served aboard it. She sent up a quick prayer of thanks to the Almighty. It would have been harder to do what she'd planned if she recognized the faces awaiting her.

"You are alone."

Grayson let the words flow over him, nothing more than a breeze. Nothing really mattered now, anyway. Jack was safe. He would never see his family again. Let Delaurier do his worst.

"Miss Lawson escaped," he said, voice as hollow as his insides felt.

Delaurier's eyebrows rose sharply, and he swung his legs around to sit up straight on his throne. There was no boredom in his face now, only the promise of punishment and a sadistic glint in his eyes.

"Did she now?" Delaurier purred.

"You lost her again?" Payne growled, emerging from the shadows.

Grayson ought to have known the villain would be lurking somewhere nearby. The fact that he had not noticed him spoke to the complete apathy that had overtaken Grayson as he descended into the cavern to meet his fate.

Delaurier held up a hand, more or less leashing his dog.

"You shall have your chance, Payne," he said softly, his eyes not shifting an inch from where they bored into Grayson. "This sort of incompetence is not like you, Thane. Not since your early years in my service did you make such foolish mistakes. I thought you had learned that lesson well enough, the price of your carelessness."

Grayson shrugged. "It seems I have not."

"And you will accept the punishment I dole out, then? For you know what it shall mean. Unless…" Delaurier cocked his head to the side. "Unless you have her secret and hope to barter with that."

Grayson's fists clenched. Jacquetta was not Delaurier's true target. He wanted to know whom she worked for, on whose behalf she had infiltrated his operation and learned his identity. He would give her over to Payne, to earn the man's allegiance. Grayson was thankful as hell that Jack was far away at sea now.

But while he would let Jacquetta go, Delaurier would pry the information she'd surrendered to Grayson from his body. By force, if he must.

So be it.

"She did not confess."

Delaurier's laughter rang through the cavern, dark and devoid of all humor. Ruthless.

Was that how *he* sounded before Jacquetta, Grayson wondered?

It was Jacquetta's voice in his head that whispered back—*No, my love.*

No—it was truly Jacquetta's voice.

"My love, be a dear and bring me something to restrain Mr. Payne."

Grayson blinked twice, struggling to make sense of the scene before him.

Payne was on his knees, Jacquetta's knife pressed to his throat and one arm twisted behind his back. The other hung at his side, dripping blood.

Christ, Jack had managed to slice him down the forearm, disabling his use of one arm, and pin the other before getting her knife to his neck. All so quickly, there had been no time for Delaurier nor Grayson to react.

He was impressed and horrified in equal parts.

She was supposed to be on a ship, sailing to safety.

"Whoever trained you, they have my utmost admiration," Delaurier said lazily, though he now stood by his throne rather than lounging in it. He made no move to rescue Payne.

Slowly, eyes darting between them, Grayson eased closer to Jacquetta.

"As they should," she said, fierce blue-green eyes trained on Delaurier. "Though I must share with you that the sentiment is not returned."

His brows rose slowly toward his hairline. "So sharp-tongued. You did not warn me, Thane."

"You did not think me a wilting debutante, surely?" she scoffed. "I would have thought a man as nefarious as yourself a better judge of danger."

Grayson was nearly to her. He tugged loose his belt, having nothing better to use to restrain Payne.

Delaurier grinned malevolently. "Ah, but it is not my mis-judgment which shall be fatal here."

A second later, Payne exploded. He'd exploited the slight loosening of Jacquetta's grip in anticipation of handing him off to Grayson to wrench his uninjured arm free. He was on his feet in a second, leveling a foot directly into Grayson's chest and sending him sprawling backward. Then he turned on Jacquetta.

Scrambling to regain himself, Grayson watched helplessly as Payne lunged, going directly for the knife. But Jacquetta was smaller and faster. She whirled and ducked, evading him easily. Free of the close quarters of the hold, she was in control, driving the altercation.

She stepped forward as if to lunge, but Grayson saw it for what it was—a feint. Payne was not as wise. He lunged forward at the same moment that she sprang back half a step. He bellowed violently in rage, but he could not move his hulking body fast enough. Not to dodge Jacquetta as she pounced and drove her knife into his gut.

"Go to hell, you bitch," Payne ground out, his legs sagging under him.

She leaned in, twisting the knife. "I shall meet you there." She raised a foot to his shoulder and kicked him down the little gravel mound, leaving him to bleed out among the seaweed and stench.

Pride surged through Grayson. He was impressed and terrified. Would it always be that way with her?

But before he could wonder further, Jacquetta's eyes landed on him. Her cry wrenched through the cavern a second before Grayson felt the steel at his own throat.

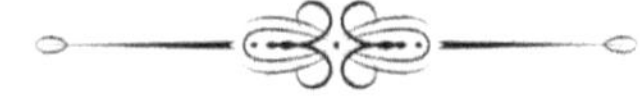

CHAPTER TWENTY-TWO

"T UT, TUT, TUT, Miss Lawson," Delaurier said, his smile widening with each second. As if he knew that with each heartbeat, her fear threatened to overcome her. "So focused on revenge against poor Payne that you neglected the true threat."

He had a knife to Grayson's throat. She doubted that Delaurier was thoughtless enough to allow Grayson a chance to wrest himself away, as she'd foolishly done for Payne. She spared not a thought for the man. He would be dead in matter of minutes; she'd felt the gush of blood on her hand and known she'd struck a fatal blow.

Grayson, Grayson.

"Drop the knife," Delaurier ordered her.

She did. It would be of no use to her now anyway.

But there had to be a way. The guards on the beach were down. Not dead, but disabled and tied up in the jungle. Payne was dead or soon would be. It was her and Grayson against Delaurier. The advantage ought to be theirs.

Except Delaurier held the one thing of value to her.

"What do you want?" she asked. Not that she intended to give Delaurier anything, but she needed to distract him.

"Your employer, naturally." Delaurier's eyes glinted with pleasure. He was enjoying this, she realized, as her stomach rolled over.

"The Foreign Office," she said easily.

"Tut, tut," Delaurier said again. Grayson shifted in his grasp. A thin line of red slid down his throat. "Do not lie, Miss Lawson."

"Why would I lie? You have me at your mercy." She eased her way down the mound where she'd taken down Payne, giving the hulking body at the bottom a wide berth in case there was any life left in it.

She had to get closer.

"At my mercy," Delaurier said, considering. "Payne was quite keen to have you at his mercy, to enjoy you as my servant Thane has. Perhaps there is something to that."

"You bastard!" Grayson lurched against him, thrashing, reaching for her. "I would rather die—"

Jacquetta pinned him with her eyes, trying to communicate without words. *Stay. Wait. Trust me.*

"Enough, Thane," Delaurier growled, tightening his grip.

The villain was truly an expert, she observed drily. It was not just a test of strength between the men, but of skill. The grip Delaurier had on Grayson was unbreakable, or near enough to it.

"I will tell you," Jacquetta said. She practically felt Delaurier's eyes snap to her. Good—she had his attention. And she now stood but a few yards from him and his throne. "For a price. A secret for a secret."

His dark laugh rolled through the cavern once again. "I have your lover in my grasp and still you try to bargain?"

She shrugged. "You are wagering my faithfulness to him is as strong as my allegiance to my cause. As I said, a secret for a secret."

Delaurier's eyes narrowed on her face. He did not see her hand moving into the folds of her skirt.

"I have a man in the Foreign Office. He was the one who warned me a spy would be placed aboard the *Agamemnon*," Delaurier said.

She nodded, as if processing that information. Indeed, it would prove valuable when she returned home. She looked to

Grayson, meeting his dark eyes. She tried to put every bit of love into that gaze, in case this should go horribly wrong and it was her last.

Grayson shook his head. "Don't do this, Jack," he whispered.

Jacquetta swallowed down the emotion in her throat and swung her gaze to Delaurier. "I work for Her Majesty, the queen."

A malicious smile slowly climbed Delaurier's face. "Tell me more," he ordered her.

"Release Grayson." It was a last attempt, before she made the move that would bring it all to an end. She was close enough now.

"Tell me more," Delaurier demanded eagerly.

"A secret for a secret," she reminded him.

Delaurier glanced to Grayson. "Then a secret it shall be. This one is for you, Thane. I bribed your would-be crewmates all those years ago. I arranged for the man's death outside the tavern. I planned it all when I heard that Lord Grayson Thane was hungry to take to the sea. I knew I had to have you."

Jacquetta watched the pain tear across Grayson's face. Master that he was at disguising his feelings, even he could not hide the devastation.

She could not wait. Another second and the enormity of it would come crashing through him and he would be flailing, fighting Delaurier.

Jacquetta ripped the pistol from the secret pocket in her skirts and fired it in the same breath.

In the corner of her awareness, she thought she heard a second shot.

But then Grayson and Delaurier were tumbling to the ground and she was scrambling over it.

Please, please, please.

The two bodies were a mass of limbs in the dark cavern, covered in water from where they'd fallen. That was blood glistening. They were moving—someone was alive.

Then a body tumbled to the side and Grayson staggered to his feet.

Jacquetta fell to her knees a yard away, her strength deserting her. A sob wrenched through her body, but then Grayson's hands were on her face. She ran her hands over his body, checking for blood. But none of it was his, she realized.

She reached for his face, catching it between her hands, ready to drag his lips down to hers and convince herself this truly was real.

"Ahem."

Grayson sprang to his feet, dragging Jacquetta with him and shoving her behind him in the same motion. But she saw the figure at the same moment he did. Even in the darkness, there was no mistaking it.

There stood little Jane Jacobson, pistol smoking in her hand.

Jacquetta had never seen her miss a shot, and today was no exception.

"We shall have to see to your marksmanship once we return to England, Jacquetta. You ought to have been able to make that shot from across the cavern," Jane admonished her.

There *had* been a second gunshot. She and Jane had fired at nearly the same moment. Which shot had killed Delaurier… Jacquetta did not care.

Her voice shook as she shoved her way around Grayson. "Jane… This is Jane Jacobson, my fellow lady knight," she stammered, realizing that Grayson was probably completely at a loss. But that was all the pleasantry she spared before she turned her eyes to her friend, her head moving side to side in disbelief. "Jane, what in God's name are you doing here?"

Jane tucked the pistol into her cropped jacket—into the special holster sewn into the fabric at her request, Jacquetta knew— and shrugged. "I received word a week after you departed that you'd been compromised. I set sail immediately—we were lucky that our source knew where you'd been taken. Once I arrived here in Bridgetown, it took me a while to work out the particulars. I followed him"—she nodded to Grayson—"from town this morning."

"How did you find a ship to take you so late in the season?" Grayson asked, shaking his head. Jacquetta would have laughed at the shock on his handsome face if it were not for the direness of the situation.

The tiniest of smiles tugged at the corners of Jane's lips. "You will find that those in Her Majesty's service have a way of getting what they want."

Grayson's eyes swung to Jacquetta. She watched the bob of his throat as he swallowed hard. "I believe I know something about that," he said quietly.

She whimpered.

Hell and damnation, a whimper? What have I been reduced to?

She forced the storm of feelings inside of her down and kept her eyes focused on Jane, who was now brushing off her hands and smoothing the dark blue skirts of her very serviceable traveling dress. Always practical, was Jane.

"What did you tell your father? You've been away for months," Jacquetta asked.

For the first time, Jane looked slightly ruffled. She pursed her lips. "My father believes I am visiting my brother in Rome. The particulars are of no importance, Jacquetta. We must take care of that"—she nodded toward the two bodies on the ground—"before someone comes looking."

Jacquetta had to look at Grayson then. "What do we do with them?"

He scratched at the stubble on his chin, considering. "We go back and get the *Agamemnon* and drag their bodies out to sea. Not a soul alive will miss Payne. Delaurier… will be more difficult."

She cocked her head to the side, nodding. "There are others who covet his power."

He nodded grimly. "There is the royal governor of Barbados, and then there is Delaurier. You can guess where the true power lies. One of his more brutal lieutenants might try to step in and take his place."

"Then it is convenient that we are trapped here until the season turns," Jane said. She'd hear no argument from Jacquetta. The mere notion of an attempted sailing during hurricane season made her nauseated.

Grayson and Jacquetta watched as Jane made her way over to Payne and toyed with him with her boot, making sure he was really and truly dead. Grayson nudged her shoulder, his dark eyebrows raised in question. She chuckled softly. There was no one as imperturbable as Jane, he'd learn soon enough.

"I will stay with the bodies while you two return to the ship," Jane said matter-of-factly.

Another questioning glance from Grayson. Jacquetta nodded subtly. Jane was more than capable of handling herself, as she had already proven.

"It will take a few hours for us to muster the crew and sail around the island," he warned Jane, though his hands were already on Jacquetta's shoulders, steering her toward the cavern's egress.

Over her shoulder, Jacquetta saw Jane wave dismissively as she settled herself onto Delaurier's abandoned throne. Tiny Jane was dwarfed by it, but she sat with all the regal grace of a pirate queen.

CHAPTER TWENTY-THREE

THEY PICKED THEIR way out of the cavern in silence, too focused on navigating the slippery ground to broach the conversation that hung waiting between them. Jacquetta was acutely aware of every movement of Grayson's body. His breathing slowly evened out as they walked. Occasionally, his hand brushed against hers. He caught himself twice from stumbling, so nimbly no one else would have noticed. She did. His body was hers. She hoped his heart was as well.

They reached the mouth of the cavern and stepped into the jungle. The forest was thick around them, but the bright midday sun was inescapable. It brought out the underlying notes of red in Grayson's dark hair and cast his tan skin in a golden glow. He took her breath away. Not just his rugged handsomeness, but the stubborn, brave line of his jaw that spoke of the brutality he'd endured and survived. The slash of his lips, so often harsh but soft now as his eyes moved to her, spoke of the goodness of the soul inside of him, despite what Delaurier had forced upon him for so long.

A good man stood in front of her. Complicated and flawed, yes. But good. And if Her Majesty's government could not see that then England was no place for them. Now Jacquetta needed to tell him as much.

She reached for his hand at the same moment that he lurched

forward, leaving her stumbling after him like an idiot.

Grayson was so determined to keep going he did not even notice.

"Your pardon, *my lord*," she sniped, planting her hands on her hips.

He turned, brow wrinkled, to find her framed by the mouth of the cavern, feet planted. His eyes narrowed and he stiffened—preparing for battle.

They had been at odds from the beginning, Jacquetta supposed. Perhaps even this was destined to be an argument.

"We must make haste. We can argue later," Grayson said, confirming her thoughts.

"We can delay a few minutes."

His feet were already starting down the path.

Huffing, she stalked after him. "You cannot avoid me forever."

"I do not intend to," he said. He did not turn, only spoke loud enough for her to hear.

"Just until you decide it is a convenient time to speak with me?"

"Once we have disposed of Delaurier and Payne and we have some measure of actual safety, then we may see to... eventualities."

"Eventualities?" That was the word he chose? Jacquetta looked for a rock to throw at him. "I am not an eventuality."

She thought she heard a dark chuckle. But the stomping of her feet was loud enough that she was not certain.

"What are you, then, Jack?"

"To you? An inevitability."

She watched his step falter and felt a surge of gratification.

"Is that so?" His voice was measured and his pace had slowed.

Good. Now she needed to get him to stop walking. She was done having a conversation with his back.

They reached a sharp turn in the path, and then they were on a bluff leading down to the ocean. Jacquetta grabbed Grayson's shoulder and yanked him back. He could not pull himself in the opposite direction or he would risk falling over the edge.

He caught himself easily, but the look he leveled on her was murderous. "Has your blood lust for the day not been satisfied?"

She chose to ignore that statement. "You are being an arse."

"Meanwhile, you are the picture of demure womanhood."

Jacquetta hit her fist against his shoulder. Not hard, really. But a show of the frustration she could not contain another moment. Grayson was going to make her scream—and not in the way she'd come to enjoy so much.

He did not so much as flinch. "Violence? I would have thought that below you, Jack."

She counted to five. She breathed in with the next wave, and out as it crashed against the shore below them. She tried to keep her temper under control. She really, truly did.

"What is so urgent that it cannot wait?" The challenge in his eyes was clear.

Jacquetta shook her head in disbelief. "Everything?"

"A rather wide net, Jack."

"We must... speak... decide what comes next." Of course, now that he was talking to her, she could not find the words.

"What comes next is disposing of—"

"Between us! Delaurier is dead. You are free. It changes things!"

Grayson's face was very serious. "Does it?"

"Of course!" she exclaimed. This man was going to drive her to distraction.

He sighed heavily. "It does not change everything, Jack. You are still an agent of the Crown—"

"Lady knight," she corrected him.

"—and I am still a smuggler with a record of misdeeds longer than you are tall."

"But with Delaurier dead, you can return to England. I can plead your case. We will be stuck here for the next six months. We can use that time to unravel Delaurier's enterprise, seek the favor of the royal governor. I cannot believe you are so easily willing to surrender!" A hint of emotion clouded his face, and Jacquetta saw her opening. "I did not believe you a coward."

"A coward?" He stepped forward, bearing down upon her. "After all that has happened, all that I have sacrificed to save the woman I love, you have the temerity to call me a coward?"

She waved her hand dismissively. "You speak of love, but you would consider leaving my side? I stand by what I said."

He shook his head, stepping back, then stomped away, running his hands angrily through his long hair. Then he turned suddenly, advancing on her once again. "If I am a coward then you are a fool! A fool to think there is any future with me—I am a criminal, Jack! Even if we managed to secure my return to England, why would you saddle yourself with me?"

She threw her hands up in the air. "Because I am in love with you, you stupid, pigheaded arse of a pirate!"

Grayson's hands dropped to his sides. Jacquetta watched as a tremor went through him. He took one step closer to her, then another, his face unreadable.

"I am not a pirate," he pointed out. "Pirates pillage. I merely ferry goods."

She pounded both fists against his shoulders in outrage.

GRAYSON DID NOT stop her. He stood still and immovable as a mountain and let Jacquetta vent her rage. Once she had, perhaps she would finally be able to see things clearly. But it hurt.

Not her petty fist falls. Given she was in Her Majesty's service, he suspected she'd had some measure of hand-to-hand training. What she was doing now, though, was not meant to hurt him. It was her heart's attempt to stop from shattering. Grayson recognized the feeling deep inside himself.

She finally slowed, her head coming to rest upon his chest

between her fisted hands.

"Are you quite done?" he asked.

She growled under her breath.

Very gently, he reached for her wrists and circled them with his hands, easing her back. Her lower lip was trembling and her turquoise eyes shone in the afternoon sun. She was very close to crying. It was a knife to his heart—throughout all she had endured aboard the *Agamemnon* and after, he'd never seen Jacquetta shed a single tear.

"I will never be done," she said emphatically.

Grayson sighed, releasing her and stepping back. He had to put space between them. The closer she was, the harder it was for him to think clearly.

"You are being dramatic." He did not pause to allow her time to interject. "We shall dismantle Delaurier's enterprise. Then, when the season turns, you and your… Miss Jacobson… will take a ship and return to England."

Jacquetta stared at him. "Where will you go?"

"I suppose it is better if you do not know."

"Because I am an agent of the Crown?" she spat.

Grayson wanted to say yes. To tell her that was the real reason they could not be together. Not because of the terror he felt when he looked at her.

"What about your family?" she argued. "You always intended to return."

"When I had the secrecy of Delaurier behind me. Now that the government knows the details of my exploits, I will never again be a free man."

"You are not listening to what I am saying at all!" She stamped her foot angrily. "Grayson, please."

He did not know how much more he could take. If she asked him again, his reserve might very well crumble.

He turned from her not because he could no longer stand her gaze, but because he was not sure he could stand at all. He staggered back toward the tree line, planting his forearm against a thick trunk for support.

He heard Jacquetta's soft steps behind him. He expected her to reach for his shoulder or his arm. But she stopped.

"You are my life, Grayson. Without you, there is no London and no future. The sun rises and the first thing I see is you. I turn in bed at night, and your body is the one I reach for." She paused to take a deep, gulping breath. When she spoke again, her words were stronger, somewhere between a promise and a threat. "Wherever you go, I will hunt you. Not for my queen or my duty, but for myself. I will sail across every damn ocean in the world until I find you, Grayson Thane. Because this—what is between us—is as inevitable as the waves lapping away at the shore. I will not lose it because you are a shortsighted idiot."

Grayson doubted he could move. He could hardly breathe, let alone make his limbs work. He might just be able to get a word out—or three.

"I love you," he said hoarsely.

"What was that?" Jacquetta demanded, stepping closer.

"I love you, Jack."

She let out an unsteady breath. "Right. I knew that," she said somewhat awkwardly, as if her bravado had chosen that moment to desert her.

When he did not speak again, she made an exasperated little sound and spun on her heel, probably to stomp back out and pout by the cliff edge. But Grayson caught her wrist.

He felt Jacquetta's gasp all the way to his bones.

"You win," he said.

"What do you mean?" she asked.

He pushed himself back off the tree to find her eying him speculatively. "You win. I shall go to the royal governor, I shall go to England—I shall do all of it." His mouth was dry, but he got the words out.

She cocked her head to the side, coral-pink lips pouted out. "As easy as that?"

Grayson dragged a hand through his hair as he coughed

hoarsely. "You think any of this was easy?"

Finally, she smiled.

Then he knew his decision was the right one. Terrifying and inevitably disastrous. But for the two of them… right.

EPILOGUE

November 1817
Six months later
Bridgetown, Barbados

ROOK TUGGED THE last oiled rope free and the mainsail unraveled, signaling that the *Agamemnon* was at full sail on the open sea. In the distance, Bridgetown was still visible, but in a few minutes it would be nothing more than a blot of brown on the otherwise lush green coastline.

A wave crashed upon the side of the massive ship, sending spray upward over the rail and covering Jacquetta's skin with a fine mist. She wrinkled her nose and squinted, shaking away the droplets. There was a faint layer of clouds overhead that made her stomach clench, even though logically she knew they were past the hurricane season.

She shivered at the thought. Three storms had hit the island directly over the past six months. Only one had been truly destructive. As long as she lived, she would never forget how it felt to emerge from the stone inn where they'd taken up residence and see the more fragile structures that made up most of Bridgetown in tatters.

As wary as she was to leave land behind, Jacquetta could not contain the thrill of excitement that sang in her belly. They were going home. Finally—to London.

She'd dispatched letters in early summer, but with hurricane season on, few ships risked traveling across the ocean. So she'd had no replies. The excitement in her belly faded slightly as she remembered the uncertain welcome that awaited them.

Soft steps echoed against the deck, coming to a stop beside her. Jacquetta did not have to turn to recognize their owner. There might be a few cabin boys aboard the *Agamemnon* as slight as Jane, but not a one who could have managed her restrained, contemplative silence.

"You have finally mastered your fear of the sea," she observed, her eyes trained on the shrinking coastline as well.

Jacquetta snorted. "Mastered might be a bit of an exaggeration. Managed, perhaps. With strong brandy and many distractions."

"Your primary distraction looks fit to burst with pride. You ought to accustom yourself to more sea voyages." Jane nodded over Jacquetta's shoulder.

She followed her friend's gaze to where Grayson stood at the ship's helm, consulting with the quartermaster and boatswain—both holdovers from Delaurier's regime of terror. He'd cut his hair during the heat of summer, but it had regained most of its length in the last few months. Several dark locks had escaped the leather thong that held the rest in a club at the nape of his neck and flew rakishly around his face.

He was not smiling. Grayson would never be a man who smiled easily. But Jacquetta could see the contentment etched into every inch of his body. The *Agamemnon* was his; the men who sailed aboard it were there entirely of their own free will.

"I am going to have to drag him away from this ship when we arrive in London," she said with a sigh.

"You ought to have intervened when the royal governor asked him what he wanted as a reward for informing on Delaurier and his nefarious lieutenants," Jane commented.

Yes, Jacquetta mused, she probably should have. But this

moment—seeing the expression on his face as the wind blew through his hair and he took command of the ship as a free man—she would not have traded for anything.

She turned back to the rail, unable to bear the burst of emotion in her chest. Jane stepped closer, her hands resting elegantly on the carved and painted gold rail where Jacquetta's gripped it desperately for some sense of security.

They watched in silence as Barbados disappeared entirely from view. The clouds that had threatened Jacquetta's peace dispersed into steady sunshine, leaving only one lingering worry—the most important one.

"Will the governor's commendation be enough?" she asked softly, finally dragging her eyes away from the horizon.

Jane cocked her head to one side. "It will be significant. Not only did Lord Thane dispose of Delaurier himself, but he also spent the better part of six months systematically tearing his smuggling enterprise to shreds. The governor offered clemency to most of the other men."

"Indeed. But they were lower-level indentures; none had been in Delaurier's service as long or risen so high in the ranks," Jacquetta countered. She did not disagree with Jane's calculations. But she knew her friend would not soften her assessment, and in that moment, she needed honesty more than comfort. "Tell me I am not taking him home to London just to see him hang," she said, voicing her deepest fear.

Jane shook her head.

Before Jacquetta could ask what that meant, the other woman reached into the pocket tucked into the folds of her gown and pulled out a folded quarto.

"What is it?" Jacquetta hardly dared to ask.

"Word from the duchess."

Jacquetta swallowed hard. "Have you read it yet?"

Jane shook her head. "Nor will I. If it commands me to deliver you and Lord Thane to London, I will never have received that order. You can boot me off on the next island and sail to your freedom. No one will be any the wiser for it."

Jacquetta grabbed Jane in a monstrous embrace. She held Jane's tiny form tight against her, squeezing so hard the other woman grunted.

"Killing me shall muck things up," Jane squeaked out.

Jacquetta released her immediately, a wobbling laugh bubbling out of her chest. "Thank you, Jane."

Her fellow lady knight looked quite put out by the overzealous display of affection. But she did smile slightly. She reached for Jacquetta's hand, deposited the letter in her palm, and then curved her fingers around it before taking a step back.

"Please do come and alert me once you have decided on whether I am bound for England's more tolerable climes, or if I shall be languishing in this unbearable heat for a few months longer."

Jacquetta nodded, heart so thoroughly lodged in her throat that no words could have made their way out.

Again, that small smile graced Jane's lips. Then she turned and strolled toward the port side of the ship. As footsteps approached from behind Jacquetta, her friend paused long enough to throw a wink over her shoulder.

"Miss Jacobson appears quite satisfied with herself."

Jacquetta's eyes closed as Grayson's arms came around her, molding her soft curves back into the hard planes of his body. He slid his hands up her forearms, pausing at her clenched fists.

"What have we here?"

She opened her hand to reveal the tightly folded letter within. "An answer, I hope," she said shakily.

He stiffened. "From London?"

"Indeed." He started to pull back, but Jacquetta caught his arm and held him in place. "Don't go. I need you here."

His body was taut. She could tell he wanted to retreat, was fighting the overwhelming urge with every muscle in his body. But he stayed at her side, faithful as ever.

"I do not know if I have the strength to read it," he admitted.

His voice was very low, his vulnerability for her ears only.

"Then I shall read it," she said. But she spun around so she could look at him, cup his face with her empty hand, and stare into those endless, dark eyes as she said, "Whatever this letter says, wherever we go, we go together."

Grayson's jaw was trembling. Her heart ached for him anew. She stood on her tiptoes and pressed a kiss to the corner of his mouth before quickly running her tongue over the rough stubble.

"Together," he murmured.

"Always," she said fiercely.

She lowered herself fully back to the deck and turned her attention to the quarto. The folds were still tight and crisp; if the letter had been read, whoever had refolded it had done an expert job of it.

Jacquetta tucked a fingernail under the first fold, and with a few expert tugs the letter was unfolding in her hands. She gave Grayson one last wobbly half-smile, and then turned her eyes downward.

It was brief, a few short paragraphs that would decide the course of her future.

No, Jacquetta told herself. She was still in control. She'd chosen Grayson. They'd chosen each other. That was the choice that drove everything else, and in the end, it was the only choice that truly mattered.

A renewed sense of calm spreading through her, she read:

Miss Jacobson,

I hope this letter finds you in good health. Your great-aunt has fallen ill and your cousin begs you come to provide succor in her care.

The message was coded, of course. Jacquetta had been expecting as much. Each lady knight had her own set of agreed-upon code words and phrases arranged with the Duchess of Guilford. They were not privy to each other's codes—there were separate ones for communicating with one another—but Jacquetta could guess that the first part of the message was a command for Jane to return to London immediately for an urgent quest. So much for dumping Jane on another island if exile proved her and Grayson's only option.

Our mutual friend Miss Scarlett has recently adjourned to the country and is expected to remain there for the duration of the year tending to her new charges. We of course wish her well, though she has requested time to settle into her new accommodations before receiving well-wishes.

That was one of Red's pseudonyms. She was in the country... with charges? Had she taken up some sort of position as a governess? The thought almost made Jacquetta laugh. Red detested children. It must be something else—she could be overseeing an exchange of valuable informants or something of the like. But the message to not attempt to contact her was clear enough.

One paragraph remained on the page.

With regard to your other request. Please inform your dear companion that we received her letter as well as several others commending her to us, including one from Monsieur Gris himself. While we cannot wait to hear the details of her adventures, please assure her of the warm welcome that awaits her and her companion in the most hallowed of London's halls.

Affectionately yours,
Matilda

Jacquetta's hand dropped to her side, though her fingers still clutched the letter.

Her eyes met Grayson's. "You wrote to the duchess?"

His face betrayed no emotion, but he nodded slowly.

"Why?"

"England is your home," he said. "I am happy to prostrate

myself before the king and queen themselves if it means bringing you happiness."

"England is your home too," she countered. "And I would very much like to hear more about how you are willing to beg." She dragged her tongue over her bottom lip, and the predatory glint that entered her husband's eyes told her he took her meaning quite fully.

"What did it say?"

"Read it for yourself." She held it up.

His eyes narrowed slightly, but he took the letter from her. Jacquetta watched as his eyes scanned the page, moving from side to side, and his eyebrows rose. "Monsieur Gris?"

"You do not approve of your *nom de guerre?*"

"It seems rather obvious. I thought your Lady Knights were supposed to be quite accomplished?" he drawled.

A giggle bubbled out of her throat. As Grayson wrapped his arms around her and tugged her against him, she knew he had understood the letter's meaning as well as she had.

She pressed her lips to his in a soft kiss. "We are going home," she said.

"Finally."

The relief in his voice... it did not break her heart. No, this time Jacquetta's heart soared.

She pressed her mouth to his, uncaring of the audience who would surely mock them endlessly for the next two months. But she could not possibly contain the emotion bursting forth from her. Grayson's grip on her hips tightened, and she unconsciously thrust her hips forward into his.

He groaned against her. "Perhaps, wife, we had best adjourn to our quarters before we become the source of every crewman's nighttime fantasies."

She chuckled again, rubbing her breasts against the linen of his shirt enticingly. He really ought to start buttoning his tailcoat if he did not intend to encourage such displays from her.

"I much prefer this sobriquet to the other," she said. She

slipped her hand inside the tailcoat, raking her nails over the thin barrier of linen between their skin, until her fingertips snagged on something firmer.

Quirking a brow, she slipped her hand into the waist of his trousers and tugged it loose. She pulled out the small black phoenix journal. Jacquetta had not seen it in months; she assumed he'd disposed of it.

"I suppose I have no need of it any longer," Grayson said, voice tinged with heaviness.

With a sharp shake of her head, she tossed it blindly over her shoulder. The vague sound of a splash was their only indication she'd hit her mark.

Grayson shook his head, that smirk tugging at his mouth. Jacquetta returned it with a raised brow.

Letting loose a low chuckle, he nipped her bottom lip then stepped back, catching her hand to pull her with him. "Come, Jack."

She wrinkled her nose. "I should not have said a word."

"I shall use both," he promised. "It is my prerogative, as your husband."

"You think yourself entitled to such liberties. But if you recall, you promised to beg."

Above them, someone snorted.

Jacquetta looked upward to where Jane stood poised on the edge of the quarterdeck. She'd never heard her friend make such an undignified sound. In fact, even now Jane looked only vaguely amused at the scene below her.

"May I take it you've good news?" she said.

Grayson tugged on Jacquetta's hand, only a few steps from the door to their cabin. She shot him a look before gazing back up at Jane. "Your great-aunt is ill."

Nothing showed on that immovable face. Jane merely inclined her head and said, "Then we ought to make haste to London."

"Indeed," Jacquetta agreed.

"Jack," Grayson said from the shadows before their door.

"Excuse me, Jane. My attentions are required elsewhere."

Jacquetta thought she heard another snort from above, but Jane's back was already turned as she strode to toward the port side of the *Agamemnon*.

"You shall never cease to annoy me," Jacquetta declared as Grayson dragged her through the door of their cabin and into his arms. She kicked the door closed behind her.

He was already unlacing her gown.

"*Now* you forget to lock the door?" she mocked, even as she tugged the tailcoat down his shoulders.

"If anyone is foolish enough to come through that door, they deserve the eyeful they will receive." He licked the swell of her breasts above her chemise. "Besides, perhaps you would enjoy having an audience as you make me beg."

Jacquetta did not bother to blush at the wave of heat between her thighs.

"I shall never be able to take you into proper society, with you whispering things like that in my ear," she said. Or nibbling her earlobe, as he did just then.

"We are already black sheep of the *ton*. Let them talk." Grayson trailed a hot line of kisses along her collarbone. "Better yet, let us give them something worth talking about."

As he slid down between her legs, Jacquetta could not have agreed more.

About the Author

A lifetime reader of romance, Cara put pen to paper (or rather, fingers to keyboard) in 2019 and published her first book. She hasn't slowed down from there. Cara is an avid traveler. As she explores new places, she imagines her characters walking hand-in-hand down a cobblestone path or sharing a passionate kiss in a secluded alcove. Cara is living out her own happily ever after in Seattle, Washington, where she resides with her husband, daughter, and two cats, RoseArt and Etch-o-Sketch.

Instagram: caramaxwellromance
Facebook: caramaxwellromance